"YOU WANT ME AS MUCH AS I WANT YOU."

"We can't go on this way," Cole said roughly. "You know that as well as I do."

Tracy swallowed and tried to concentrate on the disquieting feel of his hand on hers. She did know that they couldn't continue as they had been, yet she didn't know if she had the courage to step beyond her painful but safe boundaries.

"Go out with me," he demanded.

"Cole, find yourself a woman who's . . . who's whole."

"You're not whole?"

She shook her head. "No. No, I'm not. And I may never be."

"Well, you see, Tracy, this is where we may have a problem. I want you—whole or fractional, the good and the bad—I want the Tracy Kent sitting before me this moment." He reached for her. . . .

ABOUT THE AUTHOR

Sandra Canfield is a prolific writer of romance fiction. She lives in Louisiana with her husband, who is her number-one fan and a sounding board for the ideas in each of her books. *Cherish This Moment* is her first Superromance.

Sandra Canfield

CHERISH THIS MOMENT

Harlequin Books

TORONTO • NEW YORK • LONDON
AMSTERDAM • PARIS • SYDNEY • HAMBURG
STOCKHOLM • ATHENS • TOKYO • MILAN

Published May 1986

First printing March 1986

ISBN 0-373-70213-2

This book is dedicated to
the indomitable human spirit—
yesterday, today, tomorrow.

CHAPTER ONE

"IF I HAD ANY SENSE, I'd be in Tahiti where the women don't wear no tops," the tall, lanky, dusky-bearded young man said, speaking into the blustering cold wind that swirled lacy dots of snow.

Tracy Kent glanced at her companion, smiling into the raised hood of her heavy woolen coat as she did so. "If you were in Tahiti, you'd die of terminal drool."

"Yeah, but what a way to go," Hank Yeats drawled. "I can read the headline now—'Young Freelance Photographer Salivates to Death in Island Paradise.' "

"You fool," Tracy laughed, hunching herself farther into her coat and wishing for the warm neck scarf she had foolishly left at home. Stepping from the semishelter of the tall buildings, the two started across the street with the light that had turned an accommodating green just as they had approached the crossing. A great gust of wind suddenly tore out of the north, whipping Tracy's briefcase against her booted leg with a painful *thwack* and sending fingers of cold exploring up her plaid pleated skirt. *Ah, Tahiti,* she thought in agreement. Right this moment, it sure seemed more appealing than frigid Washington, D.C.

"How much farther?" Hank mumbled, hoisting his equipment bag from one shoulder to the other.

"The building up ahead is the Rayburn House Office Building. If we can survive the elements another two minutes, we've got it made."

"We should have taken a cab," Hank grumbled good-naturedly, and not for the first time.

"Shut up," she replied with the amiability of one good friend teasing the other. "What's happened to your adventurous spirit?"

"Right now it has an icicle growing from it," Hank griped, then added on a white puff of cold air, "You know where the congressman's office is?"

"Mmm-hmm," she answered, "third floor."

"There's a lot of offices on the third floor," he pointed out.

"Trust me, I'll find it. With Congressman Damon's reputation, we could ask the cleaning lady for directions. Sort of like asking if you know where Robert Redford or Tom Selleck hangs out."

A tingle ran down the long length of Tracy's body. Careerwise, she was excited about being granted an interview with the man who was Washington's fair-haired boy, though from the pictures she remembered seeing, Congressman Jay Cole Damon was anything but fair-haired, and at forty-two he was definitely not a boy. There was no quibbling whatsoever with the fact that the dashing politician from the state of Pennsylvania presently had the Capitol wrapped around his capable finger. He was handsome, charismatic, intelligent and had a natural bent toward politics, and, miracle of miracles, he appeared honestly concerned about his constituency and the nation as a whole. His concern was both commendable and sometimes a pain in the tush—at least to his other political cohorts who couldn't get him to bend on anything. Right now, Tracy conceded, the man's political star shone as brightly as the million and one lights glowing on the Christmas trees all over the city.

At the thought of the holiday only a week away, Tracy felt the electric sting of panic. Despite the cold her body flushed with heat, and her stomach coiled in a tight knot that strangled the air in her chest. She shuddered visibly.

"You all right?" Hank asked, turning his sensitive eyes once again to her.

"Yeah, I'm fine," she replied. And dammit, she would be! she promised herself. She'd get through this Christmas if it was the last thing she ever did! And she'd get through it by working her fanny off. "After you take the pictures, you're free to go," she told Hank in a businesslike tone as she scooted through the open door he held for her. The somewhere-distant sound of coins tinkling in a Salvation Army pan died away as the door closed behind them. "The interview probably won't last more than an hour, and then I'm heading home."

Home was a house in fashionable Georgetown, a property that she had been lucky to sublease within days after moving lock, stock, barrel and typewriter from Trenton, New Jersey, a little more than a year before. The move had been therapeutic. In fact, so was her work. Tracy had pursued her career in journalism so diligently for eight years that she was now at the top of her field and was a specialist in political affairs. Sometimes she thought that writing and living in Washington were the only two things between her and insanity.

A quick check of the wall directory revealed that Congressman Damon's office was, indeed, on the third floor. Walking to the elevators, Tracy lowered the hood of her coat and set her gloved fingers to fumbling with the coat's buttons. She sniffed in a lungful of the cavernous building's warm air, removed her gloves and rubbed her fingers across her red, numb nose. Her companion behind her, she stepped into the elevator. It had just been vacated by a group of men who were obviously politicians discussing the prudence, or the lack thereof—depending on whose voice carried—of the present government's defense posture.

With silent efficiency, the elevator started upward with its two customers.

Hank Yeats cleared his throat a little nervously. He thought a lot of the lady beside him and had ever since she'd arrived in D.C. and they'd started working together, and he didn't want to upset her by what he was about to suggest. She was a reserved, elegant thirty-four to his mellow, never-would-be elegant twenty-four—how could someone be elegant in a pair of jeans that had been washed more times than a baby's backside and a sweatshirt that proclaimed that Photographers Do It in Darkrooms? Nonetheless, he felt protective toward her. The sentiment had entirely everything to do with the nightmare she'd lived through. It was stupid, it was totally illogical, but as a man he somehow felt guilty for what some other jerk of a man, some slime of the male species, had done to her two years earlier. The fact that it had happened three days before Christmas, at a time of the year traditionally associated with happiness and joy, only added to his sense of responsibility. And to his anger.

"Listen, I'm..." he began, but started over. "I don't know what your plans are...for the holiday, I mean, but I'm going home to visit my family in Connecticut. It'll be a nice quiet Christmas, but you're more than welcome to come. Mom and Dad would love to have you. And Mom makes a great Christmas pudding," he added as an enticement, knowing Tracy's slavery to sweets.

The elevator door swooshed open at the third floor, but Tracy made no move to step out. When he realized her hesitation, he blocked the closing doors with his arm. Looking into her face and seeing the tears glistening in her big blue eyes, he cursed himself for bringing up the subject.

"You big lean lug," she said in a near whisper as she reached out to brush a swath of cinnamon-brown hair from his forehead. "That may be the nicest offer I've ever received."

His green hazel eyes still on hers, he asked, "Why do I feel a *but* coming on?"

"But . . . I'm going to stay here for the holiday. I've got tons of things to catch up on. Honest I do," she added when he looked skeptical. "Mom wants me to come home, but I just can't take the scene—four brothers, four sisters-in-law, ten nieces and nephews, one great-aunt . . ."

"And a partridge in a pear tree?" he asked with a grin.

She smiled. "You've got it. But thanks, Hank," she said, once again serious. "Thanks for being there."

"Anytime, boss," he said just as seriously as the two of them stepped from the elevator into the third-floor corridor.

Every door leading off the long hallway sported a wreath of traditional red and green, each trying to outdo its neighbor in proclaiming a happy holiday. Behind most of the decorated doors were vacant ghost-quiet offices. The upcoming Noel had scattered politicians to the four corners of the nation and beyond.

"If you change your mind about going," Hank tried once more, "I'm not leaving until the day after tomorrow."

"I'll remember," she promised, knowing full well she'd already made her decision.

In pointed contrast to the deserted offices, Congressman Damon's outer office resembled a beehive of activity with each little bee intent on doing his fair share in the making of the political honey. Two women, one a young blonde, the other a gray-haired grandmotherly type, manned the phones. At a third desk a middle-aged man sat leafing through an interminable list of computer printouts. The man appeared absorbed to the point of being oblivious to his surroundings, Tracy absently thought as she slipped from her coat and made her way to the silver-haired woman who had just recradled the phone.

"Hi. I'm Tracy Kent," she said with the authority her taller-than-usual stature and firm voice always guaranteed. "I'm here for the interview with Congressman Damon."

"He'll be with you in a minute," the woman assured her warmly. "He's clearing up some correspondence that has to go out today."

"No problem," Tracy said, taking a seat to the left of Hank. He had already slumped comfortably and sloppily into a chair.

Taking out a compact, she finger-fluffed her tawny hair. It fell multilayered to just the curve of her shoulders. She rubbed her lips together to evenly smear her peach-tinted gloss then angled the mirror upward to see if her "shy blue" eye shadow had streaked. It would more likely be frozen, she thought scoffingly, noting that her eyes, a bold blue, looked tired. The truth was she wasn't sleeping well. But the real truth was that that wasn't anything new.

"Not bad," Hank whispered, leaning against her and indicating with a raised brow the young blonde who had just moved to a filing cabinet. "She has that Meryl Streep, sorta-tragic look that I'm a sucker for."

Tracy laughed low and prettily. "Which pass are you going to use on her, Romeo?"

Hank rubbed his hand over his bearded cheek and grimaced. "Got to see if she's married first."

"Ah, a man with scruples. In Washington, no less." Despite the fact that Hank was very much a ladies' man, very much a man who lived and partied for the moment, he was, nonetheless, a man of sterling principles. Tracy respected him immensely.

"Watch this," he ordered.

In less than a minute, the young man had approached the young woman, inquired as to the location of the water fountain, which only a blind person could have missed, swallowed a small paper cup of water that he didn't want and reseated himself.

"There is a God," he said through his nearly closed lips. "She isn't married."

"Maybe she's allergic to her wedding ring," Tracy teased. "Or maybe," she added with a deliciously impish grin, "she's studying to be a nun."

"Perish both thoughts," Hank pleaded, "especially the latter."

"Which line do you plan to devastate her with?"

"Do you like the one where I confess my amnesia and can't remember where my apartment is, or the one where I simply walk up and ask her if she'd like to be the mother of my children?"

"I think you need a new repertoire of opening lines. I..."

Suddenly, without warning, the door to the congressman's office burst open. And out stepped Congressman Jay Cole Damon. Tracy's first thought was that the news footage she'd seen of the distinguished politician had failed to capture his dynamic, powerful, life-pulsing presence. Her second thought was that it had also failed to capture his...she sought for a word and had to settle on handsomeness. It was a handsomeness qualified by too square a chin and altogether too prominent cheekbones, but a handsomeness underscored by a perfect nose, a pair of friendly, sensual lips and laugh lines carelessly left behind by the years. Jet-black hair, angled back in a short, casual, no-fuss style, framed his face, and his eyes pierced life with a sharp yet sensitive awareness. She initially concluded that those eyes were black, but as he moved toward her, she was forced to amend that to the darkest brown she'd ever seen, a deep warm brown, a brown as potent as the drink Kahlúa.

"Ms Kent," he acknowledged, extending his hand for a brief but firm greeting, "please forgive the wait. My only excuse is that with the holidays coming, I'm trying to find the top of my desk." The smile he gave her flashed sincere and white in his tanned face. His confidence, though totally unpretentious, fell about him like a mantle, which she felt she could have reached out and touched.

"No need to apologize, Congressman," she replied, wondering how in the world he managed to get so tan in the pale month of December. "Congressman Damon, my photographer, Henry Yeats."

"Hank, sir," the young man corrected, shaking the congressman's hand.

"Hank it is," the politician agreed with another smile. Holding up some letters, he added, "Let me just get rid of these." He divvied up the correspondence between the blond-haired secretary and the man who was poring over the computer printouts. The man asked a question, followed by another and another. Long seconds passed before Cole Damon glanced up sheepishly. "Sorry again. When you're in the throes of a reelection campaign, there's nothing more demanding than a campaign manager." Nodding to the stout gentleman, he said, "This is Larry Seeger." The man stood, and handshakes were exchanged in friendly fashion.

"You look vaguely familiar, Ms Kent," Seeger said. His broad chest was almost equal to his broad waist. His gray eyes pinned her with a studious gaze. "Have we met before?"

At the innocuous question, Tracy's heart thudded against her chest. She had come up against the question more than once since the trial. Toward its sordid and sour end, UPI had picked up the story and syndicated it nationwide. Recognition was something she lived with daily, though she told herself that in time she would regain her anonymity. "No, I don't think so," she replied in a deceptively calm voice.

"I could swear..."

"Admit that your elephant's memory is foggy for once, Larry," the congressman teased.

Tracy felt Cole Damon's hand, large and forceful, at the small of her back and was never so grateful for being nudged out of one room and into another.

The politician's office was a testimony to the man whom Tracy suspected—and the press suggested—him to be. The dark wood paneling hinted at the man's warmth, the carpet in the wear-well color of rust at his practicality, and the expensive royal-blue real-leather furniture at his flamboyance. Two humorous prints, companion pieces, hung on the wall. One of the prints depicted a ratty, ill-kept dog leaning against a newspaper box on the corner of a busy street. The dog on the accompanying caption asks, "Know what day this is?" The second print showed the same dog, scratching his head and replying, "Me neither." She smiled to herself. She liked a man who would put such whimsy on the wall of an office where important world-vital issues were decided; it said something about that man's sense of perspective.

When Tracy dropped her eyes from the prints to the man, she found him seated on the edge of his desk, his long leg thrown casually across the corner.

"Tell me something right up front, Ms Kent," he said, folding his arms across his wide chest. "Are you going to lambaste me for my stand on the MX missile, my unshakable position on the nuclear arms race, or the fact that I voted against the last three tax cuts?" He did a poor job of hiding his smile.

Her own lips twitched. "I have no intention, I assure you, of even tackling those subjects, let alone lambasting you for them."

"Then let me assure you, you are in a minority of two, my mother being the other member."

As Tracy's smile grew wider, Cole thought it was quite the loveliest smile he had ever seen. Except that, somehow, it was incongruous with the tiny hint of sadness in her blue eyes.

"What did you have in mind in the way of an interview?" he asked seriously.

Instantly Tracy sobered. "As you know, I'm a freelancer, working primarily for political magazines. The *Political Monitor* is running a series of interviews on the East Coast candidates seeking reelection next year. I've been assigned to interview several of them, yourself included. What my boss wants is a look at the men and women making national policy. I'm not so much interested in the politics of the person as the person himself, although I realize you really can't separate the two."

"Sounds good," Cole agreed. "What do I do?"

"I thought we'd start with some pics and get them out of the way so Hank can go ahead and leave."

"Fine. Tell me what you want."

Hank was as competent and skilled as Tracy, and he had prepared his camera during the conversational exchange. "What about starting with the usual desk shot?" the photographer suggested.

Tracy agreed, but when Cole rolled down the upturned sleeves of his brown-and-white striped shirt then started to recenter the askew knot of his tie and grab the beige coat that perfectly matched his slacks, she halted him. "No, I like that casual, 'I caught you doing your job' look. What do you think, Hank?"

"Great!" the photographer replied.

Tracy watched as Hank coaxed picture after picture from the congressman. Most of the shots would be culled for the best two or three, which was a shame, she concluded, since she knew all of them would be good. Hank had that rare ability with a camera that could make anyone look photogenic. But then, Congressman Damon wouldn't need a whole lot of help. Glancing over just as the camera recorded the politician selecting a book from the wall-to-ceiling bookcase behind his desk, she noted that his hair had a slight tendency to curl, giving his face, if caught at the right angle, a boyish charm. And yet, a small inner voice added, there was nothing even remotely boyish about the strong, ultramasculine build of the man, which was well over six feet.

Ten minutes later saw the end of the photo session, and Hank took his leave, whispering to Tracy as he left that he thought he'd try the amnesia routine on the blonde in the outer office. Tracy mouthed "good luck" as she retrieved her notes from the briefcase.

"Nice guy," Cole commented.

"The best," she agreed.

Cole had once again circled the desk to perch on its edge in sprawled leisure.

Tracy deliberately forced her eyes from the arrestingly handsome picture he made. She wished that he had stayed behind the desk. A safe distance from her. Safe? *"What a ridiculous thought,"* she chided herself. And yet, he did threaten her in a way no man had in a long while. He had the audacity, sitting there with his healthy, vibrant good looks and his obvious virility—his leg, hooked across the desk's edge, stretched the pant's fabric tightly across his maleness—to remind her that she was a woman. And that was the last thing she wanted to be—a woman with normal sexual feelings. She swallowed hard and realized two things simultaneously.

The room had grown embarrassingly quiet, and Congressman Damon was staring at her. She took refuge in her notes. Clearing her throat, she checked the volume button on the small tape recorder she had asked his permission to use.

"Congressman Damon, everyone knows that you're a Pennsylvanian, that you're the youngest of three children, that your father, now deceased, was a distinguished humanities professor at Penn State. Everyone knows about your unquestionable ethics. Some say you're the greatest orator the Hill has seen in fifty years. Tell me something about Congressman Jay Cole Damon that the readers of the *Political Monitor* don't know."

He had sat enthralled by her dexterous delivery and by the way her peach-colored sweater outlined her breasts, wondering when the question would come and about its nature once it did. He smiled inwardly. He liked her style. This promised to be more than the usually boring interview. But then he'd known there was nothing usual or boring about Tracy Kent the moment he'd set eyes on her.

"Something the public doesn't know," he repeated, pondering a response. "That's difficult to say without some thought. So much has been written about me. About all politicians," he quickly qualified, injecting some humility into the comment.

"Some little something, Congressman," she urged. "Like maybe you have a penchant for eating chocolate-covered ants. Or maybe you like Garbo movies."

He trailed his hand over his cheek and jaw, which even at this late hour of the afternoon showed little trace of shadow. "Rain," he said suddenly, softly. "I like to walk in the rain."

One of Tracy's brows rose higher than the other. "Interesting. And what do you think that says about you?"

His full lips curved upward to a rakish elevation. "That I'm all wet?"

The melodious laugh she gave reminded him of breeze-tossed wind chimes.

"I'm sure your opposition would find no fault with your assessment," she said.

"No, I'm sure they wouldn't," he concurred, adding, "What do you think it says about me?"

She looked slightly caught off guard. "This is my interview," she reminded him with a smile. "I get to ask the questions."

"Aw, come on, Ms Kent, play fair. What's one question compared to all of yours?" He had once again folded his arms across his chest and sat with what looked like a challenge written all over his square-angled face. The tiny wrinkles fringing his eyes arched slightly as if in anticipation of a teasing grin.

She shrugged. "All right." Tilting her head slightly to the side in a way that caused her hair to fall forward curtainlike from behind her ear, she said, "I suppose it means you're sensitive...." She paused, groping for another word. "And sensual...I mean," Tracy quickly added, "as in appealing to the five senses, which rain certainly does. It could also mean you're romantic as in passionate, adventurous, idealistic. Of course," she added, her eyes now sparkling with teasing, "it might mean only that you have a death wish for pneumonia."

The masculine laugh he gave sounded full bodied, rich and pleasant. *Maybe too pleasant*, she thought.

"Let's see if we can't get to a more serious question," she said quickly, guiding the interview back to its purpose. She crossed one brown-booted leg over the other. In the process, her skirt rose above her knee. The action did not go unnoticed by Cole, but he forced his attention back to what she was asking. "Why should your fellow Pennsylvanians send you back to Washington for another term?"

She deserved a thoughtful answer, and the man who eased from the desk edge and walked to stare out the window at the cold darkening winter view was a man searching for the right words. He slipped both his hands into his pants pockets. Without turning around, he said, "Because I care. I care about Pennsylvania. And I care about the nation. And I'm good at being a congressman." He glanced over his shoulder. "In fact, I'm damned good."

Knowing his impeccable, achievement-oriented history, Tracy couldn't argue with his skill. And even if she hadn't known his track record, the conviction with which Cole had just announced that he was a good congressman would have persuaded her to doubt it not in the least.

"Some of your colleagues call you a conservative liberal," she continued. "How do you respond to that?"

He turned to face her. The eyes that found hers were dark and sincere. "I say they're right."

"What is a conservative liberal?"

"A conservative liberal, Ms Kent, is someone who supports a government program to give away gray pin-striped suits to the needy."

She had been expecting a serious answer, and when she heard his reply, a ripple of near-girlish laughter escaped her lips. Tracy wondered when she had last laughed so openly and unconsciously. Maybe not in two years. She decided it felt good.

Cole Damon watched and listened as the tinkling laughter bubbled up and spilled out of her lovely sensuous lips. Why did he have the feeling that such spontaneous laughter was foreign to her? Or at least limited? As surreptitiously as he could, he checked her ring finger. *Not married. How in the world could such a looker not be married? How could someone with hair the color of honey and the texture of new-spun silk be unattached? How could someone with eyes the empyrean blue of a virgin springtime sky not have a doting husband?*

The hour sped smoothly by. Questions were asked and answered, some of a controversial nature, but true to Tracy's word, most were confined to the personal realm. Cole answered fairly and honestly and oftentimes with humor. Tracy felt that, unlike some politicians whom she had interviewed, Cole Damon held nothing back. But then, the man obviously had nothing to hide. No hint of any scandal mired his reputation.

"Two more questions," she said at last. "One political, the other personal."

"Let's start with the political," he said, leaning against the desk with his trim buttocks, his long legs stretched out before him and crossed at the ankles.

"All right. What's the biggest passion of your political life? What do you want to accomplish above all else?"

"That's easy. I want to see something done for the farmers of this country. I want to see legislation enacted that's going to ease their financial burden. They work long hard hours—sunup to sundown—and for the most part, if they're lucky, they manage to scrape by. And increasing numbers of them aren't even doing that anymore. Foreign markets are disappearing, land values are diminishing, banks are refusing to extend loans, while the auctioneer's hammer is falling on land and buildings held for generations by the same families. These are men and women who feed this country—you and me—and a sizable portion of the world." He pushed himself restlessly from the desk's edge and dragged his hands to his hips, almost in a fighting pose. "If we don't stop this gross inequity, Ms Kent, we're..." He suddenly halted, a sheepish smile molding his mouth. "I'm sorry. You hit a raw nerve."

There was something about his sincerity, something about his smile, a smile she'd have labeled irresistible and all-out masculine, that warmed her. "You sound as though you have a personal interest in farm crisis," she said softly, knowing intuitively that he did.

His brown eyes merged with her blue. "I do. This isn't for publication, but I have an uncle who's losing the shirt off his work-stooped back."

"I'm sorry."

"Yeah, me, too," he added broodingly.

Seconds slipped by before she spoke again. "One last question, Congressman. It's common knowledge that your wife died in an automobile accident two years ago."

At the words, Cole's eyes faded to a dull umber, the brown of a washed-out sepia photograph. "I never talk about my wife." His tone was not harsh, but it was unswervingly resolute.

Knowing that his reticence on the subject was almost a religion with him, Tracy had anticipated his reply. "Let me ask the question, then if you still prefer not to answer, I'll accept your decision."

Cole hesitated before nodding his silent, though leery, acquiescence.

"You've been seen escorting some of the loveliest ladies in Washington. And every now and then there's been a provocative rumor. Why haven't you remarried, Congressman?"

At the realization that the question actually had nothing to do with his wife, Cole's easy mood returned. "Contrary to the old adage that politics makes strange bedfellows, it sometimes doesn't make them at all," he said, a smile once again playing around his mouth. Then his brow puckered in thought. "To be as honest as I can, escorting isn't the same as dating and romancing. It isn't getting to know a woman. I mean, really know her in a way that leads to marriage. I've been busy with politics. I just haven't had the time. And no woman has ever seemed so important that I've voluntarily set the time aside." His dazzling smile reappeared. "When, and if, the time is right, who knows what will happen?"

It was the perfect upbeat conclusion to the interview. As she gathered up her things, Tracy expressed her thanks for his time. When she started to slip back into her coat, she instantly felt Cole's hands guiding it over her shoulders. His touch was firm...disconcerting...the way that an attractive man's touch is always disconcerting to a woman. She pulled away as quickly as decorum permitted.

Cole wondered if he'd imagined her reaction. He decided he had. "Lousy weather out," he commented, "and it looks as though it's getting worse."

"Hank said that if we had any sense, we'd be in Tahiti where the women don't wear no tops."

Cole laughed. "I just got back from a few days in Martinique, and I could be persuaded to return."

"Martinique?" Tracy asked with real interest. "I was on the island about six years ago and loved it. I was there on assignment for a travel magazine. I always said one of these days I'd go back." She deliberately avoided thinking of how hard she'd tried to persuade her fiancé to go there for their honeymoon. Instead, the married couple had spent the weekend in the Poconos, trudging through snow rather than basking in golden warmth. "Are there still thousands of poinsettias growing wild on the hillsides?" Her voice suddenly had an almost childlike quality to it.

"Yeah," he said, again slipping a hand into his pocket. "A beautiful red, splashed everywhere."

Tracy smiled as if pleased at the continuity of the poinsettias, a continuity that hadn't been repeated in her marriage. A pause interrupted what had gone from a business meeting to a personal conversation. Why did she suddenly feel so awkward? And why was he looking at her with those liquid-brown eyes? "That explains your tan," she said self-consciously.

He smiled again, his eyes still on her. "Yeah, compliments of the Caribbean sun."

"Your tan looks good," she said, instantly regretting the rambling, personal remark. She grabbed her briefcase. "Well, thank you again, Congressman Damon."

"Call me Cole."

She nodded, spraying tawny hair about her shoulders. "Thank you again, Cole. I appreciate the interview."

She had barely reached the door when he spoke. "Tracy?" She turned to face him. "Could I, uh...could I buy you a drink?" At the sudden and obvious look of distress that flashed across her face, he quickly added, "Look, I didn't mean to offend you."

"You didn't offend me."

"You're not wearing a ring. I assumed you weren't married."

"I'm not. I'm divorced," she said. "I've been divorced over a year." *Why have I told him that? It has nothing to do with anything. Certainly nothing to do with him.*

"Then can I buy you a drink?" he repeated.

"No!" she said in a rush and without much tact. "I mean, I'm busy. I already have plans."

It was a lie, and he knew it was a lie. How could a woman who had exuded such confidence moments before in the performance of her job become such a basket case when dealing with her personal life? If the idea weren't so ludicrous, he could almost believe his offer had frightened her. "Maybe another time," he suggested.

She nodded, but he suspected that the gesture was a mute lie, as well.

He then said the only thing left to say. "Merry Christmas, Tracy."

For some reason he couldn't even begin to fathom, and one he pondered long after she'd left, his best wishes for her holiday seemed to distress her more than his asking her out.

CHAPTER TWO

IT HAD BEEN DELIBERATE. Tracy knew that her mother had purposely avoided calling her on December 22. She also knew that it had strained every fiber of her mother's staunch, disciplined nature not to make the long-distance call from Trenton, New Jersey, to Washington, D.C., but it was a restraint Tracy silently thanked her for. The solitude had helped her get through the day with a quiet though sometimes panic-edged dignity.

And truly, what would the two of them have said had they spoken that day? Certainly not what was on their minds. Her mother never would have said how sorry she was that her only daughter had been raped two years before on that infamous day, nor would the woman have expressed her anger at the trial's unfair verdict or her sorrow at her daughter's husband's being unable to cope with the tragedy. And Tracy never would have said that the painful memories still haunted her, but that the wound had now ceased to fester. Yes, Tracy knew it had been deliberate.

She also knew that the question her mother had just asked on the telephone that early Christmas afternoon had a deeper meaning than its surface value. "Are you having a nice Christmas?" translated to "Are you getting through it all right?"

"I'm having a lovely Christmas, Mother," Tracy responded. That translated to "I'm getting through the ordeal fine."

"Have you opened your presents?" the older woman asked.

Tracy glanced over at the ripped and ravaged paper and bows strewn about the small Christmas tree. "Yes, I just opened them," she said. "Thanks for everything." She tried to make her voice sound as light as the flakes of snow drifting past the large bay window and white-coating the yew hedge that formed the house's front border.

"I'll keep your presents the family brought with them, and you can have a second Christmas when you come home." The unspoken question was "When are you coming?"

Tracy smiled faintly at her mother's obviousness. "I'll be home in a few weeks, Mother. But only for a weekend. Okay?"

"We want you anytime you can come and for however long," Mrs. Kent said. "I'll fix that Italian cream cake you like."

"I don't need the pounds," Tracy groaned out of habit, knowing full well a little extra weight wouldn't look offensive on her slim five-feet-eight-inch frame. Eating alone had never appealed to her, and ever since the divorce, she'd skipped meals on a regular basis or simply skimped on them by snacking.

"I'll make it calorie-free."

"Sure you will, Mom."

"You did have turkey for dinner?" her mother asked suddenly, as if the thought of her daughter not having a traditional Christmas meal bordered on blasphemy.

"Yes, Mother," she answered. "I had turkey." She thought of the cardboard-tasting food she'd eaten, or at least picked at, and knew her mother would be mortified if she knew Christmas turkey had come in the form of a frozen TV dinner.

"Good," Mrs. Kent proclaimed, as if greatly relieved. There was a slight pause before her mother spoke again. "Everyone misses you, Tracy. And everyone says hello."

A lump the size of a fist formed in Tracy's throat. "I miss everyone. And tell everybody I said hi."

There was another pause, this one longer. "Tracy..." *Oh, God,* Tracy thought, her eyes shut in protest, *please don't let her say something that's going to crack the thin shell of my composure.*

"...we love you."

A warm moistness stung Tracy's eyes. "I love all of you," she managed to get out fairly normally.

"Hold on, hon, your dad wants to talk to you."

A grappling noise traveled the miles as the phone exchanged hands. In the process, Tracy heard her mother call a belated goodbye. She also heard what she thought was her mother's sniff as though the other woman, too, were fighting tears.

"Tracy, gal," William Kent's voice boomed into the line, "you taking care of yourself?"

She nodded. "Yes, Daddy." She had often wondered why she had outgrown calling her mother the more juvenile *mommy,* but had never managed to grow up enough to follow suit with her father. She doubted she'd ever be that much of an adult.

"Sure could use you here to help corral these little hellions." Tracy knew the "little hellions" were the proverbial apples of their grandfather's eye. "Jason has already smushed two chocolate-covered cherries in his sister's hair, and Nancy tried to put the cat in curlers.''

Tracy couldn't help but laugh. ''You've got to be stern.''

''I would be stern if I could catch them.'' He hesitated. ''You all right, Tracy? I mean, really all right?''

''Yes, I'm really all right.''

''You ought to be here with us,'' he proclaimed gruffly.

''Next year,'' she promised.

A silence ensued and became so heavy that Tracy thought she would collapse under its weight.

''Tracy...''

She thought she heard his voice crack. *No, no, don't let him say anything! Not the man whose control made the Rock of Gibraltar look unstable!* ''Look, there's someone at my door,'' she lied. ''I've got to go, Daddy.'' A lone tear eased from the corner of her eye.

William Kent cleared his throat. ''You get yourself home soon.''

''Yes, Daddy. 'Bye, Daddy.''

Tracy swiped at the solitary tear with the heel of her hand as she stared at the recradled phone. A sudden sense of loneliness threatened to crush her now that the vocal umbilical cord had been severed, and she struggled against the strong childlike urge to re-dial the number and listen to the comforting voices of her parents once again. Maybe she should have gone home for Christmas, she reasoned, but instantly reminded herself that she had rehashed the issue a thousand times before deciding to spend the holiday quietly. Besides, she told herself, it was too late for recriminations. Christmas Day was half over.

So far she had handled the holiday wonderfully well, Tracy praised herself as she stooped to gather up the discarded wrapping paper and ribbon. Of course, she had worked the last three days until she was ready to drop, but she had survived...coped...made it through the dark days and the darker nights.

And that's exactly what she'd continue to do, stay busy and survive, she vowed as her tricolored shoes, which matched exactly the blue, ivory, and rose of her pullover sweater, took first one step then another on the straight stairway leading to her upstairs bedroom-office. She had one more interview to write up—the last of the reelection pieces she'd been commissioned to do—and now was a perfect time. Then she'd take a walk in the flurrying snow as her reward.

Seating herself in the yellow velvet chair, which subtly accented the predominately pale-blue bedroom, Tracy turned on her tape recorder and within seconds her own voice filled the room.

"Congressman Damon, everyone knows that you're a Pennsylvanian, that you're the youngest of three children..." She finished the question and a significant pause followed before Cole Damon's voice, strong and electric, dominated the bedroom. At the sound of his rich masculine voice, a clear and quite vivid image of the black-haired dark-eyed congressman flashed before Tracy's mental eye. For a fleeting second, she wondered how he was spending Christmas.

Four hours later, when the clock on the desk read six thirty-eight, she rolled the last page of the profile from the typewriter, quickly proofed it and stacked it with the other pages. She slipped the article into a manila folder and addressed the bundle to Nathan Jeter at the *Political Monitor*. If she was any judge of her work, the piece on Congressman Jay Cole Damon was good. She had asked good questions; he had given good answers.

Could I buy you a drink?

Tracy's hand paused in delivering the folder to the mail basket. He had startled her by asking her out. He must have thought her reaction to his benign question totally abnormal. In truth, it had been. She had acted as if he had just asked her to dive off a high cliff into a narrow channel of water. She sighed. Well, in a way, that's exactly what he had asked of her. Since the . . . say it, Tracy, she ordered herself . . . since the rape and the subsequent end of her marriage, she had shied away from men. Not as much out of fear of being violated again—though it was true that she had never really again felt safe in her home—as out of uncertainty, an uncertainty as to what her reaction to a man would be should any kind of intimacy develop. And equally, what his reaction to her would be if he were to find out what had happened to her. It all boiled down to one thing. She wasn't ready to start dating again. And maybe she never would be.

She just wished she hadn't made a fool of herself with Cole Damon, for surely that was what he thought her to be.

Changing into her boots and slipping into her heavy hooded coat, she headed downstairs. She worked her fingers into warm woolen gloves and wrapped a fringed plaid scarf about her neck. Pulling the hood up to cover her hair, her face framed by soft white fur, she picked a careful path down the snow-blanketed kitchen steps and out into the already darkening early evening. Maybe a brisk walk down the block would help her find an appetite.

By the old and lonely and now leafless oak tree at the end of the drive, Tracy turned her face skyward, letting the white fleecy flakes settle on her nose, cheeks and chin. For a moment she pretended that yesterday's hurt had never happened and that tomorrow's uncertainty was light-years away. Just for a moment, Tracy pretended she was as pure as the snow dancing around her.

COLE DAMON raised his face to the fast-falling snow, hoping the nettling cold would numb his mind as it was numbing his body. He exhaled a weary sigh that instantly vaporized into a frosty cloud in the Pennsylvania air. The past few days, which he'd spent in Philadelphia with his mother, his two sisters and their families, had been nice, a treat that was getting harder and harder to cash in on. But that Christmas day, the most holy day of the year, had been nothing short of a bitch.

Late yesterday he had flown into Lancaster, where he still retained a farm that had been in his mother's family for nearly two hundred years. The eighty acres, with its two-storied square-columned white clapboard house, had become his own personal retreat from political pressures. He had crossed the state with two objectives in mind. He had wanted to spend some time alone, and he wanted to visit his uncle. Phone calls from Larry Seeger—each necessary to the reelection campaign—had smashed his hope of quietude. As for visiting his uncle, that had worked out, but, oh, how he wished it hadn't.

Cole jammed his hands farther into the pockets of his sheepskin coat and trudged off in the direction of the white barn, which had an A-shaped roof. While he didn't profess to have any training in psychology, he did, however, have enough common sense to know that Dale Schurman, his "Uncle Chigger," was in the throes of a black depression. Cole's lips tightened into a grim line as he thought of the man he'd just had dinner with. He knew that it had taken all of his uncle's courage to swallow his Lancastrian pride and tell his favorite nephew that it looked as if he wasn't going to be able to hold on to the back hundred acres of his dairy farm. Without those precious acres, there'd be no pastureland for his cattle. For a man who once said that he'd suckled the work ethic from his mother's breast, the thought of bankruptcy was repellent. As was the fact that his finances were already so depleted that he'd given his three grandchildren nothing for Christmas. It was that fact that had really broken his spirit. The man was fighting not only for his life but also for his dignity. And it was a battle both he and Cole knew he'd eventually lose—the way hundreds of other small farmers would lose similar battles.

Damn, but life was unfair!

Cole slid back the bolt on the barn's door and, slipping inside, pulled the door shut behind him. It took his eyes thirty seconds or so to adjust to the darker atmosphere. As they did, his other senses bombarded him with their keen assessment of his environment. His nose picked up earth smells, combined with the scent of hay and horse, while his ears telegraphed to his brain a slight whinnying sound and the rattle of a tin pail as it toppled over. Making his way to the far stall, Cole pulled open the door and stepped inside ... only to be greeted by a warm velvet nose.

"Hey, girl," he crooned as his hand patted the white irregular-shaped spot on the horse's forehead, the only break in the mare's otherwise rich chestnut color. The spot, recalling Shakespeare's "Out, out, damned spot..." had been responsible for the horse's name of Lady Macbeth. "Hungry?" Cole inquired, stroking the length of the animal's warm, lean body.

Looking for the oats Petey Jernigan had told him he'd find by the stall door, Cole issued up a proper meal and placed it before the ravenous mare. Cole had given the caretaker the day off, knowing he himself would be there to carry out what chores had to be done despite the holiday. Petey had expressed his profuse gratitude for the unexpected Christmas present, telling Cole he planned to spend the day with his girlfriend in Neffsville. Cole smiled slightly. Petey Jernigan, wet and with a full meal stored in his stomach, weighed all of a hundred ten pounds, while his girlfriend, if it were the one he'd courted for fifteen years without a serious commitment, weighed at least three-fifty.

Finding the wall of the stall with his back, Cole slid his body downward to sit on the soft hay covering the foor. His blue-jeaned legs bent, his spine slumped, he watched the horse's mouth circularly chew at the oats. After a while, Cole grabbed a strand of the hay and slipped it past his own lips, gnawing gently on the flavorless reed.

Somewhere in his mind, he imagined the ghostlike laughter of a young child. He unconsciously grimaced. If his wife hadn't died, with their son in her womb, he'd have someone to share this Christmas with. A beautiful, almost-two-year-old son. But . . . Dammit, *but* was a big word. Almost as big as *if*. If he and Lisa hadn't quarreled, she might never have left the house that April night, might never have lost control of the car, might not have died. And neither would have their son. But they *had* quarreled, and she *had* left. And she *had* died. And so had their beautiful, never-to-be child.

Okay, Damon, he asked himself, why don't you wallow in self-pity? Why don't you dredge up every miserable thing that's ever happened to you to worsen this already lousy day? He exhaled a long breath of air. Why don't you do yourself a favor, Congressman? Why don't you ease up on your own case? Why don't you scout your brain for a pleasant thought?

His brain surprised him with its offering. The image was tall, with a graceful statuesqueness. She had honey-tinted hair and eyes the blue color of a clear cloudless sky. The offering was named Tracy Kent. His lips pursed in thought, but at the same time his ego reminded him that she had turned down his offer of a drink. Turned him down cold. And that, no conceit intended, hadn't happened to him too many times. In fact, the number of aggressive women whom he'd turned down—women bewitched by his political career—far exceeded those who had rejected him. Then, there was the other type of woman, private and basically shy, who wanted no part of the life of a man whose every visit to the bathroom was reported by the press. But for some reason he didn't think that was why Tracy Kent had refused him. The more he thought about it, the more he thought his initial reaction was right. It had something to do with fear, not a scream-out-your-lungs kind of fear, but a subtle, insidious, low-grade fear that coiled snakelike inside, always threatening to strike but never making good the promise. He didn't understand the cause of her fear, but he knew it intrigued him. Almost as much as the woman.

The horse nuzzling her nose against his chest brought Cole back from his reverie. Stroking the animal's head, he said, "You're a lady. Think I ought to give Ms Kent another chance?" Lady Macbeth neighed a response that Cole interpreted in the affirmative. "Yeah, why not? Give her the opportunity to turn me down twice."

Minutes later, as he tracked a path through the ankle-deep drifts of snow toward the house, Cole wondered where Tracy was spending the holiday. And with whom. He grunted. Wherever and with whomever, he'd bet money she was having a better day than he was.

As if to once more mock him, his mind imagined again the trill of childish laughter. A laughter that would have been an almost two-year-old's.

WHEN TRACY FIRST heard the sound, she thought it was the laughter of a child but then realized that the shrill noise, wafting from across the street, came from a woman being playfully pursued by a man. The couple—in their early twenties, she guessed—was engaged in a ritual as old as man, woman, and snow. A ball of the frosty dust in his hand, the man circled, stalking the woman, who now held her own snowball threatening retaliation should he be so imprudent as to hurl his at her. Her warning sounded peculiarly weak, punctuated as it was with shrieks and giggles.

Finally, the man threw his snowy weapon, hitting the woman in the chest. Laughing hysterically, she lobbed her own shot and tried to run. The man tackled her and brought her none too gently to the ground. By now, both were laughing and mumbling words Tracy couldn't understand. A bit of scuffling occurred before the man pinned the woman with his solid body. His head lowered to capture the woman's lips. Tracy looked away.

The scene had upset her. She probed her mind for a reason and could settle on only one. She was lonely. The year she had been divorced stood as a poor uncomforting ratio to the six years she had been married. She had grown accustomed to companionship, to shared intimacies, to long walks and short arguments. She had grown accustomed to Dennis Webber.

Oh, Dennis, her soul cried, *why couldn't you have trusted me? Why couldn't you have loved me enough?*

The snow had increased and now fell to earth with a curtaining thickness. Tracy didn't notice, however, nor did she notice that she had begun to retrace her steps back home. She was aware of nothing except the strong, treacherous pull of the past.

The rape. It had been frightening, dewomanizing, and totally dehumanizing. It had made her feel dirty, soiled, unclean. It had made her feel anger, shame, guilt and fear. It had changed her life.

When she had first opened the door on that December 22 two years before, she had been surprised to see the blond-haired man. She instantly recognized him as someone who worked at the television station her husband partly owned. She had seen him at some of WRAP's social functions, had even spoken to him briefly at the Christmas party the week before and knew that his name was Paul Something-or-other. She concluded, and erroneously so, that Dennis had sent him. She invited him in. Almost immediately she noticed the man's agitation. He was upset about something. She questioned him subtly and discovered that he and Dennis had fought. Dennis, whose temper was well-known and carefully avoided, had raked him over the coals in front of others about a slipup. Paul Something-or-other was angry, hurt, humiliated. And he wanted to anger, hurt and humiliate someone else. He couldn't hurt Dennis, so he would hurt his wife.

When Paul's intentions became clear, Tracy tried to reason with him. When that failed, she begged him. When that failed, she fought him. God, he hadn't looked that heavy, that strong! But when he threatened her with a knife—and Tracy had believed fervently that he meant to use it—a strong survival instinct claimed her, and she did the only thing she could. She withdrew into herself. Covering her eyes with her hands, as if so doing would remove her from the scene, she'd been still, almost catatonically still, and allowed the man to do what he wanted with her. The woman on the living room floor looked like Tracy Kent Webber, but she wasn't. Tracy Kent Webber was the woman hanging frantically, and as if it were her lifeline to reality, on to every word of the six o'clock news as it filtered into the room from WRAP via the television in the den.

Over her assailant's harsh ragged breathing that moistened her ear, she heard her husband's strong, pleasant, anchorman's voice telling the WRAP viewers about some heartwarming story of holiday generosity within the community. As Paul Something-or-other speared her body, Dennis wished his audience a warm good-evening, and the strains of "Joy to the World" replaced the usual music marking the show's end. Even in her nerve-dead state, Tracy recognized the supreme irony and fought hysterical laughter. She had been raped while she listened to her husband's evening news broadcast by an employee who was angry with him.

She barely realized when Paul disjoined his sweaty body from hers. She barely saw the dazed look on his face, as if he couldn't believe what he'd just done. She barely heard him mumbling words that sounded remarkably like an apology. She had lain there on the carpeted floor for long minutes, her body jerking in nervous spasms, her teeth clashing like ivory cymbals, her heart threatening to jump from her chest. Finally clear thought returned. When it did, she fought with every ounce of her strength to keep from rushing to the shower—God, how she wanted to wash the feel of him from her! Instead, she called the police and asked them to meet her at the hospital. She then called Dennis.

As she submitted to an emergency room examination that consisted largely of semen collection, she thought how lucky she was, lucky that she was on the pill and lucky that Paul Something-or-other hadn't physically hurt her beyond his roughness. In another ridiculous irony, she later wished he had harmed her in some tangible way. Maybe then Dennis would have believed her.

The trial had been short and decidedly not sweet. At least for Tracy. Paul maintained that he had, indeed, engaged in sexual activity with Mrs. Webber—but only because she had coerced him into it. He had seen her several times at WRAP, and ever since the station's Christmas party—here, he blushed with the right amount of embarrassed humility—she had refused to leave him alone. She had made a nuisance of herself calling him. He had wanted no part of the scene, but Mrs. Webber had threatened to have him fired if he didn't come to her apartment that afternoon and, since he had had several altercations with Dennis Webber recently, he couldn't take a chance. He needed the job too badly.

He had cried. He had broken down and cried with a sincerity that would have caused even Tracy to doubt herself if she hadn't known the truth. And the sobbing of his mother and his pregnant wife had carried through the courtroom, reaching and touching every tender ear. Paul had lied. Of course, he had lied. But oh, so convincingly.

The jury had found Paul Nelson Bolden innocent. Tracy became a woman with a past. The press had had a field day.

Tracy stumbled blindly up the steps of the house, almost slipping on a patch of ice forming just at the kitchen door.

"Damn!" she cried, grabbing the door frame to steady herself.

Moving gingerly, she stepped closer and unlocked two dead bolts. Another two locks guarded the front door, while all of the apartment's windows were nailed partially closed. Throwing open the door, she moved inside. She was so cold! So cold she thought she'd never again be warm. But it was a coldness that transcended the physical sensation. It was a coldness of heart, a frigidity of soul. Mechanically, she removed her coat, gloves and neck scarf.

Within minutes, and all the while shivering, she built a fire in the living room's beige-bricked hearth. Kneeling before the nascent yellow and red tongues of flame, Tracy splayed her hands out to their warmth. Better. She felt better. At long last, she eased herself down to sit before the fireplace on the apricot-and moss-green oriental rug, and dragged her knees to just below her chin. Pinioning her legs with the band of her arms, she sat staring into the brilliantly colored blaze.

She had thought that fateful day in court that she could never be hurt again and that the rape and the unfair verdict had rendered her immune to pain. She had been wrong.

"Why, Dennis?" she spoke softly into the crackling fire. "Why couldn't you have believed in me?" Against her will, her mind raced back to the sunny June afternoon when she had ceased to truly live.

For months after the rape and the trial, she had kept going only with the support of her friends and family. Everyone wrapped her in a protective cocoon of love and understanding, everyone tried to help her deal with her feeling of having lost control of her life, and everyone shared her shock and anger at the jury's verdict. How could anyone have believed her guilty of such ludicrous charges? Though unusually quiet, Dennis seemed to offer a kind of support, too, although he made no move toward reestablishing any intimacy with her. She assumed it was in consideration of her feelings. Her emotions were raw and in turmoil. While on the one hand she increasingly longed for her husband's touch, the thought of it frightened her. What would be her reaction to the physical act that had once seemed so natural and lovely to her? Enough was enough, she had told herself finally. Life went on. Dennis had needs. And he had been so patient.

Easing to her knees on the bed beside her husband where he lay watching the end of the show credits scroll by on a golf tournament, she had begun to slowly unbutton her shirt. She refused to pay any heed to the slight trembling of her fingers.

When the delicate motion of her hands caught his attention, Dennis Webber spoke. Roughly. "What are you doing?"

The shirt unbuttoned, she pulled it from the waist of her jeans and over her shoulders. Dropping it to the floor, she moved her fingers to the front clasp of her lacy bra.

"Make love to me," she whispered. It was a silken-clothed plea.

The bra unsnapped with a sound that seemed inordinately loud, and the wispy bit of lace brazenly came away to fall beside the shirt.

At the sight of his wife's full round breasts, Dennis Webber's breath caught in his throat. Although he still made no move to touch her, Tracy saw the familiar flicker of desire. She felt her own heighten.

Their eyes locked, the pale blue of his meeting the darker blue of hers. Right that moment, with the blue eyes and golden hair that made him look like a Nordic god, he was more handsome, more desirable, than she could ever remember him being. And God, how she loved him!

"Help me, Dennis," she pleaded. "Help me to love you."

He made no move toward her.

Slowly she dragged the zipper of her jeans downward, twisting her slim hips from the denim's confines. She watched him watch her as she slowly guided the brief panties from her firm thighs and long legs.

For what seemed an eternity, she stood naked before him—physically and emotionally stripped.

"What do you want from me, Tracy?" he barked suddenly. Jerking up a cigarette from the bedside table, he slid from the bed and moved to stand before the window.

Startled, staring at his back, she answered, "I want to make love."

He didn't respond right away. When he did, she wished he hadn't. "Well, maybe I don't. I can't just tumble into bed like nothing's happened. I can't just conveniently forget you've been with another man." His voice held a note of sickening disgust.

Tracy felt the sharp talons of unreality gashing at her tender composure. "I wasn't with another man out of choice."

"The act is the same regardless of the intent."

A shaft of red-hot anger shot through her body. "If you think that..."

He whirled toward her. "Physically it's the same!"

Tracy searched her mind for a response, but her brain was too muddled to decide on anything. *Please don't do this to me,* she wanted to beg, but even those words she couldn't get out. She told herself that in a moment the nightmare would end. As she watched the face of her husband, however, his mouth slashing his face in a too-serious line and his blue eyes looking not warm and inviting, but cold and unapproachable, she knew she *was* facing reality. For the first time in their marriage, she reached for the bedspread to hide her nakedness.

Looking at her, something momentarily softened in her husband's voice. It even held a note of sad apology. "I don't think I can hack it." He stubbed out the hardly touched cigarette. "I just don't think I can hack it, Tracy."

"What is there for *you* to hack?" she asked, furious. "*I'm* the one who went through hell. I was the one who was raped."

"Were you?" he asked, his voice likewise sharp with emotion.

"What?"

"Were you raped?" His voice now sounded raw with the need for denial.

"What's that supposed to mean?" she asked in a bewildered whisper.

"C'mon, Tracy. You understand English. Were you raped or did you give it to him?" Then he spat out, "You did spend a helluva lot of time talking to pretty boy at that Christmas party. Was he right? Did you force him to go to bed with you?" He tunneled his fingers through his hair in a wild gesture. "For God's sake, Tracy, I've got to know."

A coldness that she would grow to know more intimately in the following months washed over her in glacial sheets, nearly chilling the life from her.

"Dammit, Tracy, tell me! Was the verdict a just one?"

Tracy's world spun wildly and crashed at her feet. The room grew quiet, except for the forgotten TV. When she spoke, she was surprised by the calmness of her voice. "I won't dignify that with an answer. Not to anyone. Especially not my husband."

For horribly long seconds, they stared at each other. Finally, Dennis turned back to the window and braced his hand against its frame.

With a sense of desolation, she asked, "Do you want a divorce?" As it had been during the rape and the trial, the real Tracy Kent Webber was standing some distance away, watching the woman impeccably impersonating her.

He hesitated. "I don't know."

She did not hesitate. "Well, I do."

Wrapped in a bedspread and a regal dignity she was totally unaware of, she had slipped from the bed…and out of Dennis Webber's life.

That had been over a year ago.

Tracy watched as the mature flames greedily devoured the logs, the noise of the fire piercing the solitude. Her arms were still draped almost protectively about her legs, and she began to unconsciously rock. Silent tears coursed down her cheeks and chin, dripping unnoticed onto her knees where they soaked into the wool of her pants. There she sat, the bitter past her only companion, rocking and crying, crying and rocking, long into the Christmas night.

CHAPTER THREE

TRACY GRABBED THE PHONE on its fourth shrill ring and in the middle of scribbling the word *noodles*.

"Hello?" She extended the coiled ivory cord as far as it would reach and reseated herself at the kitchen table, where she hastily scribbled the *les* to the *nood* and tucked the grocery list in her shoulder bag.

"Tracy?"

"Oh, hi, Nathan," she answered, recognizing the voice as belonging to the editor of the *Political Monitor*. "How are you?"

"Fine. How are you?"

"Good."

"How was your holiday?"

Hesitating only slightly, she said, "Not bad. And yours?"

"Terrific. Listen, I just read your piece on Congressman Damon. It's good. Real good."

Tracy had mailed the manuscript the day after Christmas and, as always, after she sent off an article, writer's paranoia had seized her, making her doubt her work. She now felt a rush of relief that her three days of anxiety had been for naught. She felt particularly pleased with Nathan Jeter's praise. He painted it on thinly and with a very small brush.

Though she had met Nathan only four times in the five years she had regularly written for his weekly publication, she had come to think of him in terms of the word *red*. A thatch of unruly, auburn-red hair topped a basically unattractive but undeniably congenial face. His eyes were bloodshot, resembling a network of roads on a map, and stared redly at every aspect of life. He edited script with a red pen that had destroyed more than one writer's fragile ego. Even Nathan joked that those who wrote for the *Political Monitor* were tough professionals with masochistic tendencies. His writers teased back that if he'd pay more, they could put themselves in analysis.

"I'm glad you're pleased with the article. I thought I had done a half-decent job."

"Better than decent. You actually managed to make the congressman look human. Most articles about him have him applying for sainthood. It seems like the printed word is always determined to make you scoundrel or saint." He paused when he realized he'd stuffed his foot in his mouth...as he somehow always managed to do. "Tracy, I'm sorry. They don't call me 'Nathan the Mouth' for nothing."

"It's all right," she soothed, ignoring the tensing of her stomach. "I couldn't agree with you more."

Though she and Nathan had discussed only briefly what had happened two years ago, Tracy knew that her employer was aware of her antagonistic feelings toward the press. It wasn't that she believed all newspaper reporters carried a hatchet. She understood that the rape of a well-known community personality's wife was news; she even understood that the rapist's being found innocent meant that at the same time the victim was found guilty, and it was too good a story for any paper to pass up. It was just that she thought several journalists, those dealing in the seamy and sensational, had enjoyed their work too much.

"Listen," Nathan said in a rush, trying to obliterate his last thoughtless comment, "I'm calling about New Year's. You got any plans?"

Tracy's grip tightened on the phone. *Good grief, was he going to ask her out?*

"If you don't have plans," he continued, "I've got a job for you."

Tracy breathed a sigh of relief and managed a slight, self-derisive smile. "What kind of job?"

"I need a piece for the mid-January issue. I had to cancel an article already scheduled, and I need a replacement faster than fast."

"What kind of article, and when do you need it?" she asked, reaching once again for the pad and pen before her. Shifting the phone to her other ear, she waited for his response with the no-nonsense attitude that made editors approach her again and again.

"Last question first. I need it by the fourth of January. Not a minute later, and sooner if possible. And as for the kind of article, I want something along the lines of how the politicians celebrate New Year's. There will be parties going on all over D.C., but I want you to concentrate on the big bash being held at The Mayflower Hotel. Just mingle, pick up the feel, talk a little here and there, and get that friend of yours to take some pictures. I'm leaving the scope of the article pretty much up to you. Whatever direction you feel is right. But bear in mind," he cautioned, "that the piece will run the middle of the month. Make the reader care about what happened two weeks before. And I don't give a royal damn who's there with whom. I don't want a gossip column approach."

Tracy's hand sped across the note pad in a combination of shorthand and illegible longhand. "Not even if the president shows up with the VP's wife?" she teased.

"In that case, interview not only the president but the vice president, as well," he quipped back.

Mutual smiles were exchanged across the miles from Washington, D.C., to New York.

"You interested?" Nathan Jeter inquired, his tone once again serious.

"You bet," she responded. "Anything else I need to know?"

"I think it's being held in the Grand Ballroom of the hotel—better check on that—and it's formal."

She groaned.

"Don't tell me a classy broad like you doesn't have something formal."

She grimaced at "the Mouth's" chauvinistic choice of words. "The broad will manage," she said, though she wondered exactly what she would wear. There hadn't been many occasions for her to wear formal attire the past couple of years, and she'd bet ten to one that her older things wouldn't fit properly because of her weight loss. "Okay, Nathan. I'll take care of it and have it to you on or before the fourth."

"Thanks," he said then added in gentle chastisement, "And, Tracy, why didn't you have any New Year's plans?"

She smiled. "I had so many offers I just couldn't make a choice." In reality, she had tactfully turned down two invitations.

"You know, that was my problem," he teased back.

Seconds later Tracy hung up the phone. Normally, she didn't like rush assignments, but this one pleased her. She had worked so zealously over the holiday that she had caught up on all her projects, and the next deadline loomed as far away as the third week of January. And even that article was already researched. This assignment would give her something to do. And she was more convinced than ever, especially after Christmas night, that her salvation lay in her work.

Christmas night. Looking back, she viewed it as a turning point of sorts. For the first time since her divorce—and curiously, the divorce had seemed more traumatic than the rape and trial, for one represented a betrayal by an acquaintance, and in the case of the jury, by strangers, while the other, and the more hurtful, a betrayal by someone she loved—she had given herself permission to cry, really cry. That night had proven to be her black pit of despair, but bleak as it had been, it had likewise been an exorcism, an exorcism of the past. Yesterday no longer chained her with its superstrength emotions. She no longer hated or loved. She did not hate her violator Paul, she did not hate the faceless jury, nor did she love her ex-husband Dennis. The past had ceased to possess her.

Assessing the job before her, she smiled. Thank goodness she had already invited Hank over for dinner. Now if only she could think of a way to tell him over beef Stroganoff that he was about to sacrifice his New Year's to business. Except, she reminded herself, there would be no beef Stroganoff if she didn't get herself to the store.

Throwing on her coat and grabbing her handbag, she headed for the back door and out into the Washington winter. Picking her way to the garage, she made herself a promise. If the streets weren't too bad to drive, and if she could finish her marketing early, she would go by her favorite dress shop in Georgetown Park to see if she could find something new to wear to the party. After all, didn't a new year deserve a new outfit?

Inside her apartment, tiny dust motes frolicked in merry play in the ribbons of sunshine tunneling through the living room window. The gold and glass clock on the mantel celebrated in chime the hour of three just as the apartment's two phones began to ring in stereophonic peals. They rang and rang and rang, with no one to answer.

COLE LISTENED with a growing sense of irritation to the incessant ringing in his ear. He checked his wrist and, when he found no watch there, glanced over at the clock on his desk.

Three o'clock. The phone rang again. And again. Muttering an oath that, if it were overheard, would have cost him the religious vote, he slammed the phone back on its stand and tried to immerse himself once again in the stack of reports on his office desk. Somewhere in the middle of a social security rescue plan, his mind returned to Tracy. Maybe she was working, he reasoned. After all, that was what *he* had flown back to the capital to do. Or maybe she was out shopping. Or maybe, he admitted with a frown tugging at his brows, she'd gone home, wherever home was, for the holidays. Pulling the booklet closer, he fought once again to engage his interest in the printed pages. This time he succeeded, but only after he promised himself that he'd call her again before he left the office.

An hour and five minutes later he was still engrossed in reports. He had just finished going over a list of proposed legislation awaiting the attention of both the Senate and the House, when he heard a tap on his door. Looking up, he saw his campaign manager peeking around the already slightly opened door. Though the two men were nearly the same age, a prematurely balding head and an overweight body that for years had seen no exercise, strenuous or otherwise, made the man now seeking entrance seem far older.

"Got a minute?" Larry Seeger asked.

Cole tossed down the report and raked his fingers through his thick black hair. "Sure, I've got lots of minutes." He motioned for the man to take the chair across from the desk. "What's up?"

"Just going over the campaign itinerary for this spring," Seeger announced, fitting his bulky frame into the indicated seat. He held up several Xeroxed papers. "I think I have everything mapped out."

Cole leaned casually back in his big, royal-blue leather chair. "Larry, you work too hard. Don't you ever take a break?"

The object of his scolding nodded toward the stack of papers littering the desk in front of him. "Is that what you're doing? Taking a break? Incidentally, I think you're the only congressman in the building today."

Cole grinned. "Touché. So we're both workaholics." Inwardly the words caused him to grimace. How many times had he and Lisa argued about just that? Every five minutes, it had seemed. She had accused him of committing bigamy when he'd married her, pointing out that he already had a wife named Politics, and that she jealously coveted every second of his life. Time and again, Cole had denied the charge, usually as he was leaving the house for some political function. Looking back, he realized—hell! maybe he'd even realized it at the time—that she had been more than half-right. It was a guilt he lived with.

His attention shifted back to the man before him. Larry Seeger was now giving a detailed account of the spring's travel schedule. Cole wanted to tell him to go home to his wife and two kids. If he had a family, that's where he'd be, instead of working so damned hard on someone else's reelection campaign. Sometimes it seemed to Cole that this campaign was more important to Larry than it was to him. The thought always made him feel a bit uneasy.

"...then we'll hit the smaller towns of Strasburg, Christiana, Paradise and New Holland. It's suicide to ignore those smaller towns," Larry intoned.

"All right," Cole spoke up, "but let's keep everything within manageable limits. I don't want to be guilty of incumbent complacency, but if my record doesn't speak for itself by now, I'm in big trouble."

"Ah, hell, Cole," the big man said smugly, "you're going to win hands down. I'll see to that."

Again Cole felt a twinge of something negative in the face of such oversize optimism. "Let's don't get too cocky, Larry. That's the same thing Jordan Adams's campaign manager is telling him. Probably right this very minute."

Seeger gave a loud harumph. "Jordan Adams is a jerk, and the people of the Sixteenth Congressional District know it."

"Could be," Cole admitted, slipping his folded hands behind his head and angling his hips more comfortably in the chair, "but then it could be that the good citizens of the Sixteenth Congressional District think I'm a jerk, too, and they'd just as soon have one jerk representing them as another.''

"Cole, you don't know your own voter power. Hell, I could run you for president right now and..."

"I know people, and let's get me reelected to Congress before we call the president and tell him to move over.''

"Nothing can stop you," the campaign manager reiterated, his cheeks aglow with the passion of confidence. "Except maybe a full-fledged scandal, so stay away from murder, rape, theft and bribery until after the votes are in.''

"Yes, sir," Cole replied, smiling.

When Larry Seeger again started to elaborate on the stumping stops he'd planned for Cole, the latter held up his hand. "Let's shelve this until after the first of the year.''

"Yeah," Larry agreed, rubbing his hand over his tired face, "I guess we could." The man rose to leave. "I think I'll go home and see if my family recognizes me.''

"Good idea," Cole confirmed. "And stay there for a while once you get there.''

"Yeah," the other man promised, adding, "But I need to take care of some of your personal correspondence before..."

"Go home!"

The man sighed. "Okay, okay."

Cole eased his chair and body into a working position. He'd just finish this report and follow his own advice. His mind was already in the middle of a column of figures when the departing campaign manager halted at the door.

"Oh, there was a note on my desk to remind you of the New Year's party tomorrow night. Does that ring a bell?"

Cole sighed heavily. "Unfortunately, yes. Thanks, Larry. I won't forget."

With the closing of the door, Cole closed his eyes, bringing the spread fingers of his hand to gently massage his shut lids. He wished he could forget the party, but socializing was as much a part of politics as anything else. Opening his eyes, his gaze lighted on the telephone. Maybe he knew a way to honey-coat the evening.

Dragging the phone to his ear, he punched in Tracy's number. The phone began to ring.

With my luck, he thought, *she'll probably already have plans.*

The phone rang again and again.

Or worse, she'd have no plans, but still turn him down.

The phone gave another unanswered squeal. Then another.

Damn! he grumbled, she must have gone out of town for the holidays. He listened to two more rings then hung up the phone so peevishly hard that it rattled in its cradle. *Hell, she might even be spending the holidays with some man! One thing's for certain, Damon, you've dialed your last time today. Maybe after the holidays are over, you'll try her again. Maybe.*

He turned his attention back to his reports and read a full three minutes before calling it quits for the day.

TRACY HEARD THE PHONE just at the very moment she started up the kitchen steps. Negotiating the snowy shelves with caution, she transferred the grocery bag to the crook of her left arm, wedging it close to her body, at the same time being careful not to dislodge the box she had tucked under her left arm. As she shoved the key into the first lock, she heard another then another of the phone's shrill summons.

Turning the key in the second lock, she threw open the door and rushed in, forgetting about the icy patch that seemed to have taken up permanent residence just at the threshold of her door. Her foot skidded, she shrieked, and the box under her arm fell to the tiled floor. Her right hand shot out to steady herself with the door frame, and she succeeded but dropped her keys in the process. They jingled to the floor in perfect harmony with another ring of the phone.

Tracy jerked the phone from its wall mounting in midring and hurried it to her ear.

"Hello," she said breathlessly. She heard the disagreeable click of the caller hanging up on her.

"Dammit!" she swore, staring at the phone in vexation. She rehung it with a jar that threatened to crack the plastic. She looked at the keys on the floor then at the box. Heaving a disgruntled sigh, she moved to the table where she deposited the groceries . . . just in time to hear the bag split and see her purchases pyramid onto the table.

"HOLY MOSES! Would you look at at this?" Hank Yeats muttered as he and Tracy stood on the outer edge of the crowd stirring about the gilded Grand Ballroom of The Mayflower Hotel.

The room was large and spacious, crammed to overflowing with people, and was lit by enormous and elegant crystal chandeliers, now casting golden light down on all the noisy revelers. A band dominated the northern quarter, playing the syncopated dissonance of jazz for the dancers on the main floor and for the onlookers sitting at tables on the second-level terrace. These tables would become premium property as the evening wore on and feet wore out. The music drifted upward to the partygoers occupying the upper wrought-iron balconies running along three sides of the ballroom. The room was richly enhanced by a burgundy-wine velvet decor and Tracy's own sense of history. The Grand Ballroom of The Mayflower Hotel had served as one of the sites of the city's several Inaugural Balls for every president since Coolidge, though only the real aficionado knew that Calvin Coolidge did not attend his inaugural ball because of family illness.

"Does that sacrilegious expletive refer to the room itself or the two billion people stuffed into it?" Tracy asked, edging herself out of the way of a man whom she instantly recognized as a senator from the state of Maine. The man had a red and silver cardboard hat sitting atop his gray hair with an elastic band strung under his jowly chin.

"Both," Hank said in an obvious state of awe. "It looks like a convention of penguins, Trace. Political penguins. In party hats."

Tracy laughed at her friend's assessment of the tuxedoed men and glamorously dressed women milling about them.

"Thank goodness I dressed formal, huh?" he added teasingly, looking down at his dress uniform of jeans. He had topped the denim with a long-sleeved beige shirt and a buff corduroy jacket that sported leather patches on the elbows.

"You're as formal as I ever expect to see you," she answered. "And don't kid me. I know you did go all out. Those are new jeans. I can actually tell they're blue. And I can see the crease the cleaners put in."

"Santa brought them," he explained, a smile peeking through the dark-haired nest of beard covering his cheeks and chin. "I was a good boy this year."

"Yeah, well, get good at taking pictures. Let's do our job and get out of here."

"Where is your sense of adventure?" he asked. The question was one they continually threw at each other when it became obvious the other's enthusiasm was waning.

"In my little toe," she replied with a grimace. "And someone just stepped on it. Come on, let's make a living."

Tracy, with Hank in tow, skirted the edge of the dance floor and with a grace and unobtrusiveness that in no way offended the party spirit—but she reasoned that not even a nuclear explosion would dent the party atmosphere—she spoke with one politician after another. Purposefully keeping her questions short and few, she soon collected comments from seven congressmen and five senators, as well as from one overly extroverted waiter who, overhearing her interview the distinguished senator from North Carolina, decided to offer his own remarks. The waiter, a dark-haired Latin type, even posed, unasked, of course, for a picture. Hank feigned total seriousness and took a shot of the beautiful tray of canapés the man held. Tracy fought back her laughter.

A little more than two hours after their arrival, their mission was completed. His camera still slung about his neck, Hank treated himself to caviar on a thin wafer while Tracy checked the notes she'd taken.

Sitting on the middle step of three leading to the second-level terrace, Tracy looked up at her friend, who was leaning against the railing, one foot crossed over the other at the ankle with his toe pointed floorward. "Well, do we stay or leave?" she asked, shouting over the loud strains of a popular song that had attracted newcomers to the dance floor the way Capistrano drew swallows.

Hank Yeats looked scandalized. "Leave? You've got to be kidding. This party's just now beginning to itch, and I want to be around when this group starts scratching." He reached out and snatched another canapé from a tray weaving past him on the arm of a waiter.

Tracy rolled her blue eyes, fringed with long, thick, mascaraed lashes, upward. "And I'm the one trying to make a living with words."

"C'mon, Trace, loosen up, disconnect, slip out of gear, enjoy yourself. Besides, it's only—" he checked his outrageously expensive watch, which always looked out of place with his otherwise unkempt appearance "—thirty-eight minutes to midnight. We've got to be somewhere to shout 'Happy New Year,' and it may as well be here."

"Okay," she answered with a resigned sigh.

"What?" he asked as the song's finale approached, and the strains of the music grew louder.

She nodded. "Okay," she shouted, "let's loosen up, disconnect, and slip out of gear."

"Now you're conversing," he shouted back, his body moving to the pulsating music.

Pulling herself to her feet, out of sheer habit Tracy dusted the bottom of her black satin pants and tugged at the black scoop-neck pullover she had bought especially for the occasion. Though she had cursed even the sale price she paid for the garment, she adored the rainbow of colors diagonally striped in sequins over half the bodice and one sleeve. The top was simple, elegant and dramatic. Slipping the note pad and pen into her black satin shoulder bag, she glanced about her. The dance floor was covered by a writhing, gyrating mob, while in her immediate vicinity people were eating, drinking champagne and talking. Occasionally some woman would shriek with uncontained laughter, while a man or sometimes a group would guffaw back. Tracy's eyes roamed to the uppermost balcony in front of her, roving idly over the people there then scanned the balcony on her left.

It was there she saw him.

Cole Damon stood with his hand thrust rakishly into the pants pocket of his tuxedo, a tuxedo midnight black in color and exactly matching the rich ebony of his hair. A crisp, white wing-collar shirt, which Tracy could tell even at this distance had a pleated front, acted as a perfect foil to the dark color and as an even more perfect echo of the white smile that seemed to be so much a part of his face—a smile he was presently bestowing on the lovely brunette beside him. Characteristic of his usual deviation from convention, a red bow tie and a red pocket handkerchief completed his immaculate dress. In that moment, Tracy supposed she had seen men who were more handsome, but she certainly had never seen one more watchable.

Her eyes shifted to the woman receiving his rapt attention. Lovely and in her mid-thirties, she was clinging to his every word. Tracy wondered if the woman was his date. The possibility gave her an uncomfortable feeling she couldn't quite label.

As if by some unseen force, Cole's eyes drifted downward to the room's main floor. Aimlessly scanning the sea of faces, he suddenly stopped. His eyes widened in immediate recognition though they sparkled with a tiny hint of disbelief. Their stares merging, he and Tracy watched each other for countless seconds. Finally he sent a smile across the distance, which she returned along with an embarrassed nod. She quickly looked away and back to Hank to whom she made some inane comment about the party that she couldn't have remembered thirty seconds later under threat of death. For the first time that evening, the music faded and was replaced in Tracy's ears with her own thundering heartbeat.

She tried to concentrate on what Hank was telling her about the liver pâté and succeeded somewhat. She even allowed him to talk her into tasting the delicacy he had proclaimed outstanding. She agreed. She also agreed to poached salmon on cracker. She did not agree to the party hat he tried to put on her head. Minutes later she braved another look at the balcony. She was relieved Cole had disappeared.

She had just turned back to say something to Hank when she heard her friend bellow suddenly, "Congressman! Good to see you." She watched him extend his hand to the one already outstretched.

Jerking her head upward, Tracy saw Cole standing before her. "Hank, isn't it?" Cole asked, the handshake already consummated.

"Yes, sir. How are you?"

"Fine," he answered, his eyes already leaving the young man to travel to Tracy. "Hi."

"Hello." Was it her imagination, or was it suddenly hot in the room?

Cole slipped his hand into his pocket, slightly bunching up his tux jacket in the process, and nodded his head at Hank's camera. "Don't tell me you two are working."

"'Fraid so," Hank replied with a tilt of his head in Tracy's direction. "She's a slave driver."

A smile captured the corners of her mouth. "Actually, we're finished."

"What are you writing now?" Cole inquired, taking in what he considered every perfect feature of Tracy's face.

"Another article for the *Political Monitor*. This one's on how you politicians celebrate New Year's."

"That could be summed up in one word," he said. "Noisily."

The band had just broken into another jazz rendition, louder, it seemed, than anything else to date.

"Pardon?" Tracy queried, turning her head to better hear him.

Cole leaned closer. "Noisily," he repeated near her ear. "We celebrate noisily." His warm breath fanned with a tickling swish the tawny wisps of hair dangling by design from the severe knot twisted on the top of her head. Her nostrils caught for one second the fresh, full-bodied scent of his cologne.

Smiling, she nodded her head in silent agreement.

"If you two will excuse me," Hank shouted, "I think I'll browse around and get some more shots." Before either Tracy or Cole could reply, he strolled off, party hat on his head, camera around his neck, as another canapé disappeared into the slit in his beard.

Tracy brought her eyes from Hank's retreating form back to Cole. She discovered his gaze already on her. She smiled almost shyly. Ridiculously, she wished Hank were back beside her.

"How was your Christmas?" Cole asked, remembering but still not understanding her distressed look when he had wished her a happy holiday.

"Okay. And yours?"

"Fine." His lips suddenly twitched. "To be honest, it was only mediocre."

Her lips curved slightly, too. "To be honest, so was mine."

"Actually, mine was the pits," he spoke truthfully.

"Actually, mine was worse than the pits," she admitted.

With each greater step of honesty, their smiles had grown broader until finally both laughed in a way neither had been able to Christmas Day. Neither of them questioned how easy it was at this moment.

Looking at the warm radiance of laughter in her eyes, Cole said the first thing that came to his mind. "You look sensational."

She answered just as spontaneously, "So do you."

Her forthrightness surprised him a little—he suspected it had even her—but he made no comment. "I like you hair up," he said instead, waving his hand to indicate some kind of upswept motion.

Actually he knew that what he liked best about her hairstyle was the possibility of unloosening pins and trailing his fingers through that honey-spun silk. He knew also that right this moment he'd love to be making love to this woman. To be honest, he'd wanted to make love to her the first time he'd seen her. That surprised him. Men were supposed to have instant libidos, but his had never worked with such a hair trigger reaction. Until now. Usually, he wanted to know something about the woman he took to his bed, but with Tracy Kent, all he wanted to know was if she was willing. Intuitively he knew she would not be. Strangely, he liked her and desired her all the more.

When his thoughts made the transition from bed to ballroom, he found she had thanked him for his compliment and now stood unconsciously gnawing the corner of her lip. He would never have guessed it from her competent interview, but the woman had a sliver of shyness in her. And damned if he didn't like it!

"Well," she said with a tiny smile, "I'm keeping you from your date."

"Date?"

Her eyes never glancing away from him, she gestured vaguely toward the balcony where she'd first seen him.

"Oh! That was Barbara Hershel...the wife of Senator Hershel." Then he added, "I'm not here with anyone." A pause followed before he spoke again. "Are you? I mean, with anyone other than Hank?"

"No," she answered quickly.

A sudden thought occurred to him, and he frowned. "You and Hank aren't..."

"Good Lord, no! I'm old enough to be his..."

"You're not old enough to be anything except his friend or lover."

"We're friends," she said, her eyes underscoring her words. "Good friends."

There was a long moment of silence before he replied simply, "Good."

She wondered about his response but didn't question it.

Abruptly pulling his hand from his pocket, he took two glasses of champagne passing by on a tray a waiter was valiantly trying to carry to the terrace. "Surely you can't object to my offering you a drink under these circumstances," he said, handing a glass of the yellow-white wine to Tracy. There was a hint of questioning in his dark eyes and maybe a tad of amusement.

Instinctively she took the glass he held out to her. She felt more than a twinge of discomfort at being reminded that she had so strongly turned down his offer of a drink.

"Let's move over there," he suggested, nodding toward a recently vacated corner of the dance floor that promised more privacy and maybe a decibel less noise. As she stepped across the hardwood floor, she felt his hand resting lightly on the small of her back. It was a comforting touch in a roomful of strangers.

Once they were sequestered in the quieter, less public spot, she sipped the champagne, her gaze finding his over the rim of the glass. She quickly lowered her eyes to the front of his shirt then slowly raised them again. His eyes had never left her.

"I'd like to explain about that," she said. "I mean, about refusing your offer of a drink."

His gaze intensified. "You don't have to." A sudden smile arced the corners of his mouth. "However, I won't stop you if you insist. A little salve to my wounded ego would feel pretty good."

She couldn't keep a slight smile from her own lips. She imagined women turned him down very seldom. "It was nothing personal. Honest."

"Then you don't categorically dislike politicians from Pennsylvania?" His eyes had picked up the smile on his lips and were now flashing their own form of amusement.

Her own smile broadened. "No," she said, shaking her head once.

He took a slow swallow of his drink. "Then why did you turn down my generous offer?"

Tracy peered into her glass of champagne as if the right words would surface there. Glancing up, she said, "I haven't dated anyone since my divorce."

He considered this. "Which was over a year ago?"

She nodded, surprised that he had remembered.

"It can't be because you haven't been asked."

"No," she admitted truthfully, "I've had some offers."

"Some" he suspected to be on the far side of humility. "But you've turned them all down."

"Yes."

His eyes, their previous amusement gone, pinned hers with a forcefulness she could only call magnetic. The brown irises appeared almost black. "Are you still in love with him?"

Tracy had no doubt to whom "him" referred and, as if the pronoun had been a conjurer, a vision of Dennis Webber flashed in her mind, but as soon as his image appeared, it disappeared, giving way to the reality of the man before her, the man waiting for her answer.

"No," she replied softly, again placing the edge of the glass to her lips so as to moisten her dry mouth. "I'm in love with some of the good times we had. I guess I always will be, but I'm not in love with him."

Cole weighed her words. He also weighed the haunted look on her face. "Maybe I'm slow, but that doesn't explain to me why you're not dating. You've been divorced for over a year, you're not carrying a torch for your ex, yet you..."

"Please..." The tone of her voice begged him not to continue. "I'm just not ready to start dating."

Quiet seconds swirled by. He watched her, watched as her clear blue eyes seemed to cloud not with tears but with memories, watched as those same eyes pleaded with him to let the subject drop...as well as the idea of dating her. She watched and waited for his reaction. In the personal silence of their conversation, they heard the band commence a slow romantic ballad.

Finally, an unhurried smile spread across his lips, and he shrugged. "Okay, so you're not ready to date. I'll settle for a dance." Without waiting for her response, he took her glass and set it, along with his, on a table. He then reached for her hand and drew her onto the dance floor.

At the touch of his hand on hers, a feeling of panic raced through her...and strangely her heart did a somersault which would have been more at home in the body of a starry-eyed adolescent.

Pulling her into the circle of his arms, he spoke, forcing her to tilt her head slightly upward despite the fact that she was tall and in heels. "Don't give me that confused look, Tracy Kent. I'm not asking for a lifetime commitment. Just a dance. Okay?"

She looked about her, at all the couples gliding by to the slow pulse of the music. "Do I have a choice?"

"No," he answered flatly.

"Then I'd love to dance."

He laughed. She smiled. The world seemed a nice place to live.

His hand settled more firmly about her waist, resting at the curve of the small of her back. His other hand gently but firmly held hers, pulling their coupled fingers to lie comfortably near his lapel. Occasionally her wrist brushed the handkerchief in his pocket. She tried to relax her other hand on his shoulder but couldn't. She felt tense. It was the nearest she'd been to a man in a very long time. Except Hank, and Hank didn't count. Cole held her closely but not intimately, and it was only every now and then that his thigh randomly brushed against hers. At those times, her body stiffened despite her resolve. She wondered if he felt her reaction.

He spoke to her only once as they moved about the floor. Without even looking at her and speaking very near her ear, he asked, "Do you have a New Year's resolution?"

"No," she answered. "I never bother. I always manage to break mine before the snow even melts." She angled her head back to look into his face. His very handsome face. "Do you?"

"Yes." She waited for him to elaborate, but he didn't. He simply said, his eyes locked to hers, "And I intend to keep mine."

For a fleeting second, Tracy had the feeling his resolution had something to do with her, but she forced the thought from her mind, telling herself the notion was fanciful. But why was he still looking at her so intently?

Abruptly the music stopped. Some group began a countdown to the new year and was soon joined by what seemed like the entire room of celebrants.

"Ten...nine...eight...seven..." they shouted, the chorus growing louder and louder. The floor now became a chaotic whirl of people, some seeking out that special person to be with at the precise moment when the old year died, and the new year with its rich promises would be born, others seeking out hats, horns and other merry-making tools. At the increasing crush of people, Cole pulled Tracy closer, his arm firmly hugging her waist.

"Six...five...four...three...two..." Someone released the colored balloons early, and the swollen balls tumbled downward, some popping in their airy descent, others being chased and batted about by a frenzied crowd.

"One!" the group cried in unison. At the magic moment, the band blasted into "Auld Lang Syne," accompanied by everyone who couldn't sing. Horns squealed their tinny sound, and people laughed, whistled and cried. Streamers of colored crepe paper seemed to fall from nowhere, and giant quantities of sparkling confetti rained on the entire ballroom.

"This is madness!" Tracy shouted up into Cole's smiling face.

"Totally!" he shouted back, pulling her closer and out of the way of an amorous couple.

Looking down into her upturned face, Cole reached out to lightly brush her cheek with his fingers. "Confetti," he explained.

Without either of them quite knowing how, his fingers moved from brushing to cradling her cheek. His eyes merged with hers, and he hesitated only briefly before he lowered his head, and his mouth took hers. Brief, sweet, passionless, it was a kiss of introduction.

There was no time for Tracy to panic. Just time to feel a wondrous, near-forgotten feminine warmth wash over her in lazy waves before he hesitantly pulled away.

"Happy New Year, Tracy Kent," he whispered, his eyes burning into hers.

A red streamer fluttered downward and fell across Cole's shoulder, while the other end settled across Tracy's, binding them together as the new year gasped its first breaths of life.

CHAPTER FOUR

"LET ME TAKE YOU HOME."

Cole's words chilled the warmth bathing Tracy's body, chilled it with ice-spears of reality.

"I . . . I don't think that would be a good idea," she whispered, her lips still wet from his.

"I think it would be a wonderful idea," he persisted, his lips still tingling from the sweet touch of her mouth.

That sweet mouth slid slowly into a smile. "I thought you were going to content yourself with a dance."

His eyes shone with a devilish light as he returned, "I don't remember using the word content. I think it was settle. Besides, all of that was last year."

"Cole," she said, her smile fading, "I . . . I thank you, but . . ."

Both Tracy's and Cole's attention shifted to the man sauntering up to her side.

"Hank, do you have any clout with this lady?" Cole asked, telling himself he'd take any advantage, unfair or otherwise, that he could. "I just asked her to let me drive her home, and the answer I got was flatter than a pancake."

Hank Yeats and Tracy exchanged glances, quick, knowing glances. She felt a keen sense of relief. Hank would get her out of this—gracefully.

Sizing up the situation, Hank made an instant decision. "Well, actually, sir, she did come with me..."

Tracy's stomach muscles began to uncoil.

"...and we usually stay together when we're working..."

Thank God for Hank! Tracy thought.

"...but it sure would be a big favor to me tonight if you did drive her home."

Tracy smiled. "Thanks just the same, Cole. I really appre—" Her eyes flew to Hank's in disbelief.

Her friend gave his best "gee I'm sorry about that" grin. "Actually, I kinda promised someone I'd stop by her party." Hank looked over at Cole. "The pretty lady in your office."

"Marisa Wisner?" Cole asked with a tilt of his brow.

Hank nodded then clarified to Tracy, "Meryl Streep. She liked my amnesia routine."

Ordinarily Tracy would have replied with something witty, but there was really nothing ordinary about that moment, a fact her wilder than wild heartbeat attested to.

"Give Marisa my best," Cole said, stretching his hand forward in goodbye. The streamer of crepe paper, dangling over his shoulder and Tracy's, fluttered to the floor.

"I'll do that, sir," Hank returned with a firm handshake. Turning to Tracy, he added, "Happy New Year, Trace." He bent forward and placed a kiss on her cheek. As he did so, he whispered, "Where's your sense of adventure?"

"It's been stabbed in the Senate, Brutus," she whispered back.

"You're going to thank me for this."

"Sure, Yeats. I'll probably take out a full-page ad in the *New York Times*." Hank chuckled, and she watched as he walked away and disappeared into the clamoring throng. She felt the last shred of her equanimity evaporate as her eyes slid to Cole's— brown and blue, gauging each nuance of emotion.

"Nice guy," Cole commented. It was a remark he'd made before.

"Sometimes," Tracy said.

Cole watched as her teeth unconsciously bit at her lower lip. He suddenly wondered if he'd done the right thing by pushing her.

"Look," he said, fighting the urge to take his thumb and free her lip from its torment, "if this is going to be a problem, I'll call you a cab."

She studied him...and her heart. Did she want him to call her a cab? The truth was, she didn't think she did. And she knew that that fact was the very reason she should insist that he do so. She didn't need this kind of complication in her life. Not such an attractive complication. And yet, a drive home was just a drive home. Wasn't it?

"No," she finally said with a shake of her head, "there's no problem. Besides, I doubt you could get a cab for hours tonight."

Cole's lips upcurved rakishly. "That was going to be my argument if you'd insisted on one."

"You're sneaky, Congressman," she said as her own lips twitched.

"Only as sneaky as I have to be to get what I want."

She didn't dare translate the implication of his words.

Minutes later Cole drove through the Washington, D.C., streets—past the obelisklike buildings of downtown, past squatty, sleepy suburbia and into the elegant charm of Georgetown. Thankful that he hadn't forced conversation, Tracy sat huddled against the cold. The droning heater was slowly battling the frigid air, but it couldn't begin to battle the turmoil in her mind. *Would he want to come in? Of course he would. What man wouldn't? Would he try to kiss her again? Did she want him to? No.* She thought about his lips moving gently over hers. She thought about how gentle kisses inescapably flared into passionate kisses. She shuddered.

"Still cold?" Cole asked at the sharp shaking of her shoulders.

Tracy's gaze met his in the darkness. Cole's eyes were as black as onyx...and as warm as a melting summer sun. She suddenly felt cheated and angry that she hadn't met Congressman Damon at a time in her life when she had been whole.

"I'm fine," she lied.

They lapsed into silence while Cole studied her. She was an enigma. Professionally she was competent. Personally she was flawed. What those flaws were he had no real idea. He'd been right, though. There was some kind of low-grade fear coursing through her veins. And it seemed to have something to do with men. Though she'd tried to conceal it, she hadn't even been able to dance with him comfortably. The only man she seemed truly comfortable with was Hank Yeats. In that moment Cole experienced a perfect case of envy, the first he thought he'd ever been guilty of. He'd give anything if the woman beside him could feel comfortable with him.

"Turn here," she said. "Fourth house on the right."

Cole angled the car into the drive, sending the headlights bouncing off a garage in the back. He made the mental notation that the house was one of the older refurbished homes that Georgetown was so famous for. He noted also that the neighborhood was one with more modestly priced homes. "Pull down, and I'll go in the back door." Cole complied and, shoving the gear into Park, left the car running.

"Thanks," Tracy said, immediately reaching for the door handle.

With lightning swiftness, he caught her coat sleeve. "Wait!"

Her eyes, just a little too wide for normal, raced to his. Slowly he eased his hold. "I have two tickets to the theater next week. Could I tempt you?"

Regret shimmied across her blue irises and settled into the deep tone of her voice. "Cole, I was serious when I said I wasn't ready to date yet."

"I know you said it was nothing personal, but I have to ask, anyway. Is it just that you don't find me—" the outstanding orator searched for the right word "—attractive? Do our chemistries just not mesh? If so, I'll leave you alone."

He was giving her the perfect out, and yet she couldn't take it. She couldn't make it easy on herself at his expense. She smiled. "No, I do not find you unattractive, and our chemistries..." She halted, then said tonelessly, "I don't have a chemistry right now."

Cole didn't pursue the comment. Instead he smiled, his lips pushed upward by pure confidence. "I won't give up so easily. Ask anyone on the Hill. I know how to fight . . . and win."

His words sent shivers dancing down her spine. She didn't think all of them had their origins in fear. Curiously, that made her feel even more vulnerable.

"C'mon. Let me walk you to the door," he insisted.

Before she could protest, he walked across the bright beam of headlights and opened her door. Mechanically she slid out. His hand at her back—brushing but not really touching—she moved the short distance to and up the steps, extracted a key from her handbag and unbolted both locks. So accustomed was she to the two dead bolts that she gave them no thought. Not so Cole. Somewhere in a tiny corner of his mind he filed the fact away...where maybe sometime it would be brought out and classified as unusual.

The door open, Tracy turned with a heart gone skitter-wild at the possibility that he might try to kiss her. She extended her hand, which he took. It was warm and large. "Thanks, Cole," she said quietly. "I appreciate the drive home. I..."

In trying to quickly step away, her foot slipped on the ever-present patch of ice. She gave a strangled scream as Cole's arm shot about her and crushed her tightly against him.

"Careful," he said as her neck angled and their eyes merged.

Brown, she thought. His eyes were drown-in-them brown. And his square-featured face was so handsome framed against the raven night and the upturned collar of his coat. And his body...so hard...so solid...so *male*. She felt her body tremble. With the heels of her hands on his chest, she pushed away from him. Uncoiling his arm, he let her go—though not with his eyes.

"You ought to put some salt on that ice," he said in a husky voice.

She stepped over the threshold and into safety— safety from the ice, safety from the man. "I...I will." Her soft voice sounded jagged, like shattered crystal smothered in satin.

Both of them sought words to fill the silence, but they found none. Finally he stuffed the hand that moments before had held her to him into his coat pocket. "Well, good night."

"Good night."

"I'll be in touch." With that promise he turned and was gone.

Closing the door, she eased her back against it and exhaled a labored sigh. *I'll be in touch.* She didn't want him to be in touch ... yet, curiously, the thought that he might sent a ribbon of excitement unfurling along sensual nerve endings that had been dormant for a long while.

COLE WAS IN TOUCH. The following Wednesday he called with a second bid for her to go to the theater with him. She again declined. He accepted her rejection with all the grace of a man who seemed to be expecting it. The following Sunday he asked her to a movie. Again she turned him down. Afterward he kept her on the phone so long that the movie had already begun by the time he hung up. For a reason she didn't try to explain, she was pleased that he had opted not to go if she didn't go with him. And with a comparable lack of explanation, she felt a little at loose ends for the remainder of that Sunday, almost as if the solitude she usually enjoyed now bordered on loneliness.

The following week, he asked her to dinner.

"No, thanks," she responded. Undaunted, he asked her to a party. "No."

"Another movie?"

"No."

"Ice skating on the C&O Canal?"

"Ice skating?"

"Sure," he'd told her, "politicians ice skate—usually on very thin ice. How about it?"

She had laughed and answered no, but it was with the first real hesitation he'd detected, brought about by Hans Brinker visions of mirror ice and cozy bank fires skating into her mind's eye.

"How about a drink after work tomorrow?" he had asked one Thursday night. Again she had turned him down. Following her refusal, they talked for hours and when she hung up at a ridiculous hour, she realized two things: Congressman Cole Damon was a warm, interesting man—a *persistent*, warm, interesting man—and he made her laugh. The next evening, as she wandered through her silent apartment, Tracy wondered if he'd found someone else to have that drink with. The thought nagged at her.

When January was in its third cold week, he called again.

"Hello?" Tracy said, stretching across the paper-strewn desk in her bedroom to grab the phone.

"I've called for my usual dose of humility."

At the sound of the voice, a voice she hadn't heard for four days, her heartbeat accelerated. "Hi," she said, clicking off the humming typewriter. As she did so, she told herself it was no big deal that he was calling. She also forced her fingers to unloosen their grip on the telephone. "What's this about a dose of humility?"

"I've had such a productive week, I'm threatening to walk on water. Thought I'd call you right quick, and let you turn me down for another date so I could get everything into perspective."

She laughed.

"Want to go out?"

"No."

"Thanks. I feel more human already."

Tracy laughed again. "Am I that bad?"

"You're pretty denting to a male ego," he replied, but she imagined he was smiling. "How's your week going?"

"Pretty good," she answered. "And I guess I don't have to ask about yours."

"I lied. Except for convincing someone to vote with me on a dairy bill, it's going somewhere between okay and fair." *Maybe even fair and lousy,* he thought with a frown as he glanced down at the article in that week's *Washington Tattler*. The tabloid, which printed journalism so yellow it rivaled sunshine, had done it again. Or rather, Thomas Lovell, who *was* the paper, had done it again. Where the hell the man got his information or rather his misinformation, he couldn't begin to guess. And where in hell he'd found out about Uncle Chigger losing his farm was an even bigger puzzle. The only thing that made any sense at all was the implication that Congressman Cole Damon was promoting farming legislation only for personal gain. It was obvious Lovell was starting a precampaign smear. But here again, the *why* was a puzzle. He didn't even know the guy. He...

"Are you there?" Tracy's question penetrated the growing silence.

"Yeah," Cole said, mentally discontinuing the unpleasant subject and tuning back to the voice he'd wanted to hear all day, all week. He switched the phone to his other ear. "Listen, Barbara Hershel's invited me to a party this weekend. She said to bring someone." He paused. "I don't guess you'd want to go?"

For the first time Tracy thought she heard a note of vulnerability in his voice. It caused a curious tightening in her stomach.

"I'm sorry, Cole. I'm going to be out of town this weekend. I'm going home to visit my parents."

"Oh. Where's home?"

"New Jersey. Trenton."

"I've never been there."

"It's nice," she said and meant it despite all the bad memories Trenton held. "I'm going home for Christmas," she heard herself explaining.

"Christmas?"

"Yeah. I didn't make it home for the holiday, so I'm going home for turkey and dressing and my family's presents. If I don't, my parents are going to disinherit me."

Cole smiled, though he was remembering how his wishing her a happy holiday had upset her. Maybe it had been because she was spending it alone. *No.* He intuitively knew that wasn't it. *Spending a holiday alone didn't pluck cords of fear.* "When are you leaving?"

"Friday morning."

"Have a nice time."

"Thanks."

"Just for the record, Tracy. Would you have gone with me to Barbara Hershel's party if you'd been in town?"

There was a lengthy silence. "Probably not."

It was the first time she'd qualified her rejection. And both of them knew it. Cole felt a warm trickle of optimism, while Tracy realized that the simple unvarnished truth was that she really had wanted to accept. She probably wouldn't have, but she'd wanted to.

"Be careful," Cole cautioned. "And I'll talk to you when you get back."

"Okay," she said, wishing he wouldn't hang up so soon.

But he did. "Bye now."

"Bye."

The phone left her ear; the phone left his ear. Suddenly he called out, "Hey, Tracy?"

She pulled the phone back. "Yes?"

"When are you coming back?"

"Sunday."

"I'll talk to you then."

After the phones had been recradled, both Tracy and Cole sat staring at them. They shared a singular thought: it promised to be a long time until Sunday.

THE GIFT ARRIVED in New Jersey on Saturday afternoon. Mr. and Mrs. Kent and Tracy were lounging around after a shopping spree in a nearby crowded mall. Surprised to see that the return address on the parcel was a little antique shop in Georgetown, Tracy ripped at the wrapping until all that was left was a white box. She removed the lid then stared at a froth of tissue, which crinkled as it bloomed open. Hidden inside was a small music box that began to play when she accidentally indented the side button. The modern romance ballad, which Tracy immediately recognized as David Gates's "If," contrasted beautifully with the restored eighteenth-century gold-filigreed box. The notes were crisp, the imagined lyrics poignant, as the music box played the song of a man who, if he could be two places at one time, would choose to be with his lover—tomorrow and today.

Tracy reached for the card and read, "Merry Christmas, Cole."

A sweet shower of warmth rained over her, misting its glow over her body and heart and flooding her with a powerful image of black-haired, dark-eyed Cole Damon.

"What is it, Tracy gal?" asked her father.

"It's..." She paused, clearing her throat. "It's a music box."

"Who's it from?" Ruby Kent asked.

"It's from...it's from this man."

The Kents exchanged glances. "Anyone special?" her mother asked with an undeniable wistfulness.

There was a pause of sweet confusion before Tracy whispered, "I don't know."

WHEN SHE GOT HOME SUNDAY, she set the music box on the bedside table...and waited. She told herself that she wasn't waiting for Cole's call, but her vigilant check of the clock said otherwise. She checked at three minutes after 7:00 as she ate a pimento cheese sandwich, she checked at 7:20 as she put on a load of laundry, and she checked at 8:00 as she plopped wet clothes into the dryer. She paced, dashed a quick note to Nathan the Mouth and forced herself to prove she wasn't waiting for Cole's call by tying up the phone with a call to Hank. She kept him talking for exactly three minutes, which seemed more like three thousand.

For heaven's sake, Tracy! she chided herself. *Stop this!*

At 9:12 she went into the bathroom, brushed her honey-tinted hair a crisp one hundred strokes, slipped out of her denim skirt and ivory underwear and stepped into the shower. She left the bathroom door open. She told herself it was to keep the room from steaming up. Hot water, soap, and a sore ear from straining to hear later, she stepped from the shower and grabbed a yellow towel. She peered through to the clock by the bed. 9:34. Maybe he wasn't going to call. Maybe he'd taken someone else to Barbara Hershel's party. Maybe . . .

She postponed going to bed as long as was sensibly possible, but at 10:18 she had to admit that she was inventing reasons to keep her travel-tired body up. He wasn't going to call. It was as simple as that. With a sigh, she deliberately didn't glance at the music box, turned off the lamp and crawled into bed. She finally even fell asleep.

The phone rang—sharply, shatteringly—at twenty-one minutes after eleven.

Thinking it was morning, a sleepy-eyed Tracy reached for the receiver and dragged it to her ear. "Hello?" she mumbled, fully expecting to hear Hank's disgustingly morning-cheerful voice. Instead she heard a protracted silence.

"Ah, damn, I woke you, didn't I? I'm sorry, but I just got in and saw what time it was and I . . ."

"Cole?" she asked the question but knew the answer. No other voice could sound so warm, so welcome.

"You *were* asleep, weren't you?"

"It's all right."

"No, it isn't. I..."

"I thought you weren't going to call," she interrupted.

There was a childlike honesty in the words, a frank admission in their tone that clearly said that she'd wanted him to call and had been disappointed when he hadn't. He wasn't sure that she was even aware of what she was revealing, but it was a revelation that caused him to ease to the side to the bed with a tender smile.

"I wanted to call earlier, but I got hung up in a meeting."

"On Sunday night?"

"Politics doesn't sleep. Bob Evans of the Associated Milk Producers Political Action Committee wanted to talk about..." He stopped. "That isn't why I called. Did you have a nice trip?"

"Yes, thank you," she said, finger-brushing the hair from her eyes.

"Your parents okay?"

"Um-huh."

"No problems traveling, huh?"

"Huh-uh. Cole?"

"Yeah?"

"I...I love the music box."

There was the tiniest of pauses. "Enough to go out with me? Now, before you say no, just listen to me. We've been going at this all wrong. What we need to do is compromise. It's a great American tradition."

Tracy could hear him switch the phone to his other ear. "Let me show you how it works. I ask you to dinner, you say no, but that a drink after work would be acceptable. That way, you don't win and I don't win. But then, you don't lose and neither do I. What do you think?"

A smile teased the corners of Tracy's sleep-slackened mouth. "I think you're crazy to call a woman in the middle of the night and lecture about compromise...about as crazy as she is for entertaining the notion."

"Does that mean you'll meet me for a drink?" he asked, holding his breath.

"Yes. But," she qualified, "the only reason I'm agreeing to this is because I'm half asleep."

A deep, very masculine chuckle wafted through the line and curled cozily in her ear. "That's obviously where I've been making my mistake. I've been trying to reason with you when you're awake."

Slowly, suddenly, the atmosphere became intimate. Both of them sensed it. It was an intimacy based on the realization that this conversation was taking place in the middle of the night, that he, in essence, had invaded her bedroom, had caught her in sleep, had caught her without the mask of makeup, clothes, and inhibitions. She felt strangely vulnerable; he felt strongly protective.

"Go back to sleep," he ordered thickly.

She scooted down into the warmth of the covers. "Cole..." she whispered but said nothing more.

He waited, waited, even wondered if she'd fallen asleep.

"...I'm glad you called."

Her words sent his heart pummeling against his chest. "I'm glad you're back."

Seconds later, after they'd hung up, her last coherent thought before drifting off to sleep was that was exactly what she'd wanted him to say.

THE FOLLOWING FRIDAY a cab pulled to the curb in front of Tulliver's Travels.

"How do I look?" Tracy asked the man sharing the back seat.

"Exactly the way you looked three minutes ago," Hank Yeats said with an indulgent grin. "Great."

Tracy pulled her heavy woolen coat about her, seeking not warmth but sanctuary. "I don't think this was such a good idea."

"Where's your sense of adventure?"

"It's just made a hard-core decision. Never agree to anything a man suggests in the middle of the night."

"I'll have you know," the young man said, a salacious grin peeking from his beard, "I've made some of my best suggestions in the middle of the night."

"Yeah," Tracy answered, "and the vice squad has them all on file."

Hank laughed, but at the sight of her teeth's brutal bruising of her bottom lip, he sobered. "It's only a drink, Trace. The man's only asking you to have a drink. Not to marry him. Not to spend the night with him. Just to have a drink." In a gesture of genuine concern, he curved his arm around her shoulders and squeezed. "Give yourself a chance. Give him a chance."

"But..."

"No buts. Now get your posterior in there!"

"You sure you don't want to come in and..."

"Get out!"

"As you said, it's only a drink."

"Woman, will you get out of this cab so I can go meet Marisa."

"Marisa, huh?"

"Marisa. Now get out."

Tracy threw open the cab door. "That's what I like about you, Yeats. You never put self-interest above our friendship." Shutting the door, she stared down at her friend, who was leaning across the seat with a smile and a thumbs-up. She returned the "go get 'em" signal with something less than an enthusiastic smile and started for the bar's door.

As the cab drove away, Hank Yeats peered through the back window and prayed—prayed that Cole Damon was man enough for the woman he was about to have a drink with.

Cole saw her the moment she walked in. But then it would have been hard to miss her. She looked like an innocent-eyed lamb who'd just arrived at the slaughterhouse. That sense of protection that she alone seemed capable of evoking in him rose once more to the surface. In that moment the only thing of importance was to put her at ease…and to make those soft, those sweetly soft lips smile. He scraped back his chair and started toward her.

Maybe he isn't here, Tracy thought hopefully as she peered through the darkened room. The New York style bar, with its checkered tablecloths, its gaslight wall sconces and its white tile floor, was alive with a Friday night crowd, a crowd that she prayed would not include Congressman Cole Damon. Why had she agreed to meet him? Why hadn't she stuck to her resolve that she wasn't ready to start dating? Why… At the sight of him, dressed in black slacks and an ivory cable-knit sweater, her heart stopped.

"Hi," he said with his usual confidence that at the moment seemed unfairly apportioned between the two of them.

"Hi," she quiver-whispered as she fiddled with the strap of the gray handbag banded across her shoulder.

The smile that walked across his lips was knowing. "It looks as though you're having second thoughts."

"And third and fourth and fifth," she answered honestly.

Taking the lead by grasping her elbow in a way he hoped wasn't threatening, he suggested, "Why don't we have a seat and you can have those second, third, fourth and fifth thoughts with me?"

"I'm not sure, but I think that's going to defeat them," she said over her shoulder as he guided her to a table in the back of the room.

"That's the plan," he parried.

She couldn't help but smile.

With his assistance, her coat fell away to reveal a copper-colored silk crêpe de chine blouse tucked flawlessly into slate-gray pants. She eased into the seat he offered.

"A Bloody Mary," she announced the moment he sat down across from her.

A grin played with one side of his mouth, and his dark eyes sparkled with instant mischief. "Just like that, huh? No proper hello? No how-are-you?"

She had the good grace to blush at her overzealous haste. "I'm sorry."

"No, no," he said, hurrying to put her at ease, "you came here for a drink, and you're going to have one."

He motioned for the waiter. "The lady will have a Bloody Mary and I'll have another bourbon and water." After the waiter stepped away, Cole added, "You're not going to gulp this down in one swallow, are you?"

Her mouth twitched, sending the corners of her copper-glossed lips upward and crinkling the fashionably taupe-dusted hollows of her cheeks. "No. I promise to evenly distribute it in two."

His smile was rich and full. "When I was practicing law, I insisted my clients get everything in writing."

The teasing brought another smile to Tracy's lips, a smile that slowly slid away. "You ever miss the courtroom?"

He shook his head. "Nope. I'm a born politician. I've got hearings and reforms and vetoes and budgets pumping in my veins the way most people have blood. What about you? You always been a writer?"

Their drinks had come and Tracy sipped at the tomato juice and vodka before answering, "Always. It's the only thing I know how to do."

"I hear you're very good at it."

She shrugged her shoulders. "I do okay."

Sensing that praise bothered her, he changed subjects. "How was your week?"

"Fine. Yours?"

"Pretty good."

He took a slow swallow of his bourbon and water. She brought her glass to her lips. They stared at each other. He purposely said nothing more.

"Bad weather this week, huh?" she asked to fill the awkward void. Her teeth began to gnaw her lip.

"Yeah."

"They're predicting snow again tonight."

"Yeah."

"They said it may break some kind of record."

"Yeah."

She opened her mouth with another inane remark but closed it. She looked down at her glass then up at him. He was watching her.

"You think we're through with the small talk?" he asked.

"Is that what we're doing? Making small talk?"

"Aren't we?" He neither expected nor waited for a reply. "I don't think either one of us is saying what we'd like to." He swished the liquid in his glass, though it was an absent gesture, for his eyes were pinned on the woman before him. "If I say what I really want to, would you reciprocate?"

The look she gave him was full of honesty, just the way her words were. "I'll try."

"Fair enough." His hand was lying near hers, and his thumb reached out and lightly traced her little finger. She looked down at the point of contact then back up. "I'm glad you came," he said, looking into her eyes.

She swallowed . . . and smiled with the shyness he found endearing. "I'm glad I came, too," she answered and meant it even though she wasn't sure what she was getting herself into.

The smile he gave outshone the golden light casting shadows in the room. "That wasn't so hard, now was it?"

"You're making fun of me," she accused.

"No, I'm not," he answered, thinking that what he was trying to do was to break through her self-imposed wall. "Let's play another round of honesty." Before she could object, he said, "You're not comfortable being with any man except Hank."

She felt the air solidifying in her lungs and tried to pull her hand from his. He captured it and held it fast. Her eyes flew to his...in panic...not at being held, but in being found out.

"Don't pull away from me," he said softly. After long seconds, seconds in which their eyes and wills battled, she relaxed her hand beneath his. "You don't have to reciprocate. You don't have to explain why you're uncomfortable. Just know that I know. And that it's okay."

"Cole—" she hesitated, wanting to say so much, knowing she'd say so little "—this drink doesn't change anything. I'm still not ready to have...to have a man in my life." She took a deep, regretful breath. "Do yourself a favor. Find yourself a woman who's—" she started to say whole, but thought it too revealing "—find yourself a woman who's ready to be found."

"And I want you to understand that this drink doesn't change anything for me. I'm still going to try to get you to date me. And I'd appreciate it if you'd let me decide on the woman I want to find."

Tracy knew that he was a threat to the safe world she'd built for herself. He was like fire—dangerous, but compelling—and in the end she'd have to back away or be burned. She knew that when that time came, she would back away—self-preservation would demand it—but right this moment she'd let herself be teased by the flames. "You're stubborn," she said with a grin that made her look so beautiful that Cole's heart skipped a beat.

"You're damned right. Oh, and incidentally, you're beautiful."

Color flushed Tracy's cheeks as she lowered her forehead into her hand. She groaned.

Cole grinned at her distress. "It's true. Ask any man in this bar," he challenged as he glanced around him. "Ask any..." His voice trailed off when his eyes connected with those of a man who was seated three tables away from them.

At the sudden silence Tracy raised her head and followed Cole's line of vision. She saw a man, probably in his mid-thirties, with strawberry-blond hair and attractive features underscored with just that perfect hint of dissipation that was guaranteed to seduce. He was a man who had lived and had loved doing so, but something in his troubled, opaque eyes said that he'd paid a price. Maybe a high one.

Even as Tracy watched, the man raised his glass in a salute to Cole and said in a voice that carried across the way, "Congressman." The voice was unmistakably British.

Cole gave such a slight inclination of his head that it couldn't even be considered a nod. He stared at the man for a penetrating moment before shifting his attention away and back to Tracy, who was now watching with an intense interest.

"I take it he's not a close friend," she said.

"Hardly," was Cole's terse reply as he reached for his drink and swallowed down a healthy draw.

"A political opponent?"

"An opponent, though not political. Actually, he's more in your line of work." Tracy gave him a look that was encouragement enough for Cole to continue.

"He's a journalist...though I use the word in its loosest form. His name's Tom Lovell."

Tom Lovell. Tracy felt an inexplicable shudder of something unpleasant.

"Washington Tattler," Cole added as if the two words clarified everything.

They did. Tracy's hand jerked, sending her copper-hued nails tinkling against the side of her glass. It tumbled, spilling the last of the drink onto the table. She instantly grabbed her napkin and began to dab at the red stain. "I'm sorry," she said, reaching for the napkin Cole handed her. "I'm sorry. I..."

"Hey," Cole said, stilling her hands in his, "it's okay. They'll clean it up." The hands, tenderly imprisoned within his, shook with a slight tremor. It crossed his mind that spilling a drink was a strange thing to tremble about. But then, had the trembling spilled the drink? Cole tilted his head in the direction of Tom Lovell. "Do you know him?"

"No! I mean, no, of course not. Just his work." It wasn't a lie. She didn't actually know Tom Lovell. She could still vividly remember his article following the trial. While he'd been careful not to state that Tracy Webber was guilty of seduction—that would have been libelous—he had carefully led the reader to that conclusion with subtle innuendo and lethal implication. And what had really galled her the most was that his only goal had been to sell papers. God help the man, she thought, who was the target of Lovell's personal grudge!

"Hey, are you all right?"

Tracy focused on Cole and pulled her hands from his. She felt obligated to repeat, "I don't know Mr.

Lovell. I just know his type—willing to take cheap shots if it keeps his byline in print.''

"Yeah," Cole agreed, "and last week he took a shot at me." At Tracy's concerned look, he added, "No big deal. It's an election year. Everyone running for re-election is fair game." The answer sounded as if Tom Lovell's attack was of an impersonal nature, and Cole had no reason to believe otherwise. He wondered then why he couldn't fully buy it? But what the hell had he ever done to Tom Lovell? With a start Cole realized that Tracy had spoken. "I'm sorry. What?"

"I think I'd better go."

"I couldn't persuade you to stay for dinner?"

She shook her head. "A compromise is a compromise."

"And a lonely evening is a lonely evening."

"Cole . . ." The one word carried a plea.

"Let's go," he said with an accepting smile.

As they rose to leave, Tracy deliberately avoided looking in Thomas Lovell's direction and conspicuously hastened to the front of the bar. There she tunneled her arms into the coat Cole offered. He then slid into his own, pushed open the door, and they walked out into the frigid night. The predicted snow had begun to fall.

"I'll have to hail us a cab," Cole said.

"Hail two. There's no need for you to see me home."

The look in his eyes said that he wanted to argue; his sigh of acquiescence said that he knew he'd better not. She'd made enough concessions for one evening. With his raised hand he hailed a cruising cab. Within seconds he'd fitted her into the back seat . . . but couldn't bring himself to close the door without saying again, "I'm glad you came."

"Me, too," she said honestly.

"I'll call."

Before she could speak, he silenced her lips with the tips of his warm fingers. "I'll call." After a long, lingering look, he closed the door.

The cab pulled away.

Inside the car, Tracy leaned her head back against the seat. Why hadn't she insisted that he not call her? She wasn't going to date him. And if she'd ever given the idea the slightest serious consideration, running into Thomas Lovell had instantly nixed it. The truth was, the past wasn't, nor would it ever be, finished with her. And with her kind of past, the future was built on shaky, shifting ground. So why then did she dance around Cole Damon's flame? She eased her fingers to her lips, lips still burning from Cole's touch. The answer, she knew, had something to do, not with yesterday or tomorrow, but with today...and the way the distinguished congressman from Pennsylvania made the present, and her, seem wonderfully alive.

Cole watched as the cab disappeared into the shark-feed that was Washington traffic. He exhaled a breath that clouded the cold air in white. The more he knew her, the less he knew her. She was uncomfortable with men, she'd been downright panicked by the Christmas holiday, she trembled in the presence of, and hid her face from, unscrupulous reporters. She'd politely told him to get lost. So why did he insist on hanging around? It was really quite simple, he thought. Unless he was very much mistaken, he was falling in love with Tracy Kent. That thought imprisoned in his heart, he hailed a cab.

Inside Tulliver's Travels, Tom Lovell hailed another drink. He'd already had too many, but what the hell? He had nothing...or no one...to go home to. That bloody son-of-a-bitch Damon had seen to that. *Easy, man, easy,* he told himself. *Bide your time and make him pay.* As the amber solace streamed down his throat, he wondered if Damon had seen last week's article, wondered also who the woman was with him, wondered if he dare have another drink. He decided he did dare.

"Another Scotch," he said, shoving the glass at Jack Tulliver, who'd walked over to serve the table himself.

"Why don't you call it quits?"

"One more."

Reluctantly the bar's owner poured another inch. "This is it."

"Yeah, yeah," Tom Lovell said, swigging the drink down in one gulp. He swiped the back of his hand across his mouth and looked up. His face suddenly softened. "You know what she told me?" There was no identifying "she," nor any waiting for Jack Tulliver's response. "She said I had the soul of a poet. That's what she said." He gave a choppy cynical laugh. "I have the soul of a poet, the heart of a mercenary." His eyes filmed with tears. "I still have her obituary. But you know what, man? Every time I see it, I see my own. 'Thomas Gregston Lovell died today of hatred. It had dined on him until it had consumed all the best parts of him. What had begun as a gentle gnawing in the pit of his stomach proceeded to a persistent, bite-snatching of his heart and ended as a ravenous, teeth-tearing feast of his soul. He was

condemned to hell. Amen...amen...'" He raised
bleary, lifeless eyes. "You didn't know I was dead, did
you, Jack?"

CHAPTER FIVE

TRACY AND COLE continued to play the dating game, but with subtly different ground rules. What had once been sporadic calls now became every-night telephone conversations that both accepted as a natural part of the day. And, while the professed goal was still to get Tracy to agree to a date, the calls themselves began to serve the purpose of dating. Slowly, and with an unfolding magic, they began to learn about each other. They learned of likes ...

"You really like sweets, huh?" he asked one February evening as snow blanketed the capital in a white and majestic glory.

"Almost as much as you like walking in the rain," she'd replied.

"You remembered."

"Of course I remembered. You're the man with the death wish."

"Will you walk with me in the rain sometime?"

"Are you asking me out?"

"No."

"Good. Then I'll walk with you in the rain sometime."

And they learned of dislikes ...

"And then the jerk turned to me, after I'd picked up the outrageous tab for lunch, and said that he'd already promised to vote against aid to Nicaragua. God, I hate wasting my time!''

"Susan Whitley."

"Susan Whitley? What's a Susan Whitley?"

"First grade. Big end-of-the-year party. I did everything I could to get invited. Even bought Susan Whitley an all-day sucker with the last of my allowance. Turns out she never intended to invite me at all. Wasted my time and my lollipop. To this day, I hate lollipops.''

"Poor baby," he'd drawled. "I'll invite you to my party."

"Are you having a party?"

"No. But I'll plan one if you'll come."

"Good try, Congressman. No points, but a good try."

After this conversation Tracy wondered why, if Cole hated wasting his time, did he continue to call her? And while she was wondering, she wondered how he had known that she was uncomfortable with men. Had she been so obvious? And why had he never mentioned it again? There were times that she almost wished he'd drag the ugly truth about the rape from her. But then, she rationalized, his knowing might bring an end to their tenuous relationship...and the nightly phone calls that brightened her lonely life.

In the days that followed, they laughed together on the phone, discussed the state of the world together, had deep and convoluted philosophical debates together. They also sometimes shared their meals. Between bites of pizza or other take-out fast foods that two busy schedules settled for, they would discuss the day, with its frustrations and pleasures. One evening, they even watched an old movie together. Cole, drawing the phone to the top of his bent jean-clad knee, sat on the floor of the hotel room he called home when in the capital, while Tracy sat Indian style in the middle of her bed. After two hours of the fiery, on-the-screen romance between Bogart and Bacall, Tracy felt vaguely unsatisfied with Cole's warm basso voice. It suddenly seemed so intangibly little when his presence promised so much. Tracy told herself she was just caught up in the backwash of the movie's romantic theme. She told herself this several times in the long hours it took her to fall asleep that night. Cole fell asleep quickly... following a cold, passion-dousing shower.

As February shivered into maturity, their relationship took on an even more personal note. When Cole called in the third week of Cupid's month, he knew immediately by Tracy's snappish, irritable manner that something wasn't right.

"What's wrong?"

"Nothing's wrong," she barked, feeling somewhere between Attila the Hun and Vladimir the Impaler.

"Tracy..."

"Nothing's wrong!" she practically screamed, her fingers pushing at the pain in her pounding temple. "I'm sorry," she added, instantly contrite. "I have a headache. I think I'm catching a cold." To prove the point, she sneezed.

"I'm sorry," he said, his concern as evident as the still-frigid weather whispering secrets against the windowpane. "Have you taken anything?"

"No." She sniffed, coughed then sneezed again.

"That's brilliant. You got any aspirins?"

"Yeah, I think so."

"Go take two."

"Now?"

"Right now. I'll hang on."

"Cole..."

"Go...take...two...aspirins. Hey, and get a heating pad if you have one."

"A heating pad?" She sounded as if she were speaking from a tunnel. "Where'd you get your medical degree from?"

"Every idiot knows a heating pad is mandatory for a cold. It doesn't really help, except that it gives you something warm to cuddle to while your cold's getting better on its own. Oh, and you need orange juice, a box of tissues, and..."

Tracy couldn't help but smile. She also sneezed.

Two aspirins, one heating pad, tissues and orange juice later, Cole ended the conversation with an order, "go to bed!" His last words were "I wish I could ease your pain." It was said so softly, so sincerely, that tears sprang to Tracy's eyes.

She wished he could, too. Along with all the emotional pain that she'd endured and was still enduring. She also wished that he were there to hold her...to just pull her into his arms and hold her tight, never-let-her-go tight. As a tear spilled from beneath her honey-hued lashes and rolled down her cheek, she told herself that she didn't really wish he was there, that being sick was causing this nearly overwhelming feeling of vulnerability and need. But as she fell asleep that night with Cole's prescribed heating pad, she pretended that the warmth was coming from his body.

Cole spent the next week in Wisconsin, meeting with troubled dairy farmers. He'd told Tracy before leaving that he probably wouldn't have time to call. He didn't. And by the end of the week she thought she was going mad. The house was so damned quiet that it was shouting. On the one hand, she told herself she was making a grave mistake in allowing Cole entrance into her life, while on the other hand, she counted the days until he'd be back. She didn't bother to try to reconcile the two opposing viewpoints.

When the phone rang Sunday night, Tracy scrambled to answer it.

"Hello?"

"I missed you," said a low throaty voice.

Tracy's knees turned to the consistency of cotton candy, necessitating that she collapse onto the side of the bed. "I missed you," she whispered. It was an honest reply that she hadn't contemplated making. But it felt right. And, it *was* true.

Her answer seemed to surprise, though delight, him. "Did you? Did you really miss me?"

"Yes," she breathed. "Did you? Really miss me?"

"God, yes," he practically groaned.

Both seemed to need a few seconds to assimilate what they'd just heard...and in Tracy's case, what she'd just admitted.

"Say something," Cole prodded at last. "Anything. Just let me hear your voice."

Tracy smiled, suddenly feeling so light that she could have danced on daydreams. "You want 'Musetta's Waltz' from *La Bohème* or my grocery list?"

Her smile traveled through the telephone wires and into Cole's hotel room, forcing the corners of his mouth upward. Simultaneously, he reached up to unloosen the knot of his green tie. His suit jacket lay draped across a worn piece of luggage. "Can you sing me 'Musetta's Waltz' from *La Bohème*?"

"No," she admitted, stifling a bold laugh.

"Then it's a good thing I want to hear the grocery list, isn't it?"

"Do you want produce or meat?"

The hesitation at Cole's end heralded a delicate change of mood. "What I want," he answered roughly, "is to see you."

Tracy's heart trembled like a dandelion in a wild wind.

"Go out with me," he pleaded. "A real, honest-to-goodness date." When the silence persisted, he asked, "Does that mean no?"

"Cole, I...I don't know." It was more of a concession than she'd ever made, but it wasn't enough for him.

"Tracy, I can't go on this way. I missed you too much this week."

Tracy's fingers tightened on the receiver until her muscles ached. "I missed you, too, but..." It was stupid, she knew, but she felt as though she were being hunted into a corner. She wanted to say yes, but she couldn't. She just couldn't! "Cole, please give me time. Maybe in time..."

"I can't," he cut her off, harshly, softly. "I thought I could give you as much time as you needed." His voice had become raggedly hoarse when he added, "But I can't. I have needs, too. And I need something more than your voice on the phone. I need you." Long moments passed, fraught with the cold tension of uncertainty. "Please, Tracy. Trust me. Whatever your problem, we'll work it out together."

She had never wanted to trust anyone any more than she did at this moment, but trust was not something that came easily now—neither trust in a stranger nor, more ironically, trust in someone she cared about.

"Cole..." It was a plea for blind understanding.

He swallowed low and painfully and as he momentarily closed his eyes to what he had to say. "If you change your mind..."

No! she wanted to scream. *Don't give me an ultimatum!*

"I won't be calling again."

The words fell about her like a sleet-silvered fog, its cold, misty fingers enfolding her in its gray, frosted embrace. She felt herself withdrawing deep inside herself to that safe, painless place where she'd retreated so many times before.

There was another silence, this one laden with the barrenness of regret.

At last Cole spoke. "I, uh, I guess I'd better go. I have to unpack and I..." His voice trailed off. Then he whispered, "Goodbye, Tracy."

IF PHILOSOPHERS ARE RIGHT that the emotional translation of hell is a state of abject hopelessness, Cole Damon spent the following week with the vilest of devils, for he knew the moment he'd hung up the phone that Tracy wouldn't call. He'd heard the finality in her silence.

Hell, Tracy would have acknowledged, was having heaven in sight and suddenly having it wrenched away, for that was precisely how she viewed the phone call. One moment Cole was telling her that he'd missed her, the next that he wouldn't be calling again. None of this, though, did she philosophize Sunday night. She'd been too stunned to think.

Monday morning, however, she awoke to the faint consolation that she'd done the right thing. She couldn't get involved with Cole or with any man, and going out with him would only have been leading him on.

Cole, on the other hand, awoke with a curse on his lips. He shouldn't have pushed her. He knew she had problems, he knew he needed to go slowly, and he knew she needed time. He'd let his own impatience defeat him.

By Tuesday Tracy found that she was no longer so certain of her decision. She missed Cole and knowing that he was only a phone call away tempted her more powerfully than gold does greed. Twice she reached for the phone, twice she backed away. Each time she told herself that Cole deserved a whole woman, a woman who was able to give of herself freely and honestly.

In contrast to Tracy's doubts, Cole reverted to his original decision. He'd been right. He did have needs, needs that could no longer be satisfied by her voice, however sweet that voice was. He was falling in love with her—maybe he already had—and if their relationship was going nowhere, it would be a hell of a lot easier on him learning that now.

On Wednesday both Tracy and Cole were so irritable that Hank Yeats and Larry Seeger respectively threatened mutiny.

On Thursday the inner battles waged on.

Maybe, Cole considered, he should call her. Maybe he should just pick up the phone and say, "Talk to me. Tell me what some man has done to you to make you distrust so completely. Tell me why you tremble when I touch you. Damn you! Tell me why you can't fall in love with me.''

Maybe, Tracy considered, she should call him. Maybe she should just pick up the phone and say, "Help me." But then, she remembered, a cold sweat breaking across her forehead, that was what she'd asked of her husband. And it had been something he couldn't do. Maybe the harsh truth was that Cole wouldn't want her, either, if he knew her past.

Maybe . . .

Maybe . . .

The calendar showed Friday, and the clock showed late afternoon when Tracy, her fingers trembling, dialed Cole's private office number. What was she doing? she asked herself. What in the name of common sense and uncommon stupidity was she doing?

"Who the hell knows what's motivating Lovell," Cole was saying to Larry Seeger as the phone on the work-cluttered desk beeped that there was an incoming call on his private line. "The man's just a snake."

"Well, I wish he'd sink his fangs into your opponent Jordan Adams," the disgruntled campaign manager said as he glared down at the latest in a series of *Washington Tattler* character smears on the man to whose reelection he was devoting day and night. "I don't like the situation."

"I'm not exactly buying it flowers either," Cole said, listening to the phone's second beep. "Don't worry," he consoled his manager, who had unwedged his stocky frame from the chair and started for the door. "The man's striking blindly. Give him enough time, and he'll hit himself."

"Yeah, well," Larry Seeger cautioned, "keep your nose clean."

Cole grinned. "I'll keep my handkerchief drawn." As the door clicked shut, Cole's smile ebbed. He gave a tired sigh before he picked up the phone and punched in the private call. "Hello?" Even as he said the greeting, his mind jumped to Tracy the way it had a thousand times that week. He'd give anything he owned to hear her voice one more time.

"Cole?"

It struck Cole that Tom Lovell's next article would probably read that the congressman from Pennsylvania was losing his mind... and that the man might be right for once.

"Tracy?"

She swiped a wet palm down the side of her faded jeans. "Hi. Am I calling at a bad time? I mean, I wouldn't want to interrupt if you were on the verge of finding an answer to world peace."

"No. Now's not a bad time. And trust me, I haven't been able to find the answer to anything today—world peace or the morning crossword puzzle. How are you?" he asked.

"Fine," she lied.. "How are you?"

"Fine," he lied.

"Look, I uh..." She waved her hand in the general direction of the kitchen stove. A sauce simmered over a low heat, filling the room with the aromatic fragrance of tomatoes and spice. "I get domestic about three times a year despite everything I can do to fight the urge, and well, this is a domestic spell, and I've cooked this enormous pot of spaghetti sauce, and I can't eat it all, and I have only a small freezer filled mostly with frost, and I was wondering if you'd like …if-you'd-like-to-come-over-for-dinner-tonight.''

There was a moment's silence before Cole uttered a base profanity.

"Oh. I see word has gotten out about my spaghetti sauce," she said with a flippancy she was far from feeling.

"Tracy, I'm sorry. Any other time would be okay, but I already have plans for tonight."

Blonde, brunette or redhead? she wanted to ask but restrained herself. "That's all right. I understand."

"I'd cancel if I could, but it's the White House. Some of the Ways and Means Committee have been invited to dinner. I can't…"

"Of course you can't. What idiot would want to pass up the White House for my spaghetti?"

"I would," he said without hesitation.

As crazy as it was, the two words made her want to see him so desperately that she actually felt weak. She eased her back against the kitchen wall for support.

"Tracy? Are you there?"

"Sure. Look, give my best to the prez, huh?"

"Will you ask me again? Soon?" When she didn't answer, he repeated, "Will you?"

"Sure."

"Promise?" There was a silence. "Promise?"

"I promise," she whispered. She felt both relief and disappointment that he couldn't come: disappointment because she really wanted to see him; relief because she realized she wanted to see him too badly. Hearing his voice again had made her realize just how much she'd missed his nightly calls, his teasing, their game of hide and seek. She realized just how much she'd missed him. Like the golden beams of dawn after a long, black night, Cole Damon had gently insinuated himself into her life. And that gentle invasion frightened her.

Long after he'd hung up, Cole replayed her last words. Her "I promise" had been as fragile as a newborn kitten, and he wasn't prepared to guess whether or not she'd keep the promise. He suspected she didn't know, either, because he'd heard confusion and conflict in her voice. All he knew for certain was that she'd made an overture that he'd had to rebuff. And the only thing he could do about it was to utter another base profanity.

STEAM BILLOWED FROM THE SHOWER, misting the bathroom with a warm humidity that clung to mirror and air like smoky teardrops. Tracy took one final turn under the pummeling spray of hot water, thinking, as the fragrant film of soapy water splattered, how flat the spaghetti had tasted and how much flatter the red wine had been. In truth, the entire evening had been flat, so much so that she'd finally decided, even though it was only a little after nine, to shower and go to bed.

Shutting off the faucets, she raked back the curtain and stepped from the tub. Reaching for the towel, she began to dry herself. Ankles, legs, thighs and buttocks were quickly relieved of beaded moisture, followed by her face and arms. The crisp movement of her wrists soon dried her back, and she dragged the towel to the slightly rounded swell of her stomach. She patted, smoothed and rubbed as she inched the towel upward to her full breasts. A wisp of an unbidden sigh whispered from her lips as the fabric connected with flesh made tender from love's long denial. As she'd done for months, she willed herself not to react to the tactile stimulation, yet her will as always was not strong enough to battle the innate nature of woman.

At the sight of her image in the dew-dappled mirror, she allowed the towel to slip from her fingers and pile like a terry mountain at her feet. Coils of hair rebelled from a topknot and curtained her pink-flushed face, while her breasts thrust fully, femininely, and her hips flared to just that perfect inch of curved roundness. With no conceit intended, she knew that she had never looked better—maturity had softened her body's more youthful angles. She knew also that her body was at its sexual peak. It was a fact she disliked, but it was a fact nonetheless. She might no longer have sexual wants—those she'd abandoned to a happier time in her life—but her woman's body still did have needs.

Needs. Even as the thought scampered through her mind, sensual prickles stung her body, puckering nipples to roseate peaks and causing sharp sensations to coil to life in the valley beyond the nest of soft honeybrown curls. Slowly, as if she were touching a total stranger, she raised her fingertips and brushed them against the hardened crest of her breast. Her teeth digging into her lower lip, her eyelids at half-mast, she sighed . . . in pleasure and protest. She didn't want to feel anything, she thought, and yet, contradictorily, she did. The feelings were a validation of her being alive, a validation of her physical and emotional survival, but at the same time the feelings scared her. Especially now that such feelings were always accompanied by images of Cole Damon—dark-eyed, raven-haired Cole Damon. Could he ease this ache?

Would he want to if he knew the truth? And considering the truth, could she ever trust him to try?

The strident peal of the doorbell shattered her reverie, sending her eyes wide open and her fingers flying from her breast in inexplicable guilt. Snatching up a pink velour robe draped across a towel rack, she threw it over her head, yanked the front zipper upward and in her bare feet started out of the room and toward the stairs. With each downward step, she listened for Hank's coded buzz but at the bottom of the staircase was forced to conclude that it wasn't her friend at the door. As always since the rape, a doorbell and an unknown caller caused ripples of fear to race through her.

"I'll get it, John," she called out loudly then demanded at the door, "Who is it?" The words were met with a deathlike silence. "Who is it?" she repeated.

"Cole." The voice sounded as deflated as party balloons the morning after.

"Cole." Tracy's repetition of the word was barely audible over the wild stampeding of her heart. Unbarring the front door's two dead bolt locks, she pulled open the door...and stood face-to-face with the man who had occupied her thoughts in a most sensual way only minutes before. So blushingly stunned, so excited, yet so confused was she at seeing him on her doorstep that she didn't notice the sack he was holding nor the agony lining his usually sun-bright face. Nor did she notice the way his eyes quickly took in the compromising way she was dressed. "Hi," she said with a shy smile. It was a smile he didn't return.

"I'm sorry," he said. "I'm also presumptuous."

So caught up in soaking in his presence was she that it took his words a few seconds to register, and then, it was more his look of dejection than his words that made her suspect something was amiss. "What do you mean?"

"I thought... It never occurred to me that you were seeing someone else." The chilled early March wind whisked a froth of hair across Cole's wide, wrinkle-etched forehead. He didn't brush it back, but left it to whip about like midnight-black silk. "Look, I am sorry." He turned and started down the front steps.

"Cole! Where are you going?" she cried, following him out onto the porch until her bare feet collided with cold concrete. "What are you talking... about?" The realization hit her even as she was asking the question. "Cole, there's no one here."

He stopped midstep and turned, his eyes finding hers through the night. His questioned, hers answered.

"I don't even know a John," she said, a small smile playing at her lips. "That's the way the Rape Crisis Center suggests a woman answer her door if she lives alone." Relief flooded Cole, while a blanching panic seized Tracy. "I mean..."

"You...you weren't entertaining anyone?" he asked as if it was Christmas morning, and he was waiting for a precious gift.

Absently she shook her head, wondering what she would say if he questioned her about her association with the Rape Crisis Center. But he didn't. Instead he smiled sheepishly and moved back up the steps.

"There is no John?"

His relief now belonged to her. In celebration of it, she smiled. "There probably is somewhere in the world, but not in my house."

"I thought... I'm not only presumptuous, I'm stupid."

And jealous? she wondered, liking the possibility immensely. "You want to come in," she asked, her folded arms sheltering her from the cold, "or you want to stand out here watching me freeze while you're holding a sack of something?" As she stepped back into the house, she said, "I thought you were at a White House dinner."

"I was," Cole answered, following her in and raking back a swath of wind-touched hair, "but I just took the president aside and told him that I couldn't stay for dessert. That I had to go see a pretty lady."

"You're lying," she teased. "You told the president of the United States no such thing."

"You're right. I lied," he agreed with a grin, "though not about having to go see a pretty lady." His face became serious, and his voice adopted a smoky huskiness. "I did have to come see you, you know, or go completely crazy." He reached out and toyed with a wisp of shower-damp hair dangling just at the lobe of her ear. "I thought I remembered how beautiful you were, but I didn't even come close."

His words, or maybe his touch, sucked the breath from her lungs. "Obviously they put something in your wine at the White House," she whispered.

He shook his head. "No. I drank only water. You're the intoxication."

Their eyes merged and held, blue and the richest of sable brown. Cole wondered what she'd do if he suddenly lowered his head and captured her mouth with his... the way he'd sell his soul to... the way he fantasized doing every night before sleep claimed him as well as later in his dreams.

"What's in the sack?" Tracy asked, breaking the silence.

"Dessert for the meal I missed." He raised his brow in mischievous seduction. "Pistachio-swirl ice cream."

Tracy groaned. "I love it." Turning for the stairs, she said, "Let me go change and . . ."

"No!" he said, capturing her arm in the vise of his fingers. When their eyes met again, he added, "Don't change. What you're wearing is fine. I won't be here long."

Tracy had the curious feeling that his last remark was defining the perimeters of the evening so that she could relax and enjoy herself. And, even more curiously—with the past's torment, the future's uncertainty—she did just that . . . relaxed and started to enjoy.

"I'll get some bowls."

Cole shook his head and indicated the sack. "I brought champagne glasses from the White House."

Tracy's brow raised, and she fought a grin. "Isn't that considered theft?"

"Only if you're caught. Besides, I'll take them back."

"I suppose you sto . . . borrowed spoons, too?"

"Naturally. You think I'm inefficient?"

"I think you're going to do hard time, Damon."

Cole laughed. Tracy smiled. She suddenly realized it was the first time she'd smiled all week.

They went to the living room, where they both sat on the floor before a restoked fire, she in her housecoat, he in a black tux. His jacket was carelessly tossed over the back of the sofa, and his top shirt buttons were open to reveal ebony hair that contrasted sexily against the pristine white of his pleated shirt. The tux tie he'd abandoned to the cavity of a likewise abandoned patent-leather shoe. Stretched out and propped on an elbow, Cole ate pistachio-swirl ice cream, talked and laughed and teased. Tracy, sitting with her bare feet curled beneath her, followed suit. Time passed without either of them knowing or caring.

"You're staring," Tracy said shyly at the first lull in conversation. She was suddenly very aware that she wore nothing beneath her robe, a fact that made her blood run hot and cold.

"I was just thinking..." He hesitated as if pondering the prudence of continuing. In the pause the fire popped a flaming ember-song. "I was just thinking how different you are from Lisa."

At the mention of his wife's name, Tracy's heart constricted into a strangled knot.

"There was no way," he explained, "that she could have ever let anyone, including me, see her without makeup, a chic hairdo, and a designer outfit. There was no way she would have ever entertained on the floor before the fireplace in a practical pink housecoat with a dab of pistachio-swirl ice cream on it." With nothing on underneath that robe, he thought as his blood approached a scalding temperature.

At his words Tracy glanced down, found the offending green spot and smeared it with her finger. "I'm messy," she said self-consciously.

"Beautifully messy," he concurred in a silk-soft voice.

His eyes, like the moon at high tide, seemed to pull her, until she was forced to look full into their boundless brown depths.

"Your wife..." Tracy tried to drag her eyes away, but couldn't.... "She was very beautiful, wasn't she?"

"Yes."

"And you...you loved her very much, didn't you?" In her heart she knew that was why Cole always refused to discuss his dead wife in interviews. It was just too painful for him to do otherwise. And right this moment, pain was something she understood, because that was what she was feeling as she waited to have her comment confirmed.

They were both silent. Finally Cole pushed up on his elbow and raised himself to a sitting position. His proximity made Tracy angle her head upward in search of his eyes. She noted, and not for the first time that evening, the raven-black sprigs of hair escaping the open neck of his shirt. She had the overpowering urge to touch them.

"The truth is," he said at last, "that I didn't love her at all."

The words were unexpected, though strangely they proved to be a sweet salve to the jealous ache in Tracy's heart.

"Let me amend that. I didn't love her in the way a husband should love his wife. We were sometimes friends, sometimes lovers, but we were never really husband and wife."

"I...I don't understand."

Cole sighed and ran his hand along the back of his head. "Lisa and I met when I first became involved in state politics. She came from a political family herself—her dad had been governor of Pennsylvania for a couple of terms. She liked moving in the political world, and I think it was my political aspirations that first attracted her to me."

Tracy seriously doubted that. The woman had probably been attracted to the same handsomeness, the same emotional warmth, the same undeniable charisma that would draw almost any woman to Cole Damon. The way those traits were drawing her to him? she asked herself.

"So you married," she said, trying to rout out the renegade thought.

"Yes. We married." He sighed again heavily. "I thought I was in love with her."

"But you weren't?"

"No." He propped his elbow on his raised knee and threaded his fingers through his hair. "But I don't think she loved me in the beginning, either. I think she, like me, just thought she did."

Tracy allowed a tiny smile at the tips of her lips. "This is a little confusing, Congressman."

He smiled back faintly, sadly. "Yeah."

"What happened?" she asked, her eyes encouraging with their sapphire glow.

"Something I've never quite understood. The very thing that had once held us together—politics—became a wedge between us. She began to accuse me of being too singularly devoted to my career. And God knows, she was right. I cheated her with too many long, lonely nights. I was an overachiever doing what an overachiever does best: working myself and my family into the ground." Pain lined his face and settled in eyes that suddenly looked older and more tired.

"But I thought she wanted the political career, too?"

"Looking back, I think what happened is that we both thought we were in love, but that neither of us was. She, however, fell in love with me, and at that point my career became her competitor. On the other hand," he said, his voice charged with guilt, "I never fell in love with her." He studied Tracy for any hint of a reaction to the question that was to follow. "Does that make me a first-class heel?"

Slowly she shook her head and smiled. "No. Only human. You can't fall into or out of love at will."

"No, you can't. God knows, I tried to love her. I wanted to love her—she was my wife, for Christ's sake—but I didn't. I liked her. I desired her, but..."

His admission of desiring another woman did unsettling things to Tracy, and she found herself interrupting, "Why didn't you get a divorce?"

"She didn't want one."

"*You* didn't want a divorce?"

He gave a self-deprecating and bitter laugh. "Maybe I was trying to keep my political image attractive. God knows that Seeger had told me to often enough." He sighed. "No, that isn't true. I wasn't trying to spare my image. I was on the verge of asking for a divorce when I found out she was pregnant."

"Pregnant? I didn't know..."

"It wasn't common knowledge."

Lisa Damon's fatal accident suddenly became a double tragedy to Tracy. "Oh, Cole, you lost your child, too."

"It was a boy." He looked away as if seeing some far distant point in the past and said in a voice that was almost inaudible, "I had a son."

The night grew quiet and riddled with regret.

Tracy touched him without even realizing what she was doing; it was the simple, consoling gesture of her hand placed on his. "I'm sorry," she whispered.

His eyes lowered, not to her face but to her hand, laid so gently, so comfortingly on his. She had touched him...of her own volition...and she wasn't trembling. Slowly, with the speed of one not wanting to frighten away a skittish colt, he turned his hand palm upward and watched as her hand settled against his. He exerted the necessary pressure to lace their fingers together. She didn't resist, though a faint, belated quiver ran from her hand to his. His thumb stroked reassuringly against her flesh as he raised his eyes to hers.

She said nothing, though her lips parted to emit a sigh that sounded loud in the silent room.

"We can't go on this way," he said roughly. "You know that as well as I do. You want to be with me as badly as I want to be with you."

Tracy swallowed and tried to concentrate on something besides the feel of his hand on hers, the wonderful, disquieting feel of his hand on hers. She did know that they couldn't go on as they had been, and yet she didn't know if she had the courage to step beyond these painful but safe boundaries.

"Go out with me," he demanded.

"Cole, find yourself a woman who's...who's whole."

"You're not whole?"

She shook her head, spilling a tendril of hair from its knot. "No. No, I'm not. And I may never be."

"Well, you see, Tracy, this is where we may have a problem. I want you—whole or fractional, the good and the bad—I want the Tracy Kent sitting before me right this moment."

"Cole..." She said his name as though it was a breathless spring song but could find no other words because his free hand was tucking the newly fallen strand of hair behind her ear. His touch was masculine and intimate and something she both wanted and did not want. "Cole..." She tried to speak again, but his body was leaning into hers, his head lowering, angling, his lips moving closer, closer, breath-stealingly closer. Her heart beat the rhythm of a wild drum, but before she could protest his kiss, his lips had butterfly-brushed against hers. There was a split second of the warmest ecstasy. His mouth only a wish away from hers, he hesitated, hesitated...

And then his lips were moving onto hers again, this time in a fully committed kiss. Their warm flesh melded, their breaths, sweet and moist and tasting of pistachio-swirl ice cream, commingled. He took her mouth again and again, at every angle he'd dreamed of, with every nuance of meeting and tasting, of giving and taking. And through it all, he watched for and felt every shade of her reaction. He noted the receptive way her mouth accepted the tender foraging of his tongue, the way she tried to restrain her own but couldn't quite keep it from dancing with his. He noted also the wanton arch of her neck as his lips left hers and found the hollow behind her ear, and he thought that it had been a long time since any man had kissed her there. The thought pleased him, just as did the small purr of pleasure that slipped unnoticed by her from her lips.

Cole's lips were so pleasing and his touch so wonderfully natural that sensation overrode Tracy's sense of caution. She felt as if she were free-floating in some sensual dream that she not only didn't have the power to wake from, but that she really didn't care to wake from. It had been so long since her body had known the caress of a man, so long since she'd felt this sweet abandon. And yet, as is nature's way, the sweetness inexorably gave way to more primitive, stronger needs.

She felt her breasts blossoming to a ripe fullness, her nipples hardening to aching summits that pierced the fabric of her robe. The long-neglected core of her femininity grew hot and heavy, painfully hot and heavy, with the need to be filled with a man and stroked and loved. She suddenly felt herself growing afraid, afraid of emotions that she wasn't sure she could handle.

"Cole...no...I..." she whispered, wrenching her lips from his.

"It's okay," he soothed quickly, as if he'd been waiting for just that moment when she'd go no further. He saw the passion-flush of her face, the jut of her sensitized breasts against her robe; he recognized the willingness of her body, if not her spirit. "Slow and easy," he promised. "We're going to take it slow and easy."

She swallowed and opened her mouth to speak. To say what, she had no clear idea.

Cole stopped her with a tender "Shhh." He held her hand, while with his other palm he caressed her cheek, smoothing the pad of his thumb against her lips as he stared into her wide, uncertain, even frightened eyes. "Whatever you're running from," he whispered, "run to me."

CHAPTER SIX

SLOW AND EASY. Had he the power, Cole thought, glancing over at Tracy, who was presently chewing a hole in her bottom lip and hugging the passenger side of the car like a lover, he'd strike the hellish words from the English language. The month of March and innumerable dates with Tracy had passed, but their relationship was still very definitely in a mode called "slow and easy." It was a mode that was unquestionably driving him up a wall.

The evening had been typical. They'd gone out for hamburgers, fries and shakes, over which they'd acted as normal as any couple on a date. They'd even been intimate in the sense that she'd fed him french fries, her fingers brushing against his lips, his tongue licking her salt-dusted thumb, intimate in the sense that they'd drunk from the same straw with no reservations, intimate in the sense that he'd teased her mercilessly about her new Mickey Mouse watch. They'd even approached a heart-deep intimacy when they'd sat for long minutes saying nothing. She had then surprised him by announcing that she thought the abundant black hair on his arms was sexy. But all that intimacy behind them, the evening was ending the way it always did. She was sitting on the far side of the car... biting her lip... afraid of what was going to be expected of her now that the evening was over.

But he knew what to expect. As always, he'd pull her into his arms, and as always, she'd kiss him with a tentative abandon. The kiss would begin cautiously, but as her lips warmed to the persuasion of his, a wild abandon would set in. The strength of her passion always surprised him as did the strength of her restraint when that predictable moment came when fear overrode passion. He was convinced that she wasn't so much afraid of him as she was afraid of herself— afraid of reacting to the sensuality he was arousing in her. He had pondered long and hard as to what road had led her to this point and always ended by dumping the blame at the feet of her ex-husband. But what could he have done to leave her this timid of her own feelings?

Cole felt the surge of protectiveness that was by now familiar and accepted; he also felt a sun-warm sensation that could only be called love. He had fallen quickly, yet not so quickly. The truth was that he'd waited a lifetime to love this way. He'd waded through meaningless relationships and through a loveless marriage to feel this exquisite pain. And it *was* pain that he felt. And his need to express that love was so powerful that it, too, had become an endless, gnawing ache.

Sometimes he'd wake in the middle of the night, his breathing shallow, his brow in a heated sweat, his body turgid and tight with need. At those times he'd roll on his side and grimace away the minutes until he could breathe normally again. Sweet heaven, his thwarted desire was worse than those first preoccupied adolescent years when he thought he'd singlehandedly discovered that his body responded in ways that no one else's did. But now preoccupation had given way to obsession. He wanted Tracy. It was that plain and that simple and that damnably complex. For he knew that even if he miraculously woke in those dark midnight hours with her beside him, he still could not show her his love. That some silent sentry would stand between them, mocking his need to join them as one, feeding her fear to keep them as two. And it was her insistent duality that caused him the greatest pain. A cold shower could ease the physical ache, but nothing could ease the emotional ache that came from knowing that someone he cared about didn't care enough about him to share herself... that she wouldn't even share the reason why she couldn't share. All in all, his life had been reduced to pain.

Pain at loving her.

Pain at needing her.

Pain at watching her teeth dig into her lip at the thought of saying good-night to him. "Don't," he ordered.

Tracy turned her head toward the sound of his voice while her eyes fought through the night to find his. The face staring at her was all dusky shadows and hollows, all masculine and all heart-stealingly attractive.

"Don't what?"

"Don't bite your lip."

"Is that what I'm doing?"

"That's what you spend a great part of your life doing." She could see the smile that suddenly captured his mouth. "How am I going to kiss you good-night if you destroy your lip?"

Tracy's heart swelled with feeling for the man beside her. He was doing it again. He was openly stating the ground rules so that she could relax and enjoy their time together. He was in effect saying that he wasn't going to pressure her into any intimacy. She knew, though, that the time was coming when the ground rules were going to have to change. She knew, just as she knew he knew, that someday he was going to push.

"Did you have a good time?" he asked, dragging her thoughts from someday to now.

"Yes," she said with a smile. "Did you?"

"I always have a good time with you."

He turned the car into her driveway and cut the lights and motor. He made no move to get out; instead he shifted his body toward her and ran his arm along the back of the seat. His fingers brushed her shoulder. Her shoulder responded with a starburst of feeling. "Come here," he whispered. "I want to ask you something. Something vitally important."

She scooted toward him, though her heart began the uneven rhythm of dread. *Please don't ask me questions that I don't want to answer. Not tonight.*

"Do you really think the hair on my arms is sexy?"

She felt a wave of surprise, relief and embarrassment. She also felt a giggle welling in her throat. "Yes," she said, glancing down at the arm that had found her waist. Even in the semi-darkness, she could see darker-yet coils of hair peeking from beneath the pushed-up sleeve of his navy knit shirt. "Yes," she repeated—not so sturdily this time—as her eyes refocused on his. She deliberately refrained from touching the curls that were under such delicate discussion.

"You're the only woman who's ever thought that."

"I doubt that," she said, wondering just how much of his chest was covered in the same ebony mat. And, irrationally, she hated all the women who knew and hated herself for not having the courage to find out.

Reading the sudden troubled gleam in her eyes, he changed the subject. "I have a confession." Before she could ask what that confession was, he'd picked up her left hand and was fingering the red band of the watch on her wrist. "I really do like your Mickey Mouse watch."

She laughed again at the unexpectedness of his words.

"Have you ever thought," he asked, his tone professorially serious, "that maybe we're all on Mickey Mouse time? Maybe all of time is just an elaborate fantasy, a comic illusion? Maybe there is no such thing as past, present and future. After all, one blends into the other so quickly that who's to say?"

Tracy's brow arched upward as she pursed her mouth downward. "I'm impressed, Congressman. I had no idea that behind that handsome face lurked such thoughts. And I suppose your watch reads half past a fantasy, a quarter till an illusion?"

He held up both hands to reveal his bare wrists.

Tracy frowned. "You don't wear a watch." It was a statement—the question she asked of herself, Why had she never noticed that he didn't wear a watch?

"No. Not since Lisa died."

"Why?"

He shrugged, the upward movement of his shoulders reminding Tracy just how broad they were. "I told myself that if I hadn't been such a slave to the clock, I could have made more time for her, for us. I guess I believed that with that time I might have fallen in love with my wife." He then added softly as his eyes caressed hers, "I know now that she wasn't the one meant for me."

Tracy wasn't certain what these last words meant, but they, and the dark touch of his eyes, left her with a warm feeling that she liked. Almost as much as she liked the warm brush of his lips against the inside of her wrist. In a reflex action, she sighed and her other hand reached out to rest on the arm at her waist. She was instantly aware of soft coils of hair beneath her palm. Sexy, soft coils of hair, she thought. She started to ease her hand upward to the safer touch of his shirt.

"It's okay to have sexual feelings," he whispered, forcing her hand to remain where it was by placing his atop it. He rubbed her fingers back and forth in the springy softness. Sharp feelings burst to life in her body.

"I . . . I don't want to feel them."

"Why?"

"Please, Cole. Don't back me into a corner. Not tonight."

"I'm not back—"

"Yes, you are," she answered, her voice rising brittlely. "I didn't falsely advertise what you were getting. I told you I had problems. I told . . ."

"It's all right," Cole interrupted soothingly and with another kiss on her wrist. "It's all right."

She lowered her head, garnered her composure and once more raised her eyes. "Why do you put up with me?"

A bittersweet smile curved his lips. "Maybe someday I'll tell you."

"Maybe there is no someday," she said, teasing him with his own philosophy. "Maybe all of time is just a Mickey-Mouse-watch fantasy."

"In that case," he whispered as his head dipped and his lips targeted hers, "I'd better show you now."

As his lips closed over hers, he felt her initial rejection, followed by a feminine surrender to his masculine temptation. As her mouth opened to his, as their tongues met and mated, he allowed himself to slip into a momentary heaven, knowing sadly that hell was all too close...as close as her first tingles of fear, as close as his realization that she still couldn't, wouldn't, share.

A SEMISUPPRESSED LOVER'S GIGGLE floated from the back seat, leading Cole to the conclusion that he'd been edging toward all that Friday evening: doubledating with Hank and Marisa had been a mistake. He'd hoped to reduce some of the strain between him and Tracy by adding the buffer of another couple, but what he hadn't realized, though he should have, was that Hank and Marisa would be innocently indulging in the very action that was posing problems for him and Tracy.

There was another giggle, followed by a man's hushed murmur. Cole glanced up and into the rearview mirror...just in time to see Hank's hand gently, and very purposely, graze Marisa Wisner's breast. It was a touch of caring, a touch of evening's promise, a touch met with a playfully coy smile. It was a touch that ripped at Cole's sanity and finally shattered his weeks-long patience. He discreetly lowered his eyes from the very natural scene in the back and sought out Tracy, who was unnaturally chewing a hole in her bottom lip and hugging the far side of the car. It was time for explanations, he thought. Dammit to a fair heaven, it was overtime!

It had been a mistake, Tracy thought. Going to the movie with Hank and Marisa had been a mistake.

Their presence was only accentuating her and Cole's problems, intensifying her confusion and Cole's frustration. If she allowed her relationship with Cole to go as far as the bedroom, what would be her reaction? Could she make love like a normal woman? Or would the act do nothing more than bring back the nightmare she'd lived through? And one question frightened her even more. If Cole knew her background, would he want her? Even now, her ex-husband's rejection still cut like honed steel; it was a rejection she didn't think she could stand to see on Cole's face, to feel in his touch. Or worse, to realize it if he didn't touch her.

"...touch." The echoing of the word, the pressure on her shoulder, startled Tracy into a jump. "Hey, you okay?" Hank Yeats whispered for her ears only as he draped his lanky, lean form across the front seat.

"Sure," she said overbrightly. "Why wouldn't I be?"

Hank pondered the question, as if trying to decide whether to give her the half-dozen reasons he could think of offhand. All half-dozen had to do with the fog-thick tension he'd sensed between her and the man beside her. "I'll be in touch," he repeated.

Tracy smiled, nodded then watched as Hank eased toward the car door in tandem with the car's pulling to the curb before an apartment complex.

"Thanks for the invite, Congressman," he said. "We enjoyed the evening."

"Our pleasure," Cole replied, hoping he was adroit at lying.

"Yeah, we did have a good time," Marisa Wisner affirmed in a sultry voice reminiscent of Marlene

Dietrich. "And I enjoyed meeting you," she said, smiling at Tracy.

Tracy smiled back. She liked the woman. She liked her a lot...probably because it was obvious that Hank liked her a lot. In fact, Tracy had never seen her friend like any woman so much. It pleased her.

"We'll have to do it again," Tracy said, praying she was making her voice sound sincere, which it really should have been.

As the couple scrambled from the car, Cole said, "You need a ride home, Hank?"

There was the slightest of hesitations while Hank and Marisa exchanged a quick lovers' look. A silent question was asked and answered. "No, sir, I...I can manage."

"Good night, then," Cole said.

"Good night," everyone chorused.

Both Cole and Tracy, held by a power neither could resist, watched as Hank and Marisa, arms entwined about each other's waists, walked up the concrete pathway and toward the apartment building. Totally oblivious to jealous voyeurs, Hank bent his head and whispered a secret into Marisa's ear. She laughed, raised her pretty face, which was framed by long, straight blond hair the color of the honey-brown of her eyes, and replied something that even at a distance sounded provocative and promising.

Cole gunned the car from the curb with blatantly unnecessary force.

"He's spending the night," Tracy said, belatedly realizing she'd vocalized what she'd been thinking. Her eyes flew to Cole's.

His were nighttime-black and heated with a restless emotion. "Probably so. That's what adult people do who are attracted to each other. They spend time together in intimate and pleasurable ways."

The crispness of his voice stung.

Cole saw her pain and hated himself for inflicting it. *Damn!* he thought, though he said nothing. He simply squared his shoulders against the flawless March night and the flawed situation. Long minutes later, he switched on the car's radio, half listened for less than a minute then shut it off with a sharp twist of his wrist. He looked over at Tracy, who was looking straight ahead . . . and torturing her lip with her teeth.

"I'm sorry," he said.

She glanced his way and opened her mouth. Nothing came out. Ultimately, she looked back out the front window. She had the curious feeling, his apology notwithstanding, that the ground rules of their relationship had just changed.

"I'm coming in," he announced once he'd killed the car engine in her drive.

"I'm tired, Cole. I didn't . . ."

"I'm coming in." The granite-hard set of his jaw said that the matter was not negotiable.

"All right," she agreed, throwing open the car door and starting for the house. As she walked, she dug in her purse for the key. Seconds later he caught up with her and wordlessly took the key from her hand. She trembled at the brush of his fingers . . . or maybe she was trembling in anticipation of what she knew was coming.

He jammed the key into a lock and quarter-angled it then turned the doorknob. The door didn't budge.

"The other lock," she said calmly. How could she speak so calmly when her heart was beating faster than the wings of a startled dove?

"Good God, how many locks are on this door?" Impatience laced his voice as he asked the question, an impatience that didn't wait for an answer. Instead he threw wide the door—it hit the wall with a subdued *bam*—and motioned for her to precede him.

She did and hit the light switch. The overhead globe light instantly showered the room in a golden glow. Laying her handbag on a high-backed chair, she moved out of habit to draw the apricot drapes across the exposed bay window. That done, she turned. And stared at Cole.

He stood, one hand braced in a deceptively lazy way at the waist of his olive-green slacks, watching her with dark, piercing eyes.

He looked so handsome, Tracy thought, wondering if the next woman in his life would think so, too. "Would you like a drink?" she asked in a reedy, unfamiliar voice. *Be social, Kent! Even if your world's about to tumble!* "I have whiskey and..."

"Forget the drink. I want to talk."

Tracy swallowed and absently ran her nervous, wet palm down the side of her red-and-white print skirt. "About what?"

"You know about what."

The gold and glass clock on the mantel ticktocked its temporal opinion of what was about to happen.

"Yes," she whispered finally and honestly.

Her ready admission took him by surprise. "Tracy..." He expelled a long breath of air, as if he didn't quite know what to say now that he'd taken this first step. "Tracy, we're not kids. We're not adolescents playing with some developing sense of sexuality. We're adults, mature adults, with mature adult needs. I lo—" He stopped, intuitively knowing that he needed to amend the word to something less pressuring. "I care for you, and I believe that you care for me. Nature has graciously given us a way of expressing that caring—touches, caresses, kisses, inter—"

"I know, Cole!" she snapped.

"Do you?" he asked with a frustrating calmness.

"I think I need that drink," she said in answer to his question. She walked to a mahogany cart and splashed a generous amount of whiskey into a glass. Not bothering with ice, she downed it in one swallow. It fire-flamed its way down her throat; she coughed at its fiery potency.

"Hank touched Marisa's breast tonight."

No words could have fallen on Tracy's ears with more unexpectedness. The empty glass still in her hand, a vacant expression on her face, she turned around. "What?"

"He just reached out, as if it were the most normal thing in the world, and brushed the back of his hand against her breast. And she let him."

Tracy now saw the point he was making; she reacted with an inappropriate anger. "Half the world's population has breasts, Cole. I'm certain if you're so interested in touching one that you could probably find in a half-mile radius of D.C. alone enough women to keep you busy for..."

"I want to touch yours."

His frankness pricked her lungs, allowing the escape of a long, thin stream of air.

"It seems...unnatural to me," he said, ignoring her obvious discomfort, a discomfort her throttle-like hold on the glass attested to, "that I can't, even after all these weeks, reach out and touch you the way Hank touched Marisa. In a way that I can't explain and in a way that may seem presumptuous to you, I feel I have that right. I've felt your breasts pushed against my chest when we kiss, I've seen and felt the nipples harden.''

Tracy felt her body acting out his words in a way that caused hard dots to be etched in the red knit shirt she wore. His eyes lowered to her body's betrayal before again joining her eyes.

"Yet I don't dare reach out my hand and sculpt that fullness, that sweet part of you, in any way. It seems particularly strange to me in view of the fact that I think you want me to touch your breasts." His eyes softened. "You do want me to, don't you, Tracy?"

She felt thoroughly embarrassed. "This whole conversation..."

"Don't you?"

"...is ridiculous! It's..."

"Don't you?" His voice was sharp but blunted with caring.

"Yes!" she screamed.

Her answer seemed to satisfy him, though only partially. "And you're afraid of your reaction to that touch. And maybe afraid of what I'll do next."

"Yes," she said in a half whisper. Oh, no, she thought, he was going to make her tell him. He was going to make her spill the whole ugly truth!

"I want to know what somebody did to you to scar you so deeply that we're forced to stand here and have this conversation when we should be upstairs making love. I want to know why I can't even touch you."

"Cole..." The word was spoken in desperation.

In a desperation that he ignored. "I don't have to touch you, Tracy, but I do have to know why I can't."

His eyes said nothing, his eyes said everything, his eyes demanded truths she didn't want to divulge. She turned away from his searing gaze and set the glass back on the cart. There was the hollow sound of glass striking wood. She couldn't tell him. She couldn't. She'd rather lose him by her refusal to talk than lose him after he knew the truth. At least in the first there was no rejection. "Find yourself someone else, Cole," she said in a toneless voice.

He crossed the room angrily, grabbed her arm in a painful clasp and whirled her around until her thighs were flush against his. "Dammit, I don't want anyone else! I want you—" He felt her cringe, felt every muscle in her body tighten into stone. He was instantly surprised and hurt by her intense, fearful reaction. "My God, Tracy, you act as though I'm going to rape you."

Rape you!

Tracy's eyes widened. Her face blanched to the bloodless color of chalk. Her body jerked beneath his strong, curling fingers.

And then he knew. In one hateful moment of clarity, he knew. And to confirm the hellish realization came bits and pieces of thought and conversation.

*She's uncomfortable with men...trembles at a masculine touch...afraid of me...afraid of her own sexuality...doors patch-worked in locks... "There's no one here. That's the way the Rape Crisis Center suggests a woman answer her door if she lives alone."
...Rape Crisis Center...rape...rape! RAPE!*

"Oh, my God," Cole whispered, slowly releasing his hold on her arm. He experienced a flash of denial, followed by a rush of blinding, scalding rage, and for the first time in his life he could have murdered some faceless man, without regret and with his bare hands. His stomach knotted into a sick coil from a strange feeling of having been somehow violated himself—as if by touching Tracy, he, too, had somehow been touched—and he also felt a totally irrational feeling of guilt. What in hell had he been doing while Tracy was being raped? Why hadn't he stopped it?

At the unreadable expression on Cole's face, a frigid cold slithered up Tracy's spine. She turned back to the cart, caressed the whiskey bottle to a leaning position—the neck of the bottle chattered against the glass—and again downed the contents in one gulp. She then poured herself another drink and swallowed it down as well.

"When?" Cole asked raggedly, taking the glass and bottle from her as she started to pour yet another glass of courage and forgetfulness.

She didn't look up but gazed at her suddenly empty, suddenly shaking hands. "T-two years ago."

An abrupt thought occurred to him. "Two years ago at Christmas?"

Her eyes grazed his, and she fleetingly wondered how he'd guessed. She told herself that it didn't matter. Nothing mattered. "Three days before."

"Who?"

Hesitating, she answered, "He . . . he worked for Dennis . . . my husband . . . they'd quarrelled and . . . and he came to the house and . . . and took it out on me."

The picture in Cole's mind tore at his gut in a way that he hadn't known his gut could be torn. He actually had to force air into and out of his lungs. The exercise was painful. "Did . . . did he threaten you?"

Tracy laughed with a flippancy that sounded macabre. "Only with my life." Her body gave a convulsive shudder. "He had a knife. I thought he was angry enough to use it."

Cole's heart accelerated to the rhythm of panic. "Did he . . . did he hurt you?"

Tracy shrugged. "Yes and no."

"I don't under . . ."

"Sexual force always hurts, but . . ." She shook her head. "No, he didn't really hurt me. Not physically." She then added cryptically, "I wish he had."

Cole frowned. "What does that mean?"

"Nothing," she said wearily, raking back her hair. "It means nothing."

An uncomfortable quiet descended as Cole tried to find a way to ask what some inexplicable force was driving him to ask. He knew the answer, and yet, as a man in love with this woman, he had to ask it. "Did he . . ." He fought back the quaver in his voice that refused to let him form the question.

Tracy's eyes found his. Defiance was carved in their cold blue depths. "Did he what, Cole? Did he do all the things that rape usually implies? Yes, he did. And did I enjoy the things he did to me? Despite the fact that I was forced, did I still get some pleasure from the physical act? No. No, dammit! I didn't enjoy it! I didn't want him inside . . ."

"Stop it!" Cole barked.

"No!" she screamed back. "You want to hear all the lurid details, so let's hear them." Her eyes wild and flashing, she added, "He was big and he was strong, and he threw me to the carpet. He ripped at my slacks until he broke the zipper. He said he'd kill me if I didn't help him pull them down. And my underwear . . ."

"Tracy, don't," Cole begged in a hoarse whisper.

"I helped him pull them down. And I'd have done anything else he asked because I didn't want to die. Anything, Cole. Have you ever been so scared you'd have done anything? I remember thinking that Dennis would kill me if I got blood on our new beige carpet. Which was stupid because I would have been dead anyway, wouldn't I?"

"Tracy..."

"And then he forced me to..." She stopped and took a deep, serrated breath. "He forced me to...lie still and..." Her voice broke. "Oh, God, he was so heavy..."

"Stop it!" Cole shouted as he hurled the empty glass across the room. It crashed against the baseboard and shattered into two dozen pieces.

Tracy froze, her breathing but a harsh rasp in the room. Cole's was but a harsh rasp as well. Their eyes merged...and held. Both of them saw pain. Cole slowly and purposely lowered the whiskey bottle to the cart...as if not trusting himself not to send it hurtling after the glass.

"I wasn't accusing you of anything. I just had to ask. I don't know why. Please, Tracy, I'm just trying to cope. Just give me a minute to cope."

The laugh Tracy gave bordered on hysteria. As if from a distance, she could hear it. As could Cole. "Well, best of luck, Congressman, in learning to cope in a minute. My husband needed slightly more time. He needed an eternity." Her eyes welled with tears, and she fought to keep them dammed. She succeeded, except for a conspicuous glazing that made her eyes shine like sapphires beneath a shallow pond. "He never touched me again. I was dirty. I'd been with another man...and that made me dirty. I tried once to make love to him, but..." A lone tear tumbled down Tracy's cheek. She didn't notice it. She was somewhere far away. When her eyes found Cole's again, they were empty and blank. "He couldn't stand to touch me."

Make that two murders I should commit, Cole threatened on some wild plane of thought.

"Tracy..."

But she hadn't finished. There was still one more thing she had to say before she lost her nerve. "The jury...they found the man who raped me innocent. He said I had seduced him, that I had threatened to have him fired if he didn't go to bed with me. The jury...the jury of fair-minded men and women believed him. And Dennis..." She laughed again, a mirthless, sad sound. "He asked me...asked me if the jury's finding had been just. He asked me if I'd seduced Paul Nelson Bolden." Her voice rose. "My own husband asked me if I'd seduced another man." She slowly shook her head from side to side. Her bottom lip quivered. "I refused to answer him. He didn't deserve to know. He..." Her hand went to her stomach, at the same time her face paled under an instant cold sheen of sweat. She swallowed long and hard. "Oh, God, I...I'm going to be sick."

Cole reached out a hand to steady her but hesitated. It was a hesitation born out of indecision. Would she want him to touch her? Suddenly the joker was wild in their relationship. Suddenly he didn't know what to do.

She saw his hesitation. And felt again the devastation of rejection. Cole didn't want her. He couldn't touch her, either. Maybe she really was dirty. She had the overwhelming urge to shower in a hot, cleansing flow of water for a thousand years; conversely, a coldness, the icy numbness she'd once before grown so intimate with, invaded her body. At the same time, her stomach cramped in nausea.

"Just leave," she pleaded as she pushed past him and rushed upstairs. Strangely, she treasured the consuming nausea whose demanding fingers were clawing at her stomach. At least it kept her from thinking about the man who at that moment was walking out of her life.

Just as she was wishing that she were dead, Tracy felt a warm palm splay across her forehead.

"Get it up, baby," Cole crooned, squatting beside her on the bathroom floor. "Whiskey and nerves are a lousy combination. Remind me to tell you about the time I drank a bottle of tequila. You've never been sick until you're sick on that stuff."

She tuned in to his soothing voice, the voice saying such normal things, accepted his touch, his warm, comforting touch. At last and with a depleted sigh, she leaned back. Only vaguely did she realize that she was wedged in the vee of his legs.

"Is that it?"

"I . . . I think so."

He released her forehead and, with his knee creaking a protest, rose. She heard the medicine cabinet opening and the sound of running water. She shifted her gaze, her eyes on the level of his trim, masculinely firm buttocks. It somehow seemed fitting that he be intimately ensconced in her bathroom, her life. The thought instantly grew uncomfortable. Why had he stayed? It was just going to make it harder when he did leave. It . . .

"Here," he said, pulling at his pants leg and squatting down beside her again. He offered her the cap of a mouthwash bottle. She rinsed her mouth, and her reward was a moist rag that he applied to her face. Tracy swayed into the cool caress as he wiped her forehead, her cheeks, her throat. "Better?" he asked.

She nodded.

"C'mon, let me help you up." With those words, he wrapped an arm about her waist and with seeming effortlessness pulled her to her feet. "Let's get you into bed. Then I'll . . ."

"Cole?"

He stopped at the pleading sound of her voice, but mostly he stopped because of the way her hands were clenching the front of his shirt.

"What, baby?"

His voice was tender. His look, gentle and caring. *Don't go!* she wanted to scream. *Please don't go! Don't walk out of my life!* Instead, she said, "Aren't you going to ask me?"

"Ask you what?"

"If I . . . if I seduced him?"

The look of vulnerability on her face was so total and so overpowering that Cole felt it, felt her, in every pore of his being. In fact, in all of his life, he never remembered feeling quite the way he did at that moment, as if somehow they had merged. He felt her every pain as though it were his own. "No," he said in a voice that rippled with emotion.

A tightness spread across Tracy's chest until her heart felt weighted down by the most wondrous of feelings. Her eyes stung with the sweet release of tears. How was it possible that this man whom she'd known for only months could believe in her more faithfully than the man with whom she'd lived for six years? In a way that only her heart understood, Cole Damon became very precious to her at that moment. So precious that, more than anything else in the world, she wanted to tell him what she had vehemently refused to tell her husband.

"I . . . I didn't," she said, the words barely able to squeeze around the tight ball in her throat.

"I know."

"I wouldn't . . . I wouldn't do something like that," she whispered, tears now completely filling her eyes.

"I know," he said, ineffectively wiping at the river now chasing down her cheeks.

"He raped me. He did. He . . ."

"Oh, baby, I know," Cole said in a rough voice as he hauled her into his strong arms. "I know. God, I know."

Her face buried in his chest, her fists clutching at his shirt, she cried giant, scalding tears that seemed wrenched from her very core. She cried because of Cole's belief in her, cried because of Dennis's disbelief, cried because it felt good and right to be sharing the moment with this man. She continued to cry when Cole finally scooped her up in his arms and carried her trembling body to the bed. And cried still when he propped himself against the headboard and held her tightly and tenderly as the room's darkness swelled around them. She babbled; he soothed her, bestowing kisses on her temple.

"I need a shower," she said, instinctively trying to pull from him. "I feel so dirty."

Understanding the origin of her strange words, he restrained her. "No, you're not dirty. What happened doesn't make you dirty."

"Dennis thought I was."

"To hell with Dennis!"

"Don't leave."

"I'm not leaving."

"I'm cold. So cold."

He held her shaking body closer. And closer. And closer.

She took his warmth and his strength, and it was only later, as she was drifting off to sleep, that she realized that Cole was crying, too.

"Cole?" she said groggily, looking up at him with translucent eyes.

He kissed her eyelids closed, one of his quiet tears spilling onto her cheek. "Go to sleep."

Exhausted, wrapped in the security of his arms, she did. And long after she slept, Cole cried. Because he didn't know anything else to do. As he drew the cover up over the sleeping woman in his arms, the woman whose breath was a sweet mist pooling against his neck, he whispered into the room the two most beautiful words he knew...the words that eventually were going to make her his.

"Slow and easy."

CHAPTER SEVEN

TRACY WOKE SLOWLY. Saturday sunshine streamed through the bedroom window. Light. She saw the sliver of teasing light from beneath heavy, swollen lids. Oh, God, her eyes hurt, she thought, moaning. Had she been crying? Yes, she'd been crying. But about what, her brain stubbornly refused to disclose. Her brain did tell her—and quickly—that she'd had too much whiskey the night before and that she'd aborted it in a most undignified fashion. She moaned again. Had she disgraced herself totally? What would Cole…

Cole!

Tracy's eyes fluttered open—as open as puff-pastry lids allowed—and her head jerked to the side. Except for an indentation in the pillow, the other side of the bed was empty. And suddenly, so was her heart.

Sitting up quickly and raking the tousled hair back from her forehead, she called out in a scratchy voice, "Cole?"

There was no answer.

"Cole?"

There was still no answer.

Her empty heart stopped beating. Hanging her head, her hair falling forward in amber disarray, she once more closed her hurting eyes and let out a deep, wounded sigh. She had thought he would be there. Foolishly thought he would. During the long night, his warm body and gentle touch, his caressing words and tenderly given kisses had promised understanding, had pledged a commitment that had obviously been for the moment only. She didn't blame him. Really she didn't. Why would any man want to get involved with her? It was just... Just what? It was just that it had seemed so right last night. It was just that his arms had seemed just her size, his kisses tailor-made for her needs. But last night obviously hadn't been right...and he certainly wasn't here...and she'd never felt so alone!

Throwing back the covers, she swung her feet to the edge of the bed. And stopped. She wore only her slip and bra, lacy confections of ivory satin that sculpted every curve. Her skirt, knit top and panty hose lay sprawled across the yellow ottoman. A mélange of thoughts scurried in the outback of her mind: warm hands on her bare skin, fingers pulling and tugging, soft words coaxing her to raise up her hips, the silken command telling her to go back to sleep. And a body, a male body, tucked close to hers all through the night. An alive feeling ribboned through her at the intimate thought of his undressing her, of his sleeping with her. She told herself that she was being silly, that he hadn't thought of either as anything more than a mercy mission. She also told herself that she had to stop this line of thinking and get up.

She had just left the bed when she noticed the note lying on the bedside table. She recognized the stationery as hers. The writing she recognized as Cole's. Her heart began to beat again. Rapidly.

Sorry I had to leave—I have an important appointment. Hope you're feeling human (you're supposed to smile here). I put some coffee on for you, which was probably ready a long time ago. I'll call you later. Oh, and Tracy, we're going to work this out. You and me. Together.

It wasn't signed, but then it didn't need to be. She knew it was from the only man who'd ever cared enough to cry with her. In recognition of that fact, her eyes blurred with stinging, grateful tears.

TRACY POURED A MUG OF COFFEE just as Cole absently palmed the Styrofoam cup on his desk. Bringing it to his lips, he sipped then grimaced at the cold, gray taste. He abandoned the cup to the outer reaches of his desk and busied himself with the stack of "urgent" correspondence that Larry Seeger had already brought to his attention. But his attention was a hard animal to corral this morning. His mind kept running back to Tracy.

Tracy. Was she up yet? He glanced at the clock, semihidden behind a listing of the Ways and Means Committee's environmental tax expenditures. 10:33. Yeah, she was probably up. How did she feel? Probably as dog-miserable as he. God, his eyes hurt! And his heart! How could she have lived with a rape firsthand when he couldn't even cope with it two years after the fact and at a secondhand distance? He'd felt sick at his stomach, sick at heart, ever since she'd confirmed his ugly suspicion. And she'd thought— actually thought—that when he learned the truth, he'd walk out on her the way her husband had. That hurt. That hurt like hell. But he couldn't blame her. She'd already experienced a lousy example of fidelity. But the question remained the same as it had all during the sleepless night. How could he help her?

His eyes again fell to the latest edition of the *Washington Tattler*...and Lovell's latest slur. The man was implying once more that the congressman from Pennsylvania had a vested interest in dairy farming legislation. This time, he'd gone a step further, though. With the gutsy wiliness he was well-known for, he had somehow managed to interview Uncle Chigger and, of course, had manipulated his every word. That his uncle had been so gullible didn't surprise him—Dale Schurman was an honest man who'd never think of deception. And to give Lovell his devil's due, he was the best at what he did. But the man may have outsmarted himself this time. He may have actually done something that Cole was pleased about. He may have given him a tool with which to help the dairy-farming issue...and Tracy. Cole reached for the phone.

Tracy yanked the receiver from the kitchen wall as the God-awful ringing threatened to split her head open. "Hello?"

"Did you find the coffee?"

A tiny smile automatically formed at her lips, and she felt a warm coziness that she knew had nothing to do with the steaming brew. "I'm having some now."

"Is it drinkable?"

"I can honestly say that I haven't the foggiest idea because my taste buds are dead."

"Other than your deceased taste buds, how do you feel?"

"Like a war has been fought in my stomach and like I have two blowfish for eyes."

Cole laughed softly. "That good, huh? Well, if it's any consolation, I don't feel much better."

Tracy immediately felt contrite. "I'm sorry."

"Hey, I didn't say that for you to be sorry."

"I know…but I am. It was because of me that…"

"Tracy, don't. Don't apologize for sharing yourself with me. Ever."

A knot of emotion formed in the back of her throat, which she tried to clear away with a deep swallow. She also pulled the phone cord to its full extension and sat down at the kitchen table. "You didn't have to clean up the glass."

"I believe I was the one who broke it. I hope it wasn't some priceless family heirloom."

Tracy's lips twitched. "I think it was a year old and cost a dollar."

"Well, heck, I can break a few more at that price. Did you find my note?" he asked, his voice suddenly soft and serious.

"Yes," she answered, considering the piece of paper on the table that had been read about four dozen times.

"Do you believe it?"

"Sure. I have the coffee in my hand."

"That isn't what I meant. And you know it."

She did know it and had deliberately avoided a serious answer.

"Do you believe that we can work this out together?"

"Cole, I…" Somehow the words wouldn't come. They were jammed in her throat, along with a heartful of raw emotions. She wanted to say "Please, please, don't leave me." She also wanted to say that he deserved something better than her problems, maybe her unsolvable problems. Instead of saying anything, she rested her forehead in her hand in a classic pose of dejection.

"What is it, baby?" he asked after an inordinately long silence.

Baby. She hadn't been sure that he'd used such an endearment the night before. She thought that maybe she'd just imagined it, maybe even willed it, while she'd been caught up in nausea, tears and sleep. But he *had* called her baby. She liked his calling her that in the black velvet of night—and in the bright reality of day.

"Cole, I..." she tried again. "Believing is very hard for me."

"I know. But will you try?"

"Are you sure I'm worth all this effort?"

"Don't you ever ask me that again." His voice was harsher than she'd ever heard it; she made the mental note that she always wanted to be on his side in a confrontation. "Do you hear me?"

A small, little-girl smile crept to her lips. "Yes, sir."

"That's better, Ms Kent. Now, you never did answer me. Are you going to try to believe?"

Was she? Did she have the courage to trust again? To open up her heart to this man? To believe that in some magical way he could glue her shattered life back together?

"Yes," she heard herself answering, knowing intuitively that if Cole Damon couldn't help her, there wasn't another man in the world who could.

"Say it again," he commanded.

"Yes."

"We must have a bad connection."

"Yes!" she cried, knowing precisely what he was doing.

"Now don't forget it."

"Why do I have the feeling you're not even going to let me come close?" she teased.

"For a lady with a rebellion in her stomach and blowfish for eyes, you're kinda smart."

Tracy's answering laughter had the quality of morning sunshine, of nascent optimism.

"And keep that up, too. Laughing, that is."

"Yes, sir. Anything else?"

"Yeah. One more thing. I want you to do an article on my uncle."

"What?"

"I got a call from the editor of *Today*. He wanted to do another story on me, but I talked him into doing one on Uncle Chigger and the farming issue instead. I also told him I knew someone who might be interested in free-lancing. I told him you'd call and approach him about it. Okay?"

"Sure. But what do you want me to do exactly?"

He spent the next few minutes telling her about Tom Lovell's latest piece and explaining the counterbalancing interview he wanted her to do. He explained also that he thought it would be best to interview his uncle in person and that the most logical thing, since his uncle's property butted up against his own, was to fly the following morning to Cole's farm in Pennsylvania, where they'd spend the night and fly home the following Monday afternoon.

"I want you to see my house," Cole admitted honestly and with an obvious pride. "I think you'll love it . . . and Pennsylvania."

There was a silence at the other end.

"We'll have a chaperone, if that's what's worrying you. My foreman . . ."

"I wasn't worried about that," she interrupted, but realized that that wasn't quite true.

"Then what is it?"

"There's something you should know. Tom Lovell...he did a hatchet piece on me following the trial."

Cole swore harshly before he added, "That explains the spilled Bloody Mary. It's also one more reason for doing this article. What do you say?"

There were a dozen reasons she could have used to justify her answer—that she wanted to get even with Lovell, that she wanted to help Cole, that she wanted to help his uncle, that she wanted to aid and abet the small-farm issue—but the truth was that there was only one real reason that she was at that moment saying yes. She wanted to be with Cole Damon.

TRACY WATCHED HIM. She watched the friendly way Cole shook hands with the pilot and suspected that this wasn't the first time the man had flown for him; she watched the play of early Sunday morning light as it bounded through the plane window and highlighted his hair until it sparkled like glittery black diamonds; she also watched the way his hand was resting, with a negligent spread of thumb and index finger, at the waist of tight, comfortably aged jeans. She then watched as he turned and walked down the aisle toward her with a smile that she was certain was dissipating the slight hazy fog that was dancing around the Dulles International Airport.

As he moved toward her, one hand rammed in the pocket of a red nylon windbreaker, the other touching the backs of the empty seats he passed, two observations hit her with the force of white-bright lightning. He was more handsome than he'd been twenty-four-odd hours before—and he had an unmistakable confidence about him that somehow instilled confidence in those around him. She suddenly allowed herself the luxury of believing everything would be all right. Somehow he'd make things right. Together they *would* work things out.

"We'll be taking off in a minute," he said, dropping into the seat beside her and automatically fastening his seat belt. He leaned across her to test the strap at her waist. As he did so, her jean-clad thigh pressed against his. "You buckled in?"

"Yeah," she answered, luxuriating in the feel of his leg against hers, inhaling the fresh, sexy fragrance of his cologne. Without knowing why, she smiled.

"Damn, you've gone and done it, haven't you?" he asked abruptly.

"Done what?" she asked. His intense sable look smothered her breath just enough to make her voice vampy.

"You've gone and gotten more beautiful since Friday."

That his comment was almost a duplication of what she'd seconds before thought about him didn't register at all. But then, nothing but his nearness was registering.

"If you're trying to get my vote, Congressman, I would remind you that I'm not even from Pennsylvania."

"I'm after something much more important than a vote," Cole replied, his voice the consistency of thick golden honey. The fact that he didn't define just what he was after caused Tracy's imagination to go wild and her heart to accelerate. She liked the flying-without-a-net feeling. "I missed you," he whispered.

"I missed you," she whispered back, thinking how long and miserable the night had been. And how unsatisfying his three phone calls had been.

"I wanted to come over, but I had to try to get ahead on some work if I was going to be out of the office."

"I understand."

"Do you? Lisa never seemed to."

"I'm not Lisa."

His eyes leisurely scanned her face, absorbing its every feature—her pastel-blue eyes, her slender, straight nose, the way her jaw impeccably sloped upward into her rose-dusted cheek, the way her lips seemed parted and poised for the touch of his. "No. No, you're not. And I'm not Dennis."

She considered this, with all its implications. She shook her head slowly but certainly. "No. No, you're not."

He had promised himself that he would wait to kiss her, that he would wait until they'd been together awhile, but his promise went the way of snow under a sweltering desert sun. *Sweet heaven,* he prayed, *let this be the right thing to do. And the right time to do it.*

With his index finger hooked under her chin, he tilted her face upward until her lips were just under his. Slowly his eyelids shuttered and slowly hers shuttered, then he inched his mouth downward and brushed, oh so lightly, his lips against hers. It was a tempting, tempting taste. At contact, he felt her tense.

She felt herself tense as well, the way she always did when his lips first touched hers. But now she felt some other reaction. Some inner part of her reassured her that it was okay to relax, okay to enjoy this man's kiss. That it was okay to trust this man.

Cole felt her lips relax and part and respond with a sweet seeking of his mouth, drawing his lips back to hers as she never had before. Always before, it had taken the oblivion of passion to make her respond. Now he felt her lips' gentle beckoning. It was the headiest experience he'd ever known. Pulling back, he searched her eyes, blue and filled with this new feeling of unqualified trust.

"Kiss me," she whispered.

Kiss me. He'd never heard her say the words. He closed his eyes and for a moment thought that he just simply wasn't going to be able to breathe.

"Do you know what you said?"

She nodded, a curt movement that sent her hair bouncing. "Cole..."

He sensed that she wanted to say so much, maybe to try to explain the conflicting emotions warring inside her body, but he realized, as did she, that she couldn't find the words. Not yet.

"It's okay," he whispered, tucking a wisp of hair behind her ear. "I know a much better way to communicate, anyway." With that, he cupped her head and drew her lips to his.

"Sweet," he mumbled, lost in the enchantment of her willing participation. "Your kiss is so sweet. Your mouth is so sw..." The word was lost in the rejoining of their lips. When finally they pulled apart, both were breathless. They studied each other, eyes wide and full of wonder.

"When did the plane take off?" he asked.

"It hasn't," she answered with a smile.

"Funny, I could swear I'm flying."

Her smile slowly disappeared. "Funny, I could swear I am, too."

And minutes later, they truly were, though not nearly as high as before. The rented Cessna, its engines thrumming a flight song, climbed higher and higher and finally leveled off in search of a path to Pennsylvania.

As the plane settled, so did Cole. He unfastened his seat belt, unzipped his windbreaker, shoved the dividing armrest up between them, and, rearranging his rear end until he slumped comfortably, stretched out his legs as best he could. He then looked over at Tracy, who was following his every move with interest.

"Good night," he said.

"Good night?"

"I haven't slept for two nights. Do you mind if I catch forty winks?"

She shook her head. "No. Go ahead."

"Good," he said, reaching for her hand and bringing it to his lips. He kissed her open palm, then, as if it were the most natural thing in the world, he laid her palm flat against his jean-sheathed thigh and trapped it there with the weight of his hand. He closed his eyes, twisted his shoulders into the seat, and immediately grew still.

In pitiful contrast, Tracy's every muscle tensed to a tremble. She stared at her hand lying so familiarly, so intimately, against Cole's leg. If she were to move her thumb, in even the slightest way, she would brush against his... Her eyes moved to that powerful part of him that designated his gender as male, that part of him that was unaroused, but still straining against tight denim and zipper metal. She felt an immediate tingling in dark feminine places; she also felt the razor cut of fear. She fought the urge to pull her hand from beneath his and return it to emotional safety.

She heeded the inner voice that reminded her that this was Cole, not Paul Nelson Bolden, not Dennis Webber. This was the man who had held her Friday night, when her world had shattered again; this was the man who had stood by her, the man who had promised her that things would be all right. He was the other half of the "two" in the word together. Slowly she forced a normal breathing pattern; slowly she relaxed the wall-tight muscles of her stomach; slowly she relaxed her hand, allowing it to soak up the feel of firm male muscle. Slowly she, too, drifted off to sleep.

Cole's eyes opened, and he smiled lovingly at the child-woman next to him. His ploy had worked. Forcing her into this gentle intimacy had taken their relationship one small step further. He wanted her to grow as familiar with his body as possible. He wanted her to feel that touching him was natural. He would need something natural to fight her unnatural fear when they finally made love. And they would. Sooner or later. And her falling asleep in his arms, while her hand rested so near—so very near—that part of him that she most feared, only served as confirmation.

A long while later, Cole's head dipped, and his lips brushed lazily against hers. "We're here, baby. Welcome to Pennsylvania."

FROM WHERE TRACY STOOD, atop a slight grassy knoll on Cole's sixty-acre farm, the world looked green, that clean crinkly fresh green of early spring. Nearby stood a white barn and maybe a quarter-mile away was Cole's house, a beautiful two-story white clapboard that combined the Old World with the new in a way that seemed to characterize all of Lancaster County. It was there that yesterday cozied up next to today, there that the simple Amish lived next door to modern technology. In the far distance Tracy could see Uncle Chigger's farm—his house, his barn, his pris-

tine-white silo rising heavenward like a giant mono-
lith in praise of the gods of verdure. In the far, far
distance, only tiny specks of black and white outlined
against a sky of gray-blue, were Holstein cattle graz-
ing and lazing in what was left of the Sunday
afternoon.

The day had been a hectic one. After landing in
Lancaster, she and Cole had gone directly to his
uncle's, while Petey Jernigan, who'd met the plane
and who weighed little more than the luggage he'd insisted on carting off, had taken their things on to
Cole's farm next door. The interview had been a good
one but an emotional one for Tracy, for she had instantly liked Dale Schurman. He'd insisted she call
him Uncle Chigger, and Tracy had immediately felt his
problems as if they were her own. That they were also
Cole's problems was undeniable, and she found herself hurting for him as well. They had stayed for lunch,
a simple meal prepared by a simple man, and had then
taken their leave but only after promising to stop by on
the way back to the airport the next day. Cole had then
spent the afternoon showing her his private bit of
Pennsylvania, or, as he'd put it, that portion of William Penn's land of promise that had become his land
of retreat.

They now stood in the elder hours of the afternoon
atop a grassy knoll, basking in a cool, moist breeze
that, along with the gray clouds dusted across a blue
velvet sky, heralded the possible arrival of rain. Tracy
shivered at the chilled breath of the new spring. Without a word—in fact, neither of them had spoken for a
long while—Cole stripped off the red nylon windbreaker that he wore over a white long-sleeved shirt
and fitted it on her much smaller frame. It swallowed

her and fell midthigh to her jeans. He smiled, as if he liked the way she appeared to be lost in his jacket. She smiled simply because he did.

They walked on.

Several minutes later, with the leisureliness of a nap-stretching cat, Cole bent at the waist, his jeans hugging his rear end in an enticing way and snapped up a fluff of pink growing in the adolescent grass. He handed it to her wordlessly.

With a tilting of her lips, she took the precious gift as silently as it was given. The small pink asterlike petals radiated from large yellow disks, and all was contained on a stalky, hairy stem. Holding the pink petals to her nose, she inhaled. There was no fragrance, except a hint of wild bitterness.

Cole slid his hands in the back pockets of his tight jeans and slowly wandered off. Tracy fell into step beside him. As she walked, she played with the delicate flowers and let her mind drift to the beat of a lazy April afternoon.

"He's going to lose his farm, isn't he?" she asked finally.

Cole glanced in her direction before focusing his gaze on a distant trio of ash trees, whose ridged gray trunks nature had braided together. "Yeah," he said flatly.

"Why?" It was such a simple word with such a complex demand.

"Lots of reasons, I guess, but they all translate to 'being in debt.' Plain and simple, the bank's going to foreclose on some outstanding loans."

"How did he get so in debt? You said this morning that he's good at what he does."

One hand still in his pocket, Cole stooped and slashed up a blade of grass with the other. He never missed a step. "He is, but unfortunately, that's not enough anymore." He gave a weary sigh. "Maybe it never was." He threw her another look, explaining, "Basically a dairy farm, any farm, succeeds when product exceeds production costs. A fluctuating market, a floundering economy—both of these play havoc with the sale of dairy products and can result in lower prices. In other words, the farmer has less money to put in his pocket. And at the same time, technology is such that the farmer has to make expensive outlays to stay competitive. Then there's always labor prices, equipment replacement, facility upkeep—the electric bill alone can run as much as six to seven hundred dollars a month. Suffice it to say, it's hard to keep a positive net cash income."

"Why not just buy more cows to produce more milk to make more money to offset more bills?" Tracy asked, adding with a smile, "Or does that sound like a city girl talking?"

Cole's lips arced upward. "I'm afraid that's too logical, babe. Life's just not that accommodating. First of all, you only have so much land to support your herd—you can put only about sixty head to one hundred acres—plus, increasing productivity increases operation costs."

"Oh. Well, I never said I was an economist," Tracy said in sheepish self-defense, though the seriousness of the topic quickly took her mind from herself and back to Cole's uncle. "So what did he do wrong? There are obviously productive dairy farms in the state."

"Uncle Chigger made his mistake by trying to support two families with a farm that had originally supported only one."

"His son," Tracy said, remembering the earlier interview and how the father had tried to bring his son into the business.

"Exactly. It was just too small a tract of land, too small an operation, to give livelihood to two families, which is what family farms often try to do. When times began to get rough, he borrowed money that he eventually couldn't pay back. That's happening all over this country. Loans, borrowed for one reason or another, can't be paid back."

"And what do you want to do about it, Cole? I mean, in Congress?"

"Agriculture needs to be weaned from dependence on the federal government, but it needs to be done in fair steps, in an equitable process, so the Uncle Chiggers of this country can survive. So they can keep their dignity." He stopped talking and faced Tracy with a resolute expression. She could see his dedication in the sheen of his coffee-brown eyes. "I want to issue some legislation to guarantee those fair steps." As he spoke, he reached down and scooped up a handful of earth.

"And my interview will help?"

"It'll help. I'll use Dale Schurman as an example." He suddenly looked uncertain. "I don't know, Tracy. Maybe Lovell is right. Maybe I am biased. Maybe I'm too close to Uncle Chigger, maybe I'm too close to this land." He studied the earth in his hand as if it had suddenly come to life.

"There's nothing wrong with being biased, if you go about it in an unbiased way," Tracy said softly.

He glanced up and, not commenting, shoved out his hand. "What do you see here?"

"I've got to do better than dirt, right?"

"You know what I see?" he asked, ignoring her teasing question.

"What?" she asked, caught up in his serious mood and more than curious about his answer.

"I see a handful of time. This land has been in my family for three generations—two hundred years. I'm holding yesterday, today, tomorrow. And as farming land, that's especially true. What happened in the past affects the present and what happens in the present determines the productivity value of this soil for the future. It's all so interwoven that there's no separating it." His eyes lifted and held hers. "I'm holding time, Tracy. And we stupid mortals think that it's marked by clocks and calendars."

"But you and I know that clocks and calendars mark only Mickey Mouse time, don't we?" she asked with a slow grin.

"Exactly," he said, grinning back. "This—" he let the dirt sift through his opened fingers like sand running through the jaws of an hourglass "—is the only real time. It's measured in heartbeats, joys and sorrows, and it's played out on a stage called *now*. I can't touch this in the past, and I can't touch it in the future. I can only feel, see, smell this earth right now. This moment is the only one that's real."

She sensed strongly that he was saying that her past with its nightmares and her future with its fears were nonexistent. That only this moment had reality. She wanted very much to believe him. But she wasn't quite sure she could.

"You're not doing it," he said softly, drawing her from the talons of doubt.

"I'm not doing what?"

"You're not trying to believe. But then," he added as at the same time his hands reached out to span her waist, "it's understandable that you wouldn't believe me, standing so far away." With a gentle pressure, he drew her near until her thighs were flush against his, the red windbreaker scraping against his shirt. "There," he said in a voice as soft as the flowers that fell gently from her hand to the green at her feet, "that's a much better believing position."

Because it was really only the logical thing to do, her arms slid up and around his neck. "You're a little weird, Congressman," she teased.

"You've been talking to my opposition again."

"You're also..." She hesitated, but decided to share the feeling in her heart, something she'd wanted to do ever since he'd held her on Friday night. "You're also special."

His eyes darkened in a response so infinitesimal that it might have been nothing more than imagination. "How special?" he challenged.

"How special do you want to be?" she challenged back.

His heartbeat increased. "Very."

Her heartbeat increased. "That might be arranged."

"Ah, Tracy..." he whispered.

His head lowered, hers tilted upward, and their lips met. Tracy felt shivers of excitement at the moment of contact. She wondered if it had been only that morning that they had last kissed. It seemed forever since she'd drunk at this sweet well. She wondered also what

Cole was doing to her mouth because, with just the nibbling, the gentle biting, the thorough tasting of her lips, he was causing her senses to soar to that point where sky became infinity.

"Sweet...sweet..." he murmured, his tongue tracing the seal of her lips and tenderly, but purposely, slipping inside. She moaned as he filled her mouth with warmth and moistness. And as if it were more natural than the thunder rumbling through the sky, she wanted him to fill all of her, her woman's heart, her woman's body. And yet some inner demon taunted that maybe she would never be woman to his man. Maybe she could no longer be woman to any man. She buried the thought in the feel of his lips taking hers.

Another round of thunder growled through the sky and, as if by magic, a gentle rain began to fall. Downward from the sky came the misty crystalline drops, sending up the scent of wet earth and damp grass, moistly tangling with hair and clothes. Raindrops fell, striking the ear with the sound of a rhythmic secret shared between nature and man. The world smelled of spring. It smelled of peace.

"It's raining," Tracy said thickly, reluctantly pulling her mouth from Cole's, unable to hide her surprise that the afternoon had so drastically changed sometime during their kiss.

"Good. You owe me a walk in the rain. I'll collect on the way back."

Her lips danced with teasing. "You're going to force me to die of pneumonia with you, huh?"

"Uh-huh. I'll keep you warm." The firelight that flamed in his eyes promised that he could. "You're so beautiful," he whispered. "So damned beautiful. Did you know that your hair is straight when it's wet?'' he said as his fingers slid through the wet straight strands of her honey-satin hair.

Her fingers brushed back a wisp of black hair from his forehead. ''Did you know that yours is curly?''

''Did you know that your eyes are an incredible shade of blue?'' As he spoke, those eyes were momentarily shuttered behind the blink of rain-dewed lashes.

''Yours are the color of Kahlúa. I noticed it the first time I met you.''

''I noticed how great you looked in that peach-colored sweater.''

''You did?''

''I did.''

His hand settled at the side of her neck, where the ends of her hair brushed the back of his hair-darkened wrist. His eyes were as cloudy as the spring-stormed sky, his voice as thick as the now fast-falling rain. ''I wanted to be your lover the first time I saw you. We *are* going to be lovers, Tracy. Someday very soon.''

With a groan Cole's lips crushed hers, and they were instantly lost, lost in the vortiginous waves of passion, a passion he held tightly in check, but a passion he encouraged in her until she moaned under the masculine manipulation of his mouth and hands.

Breathless, she withdrew. She felt the rain sprinkling her upturned face, felt the clean, cool taste of it on her tongue. *Alive...alive...oh, God, she felt so alive...it had been so long and her body needed...needed...needed...* But when his hand slid down her spine, drawing her into the vee of his wet jeans, into intimate contact with a part of him hard and straining from their kiss, she reflexively froze.

"Don't!" he whispered hoarsely. "Don't pull away from me. I won't hurt you. I'd never hurt you." His hands at her hipbones, he gently pulled her closer until his arousal fit snugly against her belly. "It's only me. Only me wanting you."

She peered upward into his eyes with an expression he couldn't read, but he could feel her heart pounding against his chest—the beat of fear. He wondered if he'd gone too far and was cursing himself that he probably had. Her body began to relax, almost as if she'd sent a forced message to muscles that didn't want to obey. Tracy was giving him the gift of nearness, the gift of trust. He suddenly felt very humble.

"Cole..."

"What, baby?"

She swallowed deep and hard as she stared into his bold brown eyes. "I want you—I've never wanted anyone so much—but...but I'm afraid of making love to you."

The honesty of her desire, the honesty of her fear, touched him. "One day," he said in a voice he had trouble controlling, "the wanting is going to be greater than the fear."

"But what if it never is?"

"It will be," he whispered. "Trust me."

When his mouth moved over hers, when he pulled her still tighter, when he folded her in a close, loving embrace, she did believe. The way people who want something so desperately do. She believed with her irrational heart...if not with her rational mind.

CHAPTER EIGHT

THE ROOM WAS WARM AND COZY and filled with the sound of a gentle rain showering roof and eaves. A fire blazed in the stone hearth, dispelling the chill that had invaded the spring evening.

Overhead, a modern chrome and glass chandelier cast its glow on a room that was a pleasing blend of old and new. An ornate wood-framed portrait of Cole's grandmother, a dark-haired woman in virginal white lace and an ivory cameo, hung on the royal-blue wall above a fireplace bedecked in copperware, while a stereo system fit neatly into a built-in bookcase. Antique mahogany armchairs were clustered around a contemporary and invitingly worn sofa with red, white, and blue flowers, while a matched pair of long narrow Adam-style side tables and Georgian mirrors with gilded frames flanked the doorway. Inexpensive braided rugs in a rainbow of colors lay scattered on the shining hardwood floor. On the coffee table lay an outdated *TV Guide*, Robert Ludlum's current mystery-suspense and a chess set.

Cole's feet, which sported only socks because his tennis shoes were soggy wet, were propped on the coffee table. Tracy was buried in the opposite end of the sofa, her bare feet neatly tucked beneath her. She was going over her interview. Cole was involved in some dull-looking political papers.

They looked as though they were an old married couple settled in for the evening. The fire crackled. Popped. Spoke of things toasty and warm.

A slow love song drifted from the stereo.

Cole uncrossed then recrossed his feet at the ankles.

Tracy readjusted a pillow behind her.

Looking down at the words on the page, Cole tried once more to read them. "To advocate such a policy position would be tantamount to shouldering..." Shoulders... Her skin was the color of sun-sprinkled peaches dipped in the smoothest of cream. Not that he could see her shoulders beneath the pink sweater she wore. He couldn't. But he didn't have to see her shoulders to know their gold and ivory shading. All he had to do was close his eyes and remember how they'd looked Friday night. Taking off her skirt and top had almost driven him crazy. And the panty hose...
Even now he could feel the way her hipbones indented slightly, the way her legs went on for mile after beautiful mile, the way she'd arched her hips upward at his softly given command. He could imagine those hips arching upward in the act of loving, and he doubted seriously that there was anything in the world to compare. Except maybe her hair clinging to his fingers. From the moment he'd first seen her hair up, he'd wanted to take it down. Pin by pin. Heartbeat by heartbeat. He squirmed uncomfortably. Thank God his foreman, Petey, was in the house. Otherwise...

Tracy raised her eyes just as Cole lowered his. Adverbs, she thought absently. She had too many adverbs. She'd have to crisp up the interview. Crisp up... Her eyes fell to the crisp ebony-black hair sprinkling the backs of his hands and darkly matting the forearms extending beneath the rolled-up sleeves of the blue oxford-cloth shirt. Why did that hair fascinate her? Because it was so different from Dennis's Nordic-gold down? Maybe. All she knew was that it fascinated her to the point of near-obsession. She'd felt it with her fingers. What would it feel like next to her lips? And how would that patch of black at the throat of his shirt feel? Crisp? Or soft? Kisses-in-the-night soft? *"One day the wanting will be greater than the fear."* Did she believe that? She didn't know. All she knew was that she was glad that someone else would be present that evening.

"Congressman..."

Both Tracy and Cole glanced up. The man who'd just been occupying their thoughts stood in the doorway.

"Ma'am..." Petey Jernigan said, nodding and smiling in acknowledgment of Tracy.

She smiled back.

Petey's attention returned once more to Cole. "I thought if you didn't need me anymore this evening that I'd..." The little man, who looked a lot like a jockey in search of a horse, shuffled from one foot to the other. "That I'd...well, that I'd run over to Neffsville for the evening." He added, "I'd be back by noon...in plenty of time to get you to your plane," but neither Cole nor Tracy heard. They were too busy jerking their heads toward each other, too busy staring with too-wide eyes. *Damn!* both thought simultaneously.

"Unless there's something else you wanted me to do around here," Petey suggested, obviously feeling the sudden tension.

"No...no...I...no...you..." stammered Capitol Hill's eloquent orator.

Petey Jernigan stared at his employer with a look that seemed to ask, "Am I supposed to understand that?"

"No," Cole said, trying once more, "there's nothing more to do here. You, ah...you go on to Neffsville."

"Thanks," Petey returned. "I'll see you tomorrow."

"Yeah," Cole answered. "Enjoy yourself."

Petey nodded then smiled once more at Tracy. "Good night, ma'am."

"Good night," she said, but it was only a thin sliver of sound. She cleared her throat and tried again. "Good night."

There was a loud silence after he left.

"I'm...I'm sorry," Cole said finally to a Tracy, who was busy gnawing her bottom lip. "I didn't know what else to tell him. He stays around here week in, week out with seldom any time off and..."

"I understand," she interrupted.

"I just don't want you to think I planned this because..."

"Of course I don't think that," she said. "It's all right, Cole. I'm not afraid to be here alone with you." Only afraid of having to make a decision, she added silently.

Jerking his feet from the coffee table, he rose in one swift motion, muttering something that sounded like "Maybe you ought to be."

"What?" she asked.

"You want a brandy?" he called over his shoulder as he almost ran to the bar in the corner.

"Yes," she answered, thinking that she could use at least a couple. A couple of dozen.

Seconds later he walked toward her with two snifters. She reached out to take one, but he deliberately avoided contact and, instead, set her glass on the table.

He brought his glass to his lips, took a hearty swallow of the ruby-red liquid and, at the same time, turned and stuffed his free hand into the back pocket of his jeans. He padded in stockinged feet over the hardwood floor and the puddles of braided rugs to stand before the window. It was still pouring.

Don't touch her, he told himself. *Just don't touch her, and you'll be all right. And keep talking. Prove you're a damn orator!*

"It's still raining," he said. "Rain this heavy is a bit unusual for this time of year. The state usually sees about forty-two inches of rainfall in the span of a twelve-month period, but . . ."

A perplexed look on her face, Tracy settled in to fifteen full minutes of nonstop talk about Pennsylvania's climate. Afterward Cole stepped back to the liquor cabinet, and with hardly a glance in her direction, he poured another short brandy then started in on the history of his house.

"My great-great-grandfather acquired the land somewhere around 1780. No one's really sure when the original structure went up, but my grandfather restored sections of the house and built others sometime around . . ."

Ten minutes later as the clock struck eight-thirty, he was still talking.

". . . Petey stayed on as foreman and . . ."

"Cole?"

He jerked his head toward the soft, sweet sound of her voice.

Tracy still sat on the sofa, while Cole stood at the window with the empty brandy snifter in his hand.

"What are you doing?"

"What do you mean?"

Slowly she unfolded her feet from beneath her and stood. She started toward him. "You don't have to do this for me. I'm not uncomfortable being alone with you." She smiled and ran her hand down the side of her white slacks. "Well, maybe a little, but . . ."

"What makes you think I'm doing this for you?" His voice was slightly hoarse.

A crease cleaved through the smoothness of her forehead. "Why else?"

An uneven breath, married to a hint of a mirthless laugh, shuddered from his lips. He had already drawn the snifter to his mouth before realizing it was devoid of drink. He set the glass down. "Tracy, don't you have any idea how much I want you? How much I've wanted you for weeks? How hard it is for me to go on touching you and having you touch me yet to know that I can't make love to you? Not now, not until you're ready to trust me."

His words startled her, and yet she asked herself why they should. Hadn't she known all along what he, as a man, must be going through? Hadn't she been too caught up in her problems, her fears, her doubts, to realize the thin rope he'd been walking? Suddenly she had to ask the question that she realized had been at the back of her mind for a long time. "Am I going to lose you if I don't . . ." She hesitated, searching out the right words.

"If you don't go to bed with me?"

"Yes."

For a heart-stopping moment, he said nothing. She felt a part of her die. "No," he said in a low voice as a you-ought-to-know-better smile curved his lips. "You're not going to lose me if you don't go to bed with me. In fact, nothing you could do would 'lose' me."

Tracy felt both her eyes and her heart sting, her eyes with tears, her heart with deep emotion. "Oh, Cole. What did I do to deserve you?"

She stretched out her hand with the intent of resting her palm against his cheek. His fingers eased around her wrist, however, to stop her in midair. It was a manacle of softest velvet.

"Don't," he whispered. "Don't touch me." She saw his Adam's apple bob slowly. There was pleading in his next words. Pleading in the dark of his eyes. "Please don't."

There they stood, both wanting, both needing, neither of them knowing quite what to say or do. And in the quiet, the soft love song wafting from the stereo was taunting and teasing.

"Go to bed," he begged. Slowly his fingers unchained her wrist, and he stepped around her and toward the fire, where he stood, his hand against the mantel, staring into the dying embers. "Sleep late in the morning, if you can," he said in a voice struggling for an even timbre. "We'll leave for Washington at about three. If you need anything, just ask."

For the longest of moments, she just stood and stared at him. At the back of his bowed head. At the width of his slightly stooped shoulders. At the hard evidence of his wanting that was distinctly profiled in denim. Some emotion that she'd never experienced before curled and ribboned in her heart.

"Cole . . ."

"Good night," he said without turning around.

Her foot had taken but one step of the stairway when he spoke again. "To answer your question . . . being born was all you had to do to deserve me."

Her eyes found and mated with his across the short, the long, distance of the room.

"That's all you'll ever have to do."

TRACY HAD BEEN IN BED for almost thirty minutes when she heard Cole's step on the stairway. She listened as he hesitated at her door before moving down the hall. Rolling over, she sighed into the deep down of the pillow.

Tugging the shirt from his jeans, Cole unbuttoned it and shrugged it from his shoulders. He dropped it onto a chair then plopped onto the side of the bed and peeled out of his socks. He threw them at the chair, watched as they fell short and landed on the thick caramel-colored carpet. He didn't pick them up. He just wanted to go to bed and try to get some sleep.

All she wanted, Tracy thought, was to get some sleep. It seemed like forever since she'd slept. She turned, her legs thrashing at the covers and tangling her nightgown beneath her. *Damn!* she cursed, closing her eyes and calling for sleep.

Cole unsnapped his jeans and reached for the zipper. He stopped, rose from the bed and walked to the fireplace. Stooping, he took some logs from the enormous cast-iron pail located hearthside and with a *chunking* sound stacked them in the grate. He lit the

fire. He wondered if Tracy was cold. Maybe he should
have given her his room with the fireplace. Maybe he
should have laid out an extra blanket in the guest
room. Maybe he should go to bed and stop thinking
of her. The fire crackled.

Tracy tossed. And listened to the rhythmic beat of
the clock. Ticktock...ticktock... And to the lulling
spatter of the rain. Pitter-patter...pitter-patter... And
the images of her heart appeared. Cole holding her
while she cried. Cole crying with her. Cole telling her
that they'd work it out together. Cole on the plane.
Cole in the meadow. Cole... Cole...Cole...

She cried out, a half whimper, half agonizing plea
to something, someone, anything that could ease this
ache.

Her body ached for his touch. Her heart ached just
to be near him. Her soul ached for an interchange with
his. A vision of him standing before the fireplace
downstairs drifted through her mind. He needed her.
He wanted her. Man to woman. Lover to lover. He
wanted...

One day the wanting will be greater than the fear.

Tracy threw back the covers, eased her feet to the
side of the bed and stood. At that moment only one
thing in all the world mattered: being with Cole.

HE FELT HER—in the same way that he felt the warmth
of the fire, in the same way that he felt time stop. Still
crouching before the fireplace, he lifted his eyes,
knowing what he'd see before seeing it. She stood in
the partially open doorway—an angel, a siren, a child-
woman eating at her bottom lip. Her hair was still
piled atop her head, but careless tossings had tugged

loose myriad tendrils until it was severely mussed...
and undeniably sensual. A pale blue gown, sus-
pended over her bare shoulders with narrow hints of
straps, hung long and flowing to the floor. The tips of
her toes peeked from beneath. Lamplight and firelight were such that he could see shadows through the
fabric—a silhouette of her long, slender legs, a darker
shadow where those legs veed beneath a nest of curls.
She was beautiful. She was woman. She was a woman
in search of a lover. Cole's breath trickled from his
lungs.

She watched as he pushed from the balls of his feet
and rose from the floor, slowly, mesmerically and with
a dark magnificence. He wore only jeans—tight jeans,
jeans that appeared unsnapped at a point that was
level with the indentation of his navel. His arms were
peppered in night-black hair, coils and swirls that
seemed to have gone crazy and, before they could be
stopped, had forested the whole of his chest—from the
hollow of his throat to the yawning waist of his jeans.
His feet were bare, his hair tousled. His eyes, onyx-
bright and staring, were full of emotion; those same
eyes questioned and assured and waited...

"You were right," she whispered, the sound feather-
dancing across the distance.

"Ab..." He inhaled over the fury of his breathing.
"About what?"

"The wanting *is* greater than the fear," she said,
slowly moving step by sure step toward him. "You said
it would be. And it is." Except, she thought, it was not
the wanting that she had expected, nor the wanting she
suspected he'd meant, but how could she explain to
him what was only lacy bits of thought in her own
mind? Yes, she needed—her body pleaded for his—

but the greater need was to assuage his need. No, she couldn't explain. But it had something to do with the mysterious, nameless burning in her heart. Standing before him, their bodies mere inches apart, she arched her neck upward. Their eyes melded, the ebony of his swimming with the shaded blue of hers. "Help me. Help me to love you."

He reached for her and crushed her to him. His embrace was rough. And tender. It was a million shades of each.

She buried her face in the curve of his shoulder, while her arms crossed his back with all the strength she had. The silken hair of his chest pressed against the softness of her gown. His breath was a moist storm against her ear; his lips trembled in the tempest's wake. He was so warm, so masculine, and she was so frightened.

"I'm scared," she whispered. It was only when the mumbled words competed with the low crick-crackling of the fire that she realized she had spoken.

Cole's hold tightened, pinioning her as close to him as humanly possible. "I know you are, baby." He eased back until his eyes could gently confront hers. "Tell me what's scaring you." As he spoke, he brushed back a strand of hair from her cheek.

Her eyes were dark and hauntingly sincere. "I don't know if I can."

"Yes, you can. Together we can do anything." Releasing her except for her hand, he eased to the floor before the fireplace. He tugged until she had no choice but to follow. Firelight danced across their bodies. "Now, tell me what frightens you."

She shrugged her bare shoulders. It was a gesture that made her look vulnerable. "Everything... sexual."

"That's too general," he said, stifling the urge to react to her vulnerability by pulling her into his arms and never letting her go. "Be more specific."

"Cole, I..." She lowered her head.

With the tip of his finger under her chin, he raised her eyes to his. "I can't fight faceless demons. Help me to help you. To help us." His eyes bore more deeply into hers. "Please."

She had no armor against the simple but powerful word. She had no armor against the man. "I'm afraid..." Her eyes lowered, then raised to meet his. "I'm afraid that... that I'll get it all confused in my mind. That I won't be able to tell..."

"To tell the difference between making love and rape?"

"Yes," she said, nodding once. She also closed her eyes. "The counselor said that that isn't unusual. Flashbacks are common, and most women are afraid to be... to be intimate again."

"Did you see a counselor?"

Her eyes could meet his levelly for this. "I saw one at the Rape Crisis Center. For a few sessions."

"Good." His voice lowered; he swallowed. "Do you have flashbacks?" He felt her fingers tighten in his. He tightened his around hers.

"In the beginning I had nightmares, but not anymore. But I'm still afraid of... being intimate."

"I can understand that," Cole said, his voice so soothing that she felt her tension obeying its relaxing command. "It is the same act, isn't it?" His voice faltered slightly. "Just done for different reasons. Very different reasons."

"Cole?"

"What?"

She glanced up from their entwined fingers. There was a glassy sheen to her eyes. "You deserve better than this. Better than me."

The room was quiet, so quiet that the fire's popping sounded like a cannon, so quiet that when Cole leaned forward, she could actually hear the stretching of his jeans. "Nothing's better than you. Nothing." He kissed one eyelid then the other.

Tracy felt cherished.

Cole took a deep, full breath. "Let's assume the worst. Let's assume that you do get our loving confused with the...with the rape. Let's assume that you do have a flashback. What happens then?"

"I don't know," she said so quietly that he read her lips more than heard her. Her fear, though, he felt in his heart like the prick of a sharp, ruthless knife.

"It seems to me that the worst that could happen is that you're going to be scared again," he said. "You'd be forced to relive it. But I'd be here with you. I'd take every step with you." He drew her hand to his mouth, and his lips left a warm kiss on it. "I'd be here, Tracy. I promise you that."

"I don't want..." She hesitated, then forced herself to find his eyes. They were watching her closely, sympathetically. "I don't want to make a fool of myself. You want a lover, not a hysterical..." Her voice rose to match the sentiment of the word.

"I...want...you," he interrupted, tightening his hold on her hand until it was painful for them both. "Now," Cole asked, "what else frightens you?"

A memory of rejection swept over her. In her mind's eye, she saw a vision of Dennis turning away from her as if she were dirty, soiled. She was suddenly seized with a heart-freezing panic. Instinctively she tried to pull her hand from Cole's. .

He refused to let her go. "Tracy?" She struggled but finally relented to his superior strength. "What is it?"

Her eyes were flecked with pain, while her voice quivered. "What if...what if you just *think* you want to make love to me?"

He knew immediately where her line of thinking was headed. And so he tried to stop it. "No," he said firmly.

"What if you can't?"

"No."

"What if at the last minute you realize you can't..."

"Dammit, no!" He grabbed her chin in his hand, painfully forcing her head up and her eyes to make contact with his. "No!" Their chests were heaving; their hearts were beating a too-fast rhythm. Slowly Cole took a long, sobering breath. "Do you really think I'd take you this far, knowing what you've been through, if there was any doubt in my mind of my reaction? Do you really think I'm capable of that kind of gross callousness?"

She shook her head in a curiously victorious defeat of her suggestion. "No."

"Tracy..." Cole's fingers touched her cheek in a leisurely caress. "I've never wanted a woman the way I want you. Never."

"Never?" It was a breathy plea for confirmation that only another woman could truly understand.

"Never," he confirmed. Though his eyes still shone gravely, one corner of his mouth slowly quirked into a smile. "Another fear bites the dust. Any more?"

"Cole, what if..." Uncertainty moved across her blue irises like clouds streaking across a blossoming sun.

"What if what?"

Unconsciously she bit her bottom lip. As he'd wanted to do a thousand times, but never had till now, he reached out to stop the gentle brutality.

"Don't," he breathed as his thumb gently pried her lip from beneath her tooth. That's all he had intended to do, but the thumb had a will of its own. It hovered over her sweet flesh then whispered across the fullness of her bottom lip. The rough pad dipped inside her mouth to find a warm moisture.

It was such a simple act. But such an erotic one! Sensations ignited along the length of Tracy's body, exploding sensual capsules of hunger in every feminine cell. "What if..." His thumb glided over a tooth, hampering her words. "What if I can't..." The thumb deliberately found her tongue. She moaned as he raked across the granular surface. Unable to stop herself, she licked, rubbed her tongue against this daring invader. "What if I can't respond...like a normal woman?" The thumb, wet with her, withdrew, brushing one corner of her mouth before taking a slow journey to the other corner. It then sensuously rolled her lower lip downward, as if exposing her in an extreme intimacy. She closed her eyes and allowed the intoxicating feelings to claim her.

"You can't be serious," he whispered

"Cole..."

"Oh, God, Tracy," he breathed as he bent forward to replace his thumb with his mouth. His lips were tender but hungry; the fingers seeking out the pins in her hair were gentle but insistent. The pins found, he scattered them to the floor and just as his fingers threaded through the silken mane of her hair, his tongue slid past her lips. "Trust me," he pleaded. "Please trust me." Pulling back, his lips as wet as hers, he pierced her eyes with his. "We'll take it slowly. And we'll stop at any point you want. We don't have to have intercourse. There are a thousand ways to make love. Kissing, touching, just holding each other. We'll do whatever feels right. Okay?"

It was the confidence in his eyes, coupled with the undeniable need of her body for his, that convinced her. Slowly, she nodded, spraying a wisp of hair onto her cheek. He nuzzled it back with his nose.

"It's going to be okay," he whispered. "I promise."

CHAPTER NINE

COLE'S PROMISE WAS GOOD AS GOLD. Tenderly he
loved her with kisses and caresses, soft touches to body
and soul, until she would have breathlessly sworn that
she'd neither been kissed nor caressed before.

"Your mouth," he whispered as his lips rolled onto
hers. "Oh, God, Tracy, your mouth's so sweet ... so
sweet." His tongue probed the moist crease of that
sweet heaven, entered with tender authority, and
dueled with her tongue.

"Is it?" she whispered, trembling.

"Yes. Oh, yes ... and I'd like to do a thousand
wicked, wonderful things to it."

She pulled back. Her mouth was wet ... beginning
to swell ... and so consummately desirable that Cole
felt the overwhelming urge to grab her, clutch her to
him and kiss her until neither could remember time or
place. He chained the urge and concentrated instead
on the speck of a smile, the dash of a dare that shone
in her eyes. "Name one," she ordered.

His heart rejoiced that she was feeling comfortable
enough to tease. Both of his large hands cupped her
face, and he drew her to him. "This is number five
hundred and one," he breathed, kissing her lips once,
twice—quick, suckling unions—then, after a heartbeat's hesitation, he settled his mouth fully on hers.

She moaned. And angled her head to better receive his kiss.

He groaned. And initiated the silken communion of tongue to tongue.

"Wicked...wonderful," she whispered.

He made a low guttural sound that would have translated to agreement in any language known to mating man and woman.

The kiss ended. He smiled, a lopsided twisting of his mouth. She smiled, a slight crescenting of her thoroughly kissed lips. Her smile, however, slowly slipped away.

He sensed her sudden self-doubt. "It's our game, Tracy. We'll play it by our rules. And at our pace."

"I want you," she said honestly.

"I know." Placing his hands at her waist, he drew her to her knees and pulled her into the valley he formed by veeing his legs. "Come here," he said. "You're always too far away."

Standing in the shelter of his legs, staring down into his face, she felt safe. She reached out and placed two fingers against his lips. "I like being with you, Cole Damon. I like touching you."

His teeth bit gently at her fingers. "Then be with me. Touch me." In invitation, he released her waist and, planting both hands behind him at an angle, leaned back with his legs still bent upward at the knees. "Touch me all you want."

All she wanted. She wasn't certain that she could ever touch him that much. But she was certain that she wanted to try. In a lazy investigation, she trailed her fingers across his cheek, his smooth, only stubble-hinted cheek, down his throat—she felt his Adam's apple slide up and down in a swallow—and over the curve of his massive shoulder. His skin was warm and clean, and she wanted to touch more...and more...and still more of him. Lowering her head, she brought her lips to the patch of hair just below his throat, the patch that had so tantalized her earlier that evening. She cherished it with a kiss. The midnight swirls were soft...crinkly soft...sensually soft. A flood of warmth laced through her; Cole's response was to loll back his head in total submission.

"Ah, Tracy," he groaned, the name strained, pulled from somewhere deep in his throat.

She kissed the spot again, warm lips to warm hair-dusted skin, before raising her head to seal his mouth with hers. Shifting his weight, he rose to his knees and pulled her into the circle of his arms. His lips worshiped her lips, her face, her neck and shoulders, while his hands adored the smooth, honey-velvet of her bare back. With gentle insistence he pulled her flush against him. Full breasts flattened against the hard, inflexible wall of a male chest.

"I want to see you," he rasped, the whisper-sound an urgent plea in her ear. "I want to touch you. I *need* to touch you."

Need. She felt his need in his trembling body. She felt his need sheathed in denim and pressing into her belly. She felt her own body's need and was frightened by neither his nor hers.

"Touch me," she pleaded, her breasts begging for his caress. With no reservations, she nudged his hand downward.

Pulling back, he found her eyes. He saw in them the hazy glow of invitation. Slowly, with exquisite gentleness, and with his eyes never leaving hers, he brushed the back of his knuckles against the side of her breast.

The action caused her eyes to darken to the deepest of sapphire. He then swept one bent knuckle against the nipple; it instantly contracted to a hard, painful bead beneath the gown. She sucked in a deep gust of air.

"Easy, baby," he soothed. "I know it's been a long time."

The fact that he was aware of the sensually heightened state of her body after two years of denial bonded her still more closely to him. He was a man of sensitivity, a man she could trust, a man she could share inner thoughts and feelings with.

"It's been so long," she repeated raggedly. "Sometimes . . . sometimes I think I'm going to explode."

"I know," he said, scooping her face in his hands and bringing her lips to his. "Sometimes I think I'm going to, too."

With his cheek he nuzzled the strap from one ivory shoulder and at the same time lowered the other filament of fabric with the feathery touch of his fingers. He pulled the thin straps down and off her arms. The gown slid toward her waist, stopped only by the pebbled crests of her breasts.

"I've dreamed about how you'd look." Cole spoke quietly as he released the gown from one peak with the tip of his finger. That side of the grown draped waistward, but he kept his eyes on hers. "I've decided that you're the color of roses at twilight." His finger released the other side of the gown, and it tumbled to her waist, pale blue silk slithering downward. His eyes reassured her, begging for trust, before his hungry eyes lowered to see her kneeling before him, her gown bunched at her waist, her breasts full and pouty in their thrust.

Tracy waited, hoping, praying, that her body was pleasing to him. When he said nothing for long moments, though, she began to doubt his pleasure.

It was at the moment of supreme doubt that he spoke. "Look at you," he said reverently and in a voice as hushed as a spring breeze walking over reedy blades of grass. "Oh, God, just look at you." His hand reached out and delicately molded the lowest, fullest part of one breast.

It was a touch that sent ripples purling through Tracy's body. Hot, electric ripples of delight and near-pain. Her nipples tightened, her breasts seemed to visibly swell, and deep, deep within her began a craving that only this man could satisfy.

"I knew it," he breathed. "You *are* the color of roses at twilight." Cupping the underside of one breast in his hand, he lowered his head.

Tracy waited impatiently for his lips. When she at last felt them, she could have easily died at the simplistic beauty of his touch. He kissed the ivory orb, over and over, making smaller and smaller circles around and toward the breast's center, then pressed his lips to a distended peak, bathing it in the moistness of his breath, laving it with the tender roughness of his tongue. Gently he closed his mouth over the aching summit and with a slow, mind-shattering rhythm suckled...suckled...until Tracy's world exploded. She shivered then with a low whimpering cry laid her cheek against the top of his head.

At this, he scooped her up into his arms and carried her to the bed. Still holding her, he yanked back the spread and laid her on the pristine whiteness of a fresh-smelling sheet.

"Lie with me," he said, the three words more powerfully delivered than any speech he'd ever given. Still wearing his jeans, he slipped in beside her, loomed over her for the span of a rich melding of their eyes and their mouths, then eased to his side, pulling her into his strong embrace. He gentled her bare, sensitive breasts into the dark cloud of hair on his chest and, with a nudge of her hips, arranged her thighs flush with his. He buried his face in her hair then laced his arms across her bare back.

"You feel so good," he praised. "So good. Do I feel good to you?"

"Yes," she breathed into the hollow of his ear. She burrowed her breasts more deeply into the black hair of his chest. "Oh, yes."

Boldly his hands began to roam—over her back, over the gown bunched at her waist, over the swell of her hips hidden within the folds of the gown. Splaying his hand wide, he cupped her buttocks and gently shimmied the fabric back and forth.

Her hands traveled his shoulders, his back and finally edged lower. She slid her fingertips into the waistband of his jeans. His skin felt warm there and secretly forbidden; she again felt herself growing unsure.

He sensed her cruel doubts. Rolling her onto to her back, he took her hand and drew it to his mouth, where he kissed the palm before planting it in the dark hair of his chest. There he rubbed it in the raven swirls of hair. He then pushed her hand lower.

She tensed.

"It's all right," he said as he placed her hand on the hard muscles of his inner thigh. Slowly he rotated her hand over the denim of his jeans. "It's only me,

Tracy," he spoke softly as his hand guided hers. "Only another part of me." With slow deliberateness he molded her hand over his swollen manhood.

Air seeped from both his and her lungs.

"Does that frighten you?" he asked, his voice quivering with restraint.

"Yes...no...I don't know." She had spoken the truth. She didn't know what she was feeling. Only that she didn't want to move her hand even when the trap of his hand freed hers. Timidly, brazenly, she stroked him. She heard his breath gush forth in tattered wisps; she saw pearls of perspiration pop on his upper lip. She heard the sweet calling of her name as he arched into her touch.

"Tracy...oh, Tracy."

Her hand moved to his jeans.

"Yes," Cole encouraged. His voice was unnaturally strained. "Unzip it."

Her breath wavered, as did her resolve. He pushed her hand to the task. Slowly, with trembling fingers, she found the tab and pulled downward. In the open vee of the jeans, she saw the deep tan of skin, the pelt of coal-black hair as it disappeared in the band of low-cut, white knit briefs.

"Cole..." The word was fringed with fear.

"Don't, Tracy. Don't run now, baby." His eyes on hers, he slowly stripped the jeans from his legs. He followed them with the underwear. Tossing both garments on the floor, he eased to his knees before her. He watched as a crazy pulse beat in her temple, watched as her eyes dipped from his to lower regions. He prayed that she would find him pleasing...and not frightening.

She had been right, she thought. He frightened her. He excited her. He made her want to run. He made her want to run to him.

He watched, his breath only a drizzle of air, as she slowly slid her gown down her hips...lower... lower...until an ivory belly, honey-golden curls of hair and long, slender legs came into view. She lay back, her eyes finding his.

"He hurt me," she whispered.

Cole's eyes squeezed shut. Forcing his voice to be calm, he spoke. "You weren't making love." He lowered his body beside hers. "That won't happen now. I know you want me. Your body has to be ready."

The eyes that found his were those of a child-woman. They looked young, old, sensual, yet in need of protection.

His hand eased onto her stomach, then downward. "Let me prove it to you." He touched her thigh, her inner thigh, urging her legs apart with gentle fingers. She gasped and instinctively moved to stop him. "No," he commanded softly, pushing her hand away and continuing with his mission. His fingers caressed her intimately, slipping between the petals of her silken womanhood.

Tracy writhed as she felt a million red-hot sensations.

Suddenly Cole's lips were claiming hers, sealing her body's moistness between them like a preserved promise, kissing her with a fever that enflamed them both.

She wanted him. She needed him. She wanted him to ease his need.

"Make love to me," she urgently breathed against his lips.

He pulled back. The eyes that studied her were midnight-bright, and they watched her for every nuance of reaction. Seconds passed...rain fell...time ticktocked its way from present to past. Suddenly, Cole took command. He began to talk calmly, soothingly, as he moved downward over her body to ease himself between her legs. Always he watched her face. Never did his eyes waver from hers.

"Listen to me, Tracy. Listen to my voice. Listen to what I'm telling you." She let him move her body as he would and tried to follow his every word. She tried not to tremble...though she knew she did. She was scared. More scared than she could ever remember being. Her instinct was to fight him. Yet she didn't, because she knew in her heart that it was now or never.

"I won't hurt you," that voice was whispering. "I promise. Listen to me. Listen to what I'm telling you. I love you. I love you, Tracy. I..." He lowered himself between her legs. "Love..." Her heart went wild as his maleness pushed against the tender threshold. "You..." The word filled the room as he decisively entered her.

She gasped and arched.

He gasped and remained absolutely still.

Her eyes never left his.

His eyes never left hers.

Both waited, waited for flashbacks and fear, waited for a nightmare reaction that never came.

Instead of fear, Tracy felt the most incredible sense of triumph. And peace. And the most incredible of sensual feelings, feelings that bombarded her body with jolts so powerful that they themselves were frightening...or would have been had she not so trusted this man.

"Cole, I..." She started to tell him how good he felt inside her, how right he felt there, how the word *love* on his lips had speared her heart with a joyous warmth, but just as she would have told him this, the world stopped.

Tiny, unexpected pulsations began deep inside her, deep inside where Cole was buried. Pulsations that quickly erupted into shudders of orgasmic freedom.

She gasped. Then gasped again and whisper-cried his name.

Cole felt her release and surprise flashed in his eyes. He hadn't expected her to climax at all—not without coaxing—but that it was happening now startled him...and pleased him in a way nothing ever had.

"Oh, baby," he crooned. "Don't fight it. Just let it happen."

Her eyes closed, she arched her hips into his... slowly...in the purest of rhythms...over and over. Cole remained still, letting her take as much or as little of him as she needed. Only his hand on her lower stomach urged her forward in her undulation. In some distant quarter of his mind, he told himself that he'd been right. The sensual movement of her hips when making love was the most beautiful thing he'd ever seen.

Her hands twisted into fists in the sheet as warm sensations bathed her. She felt warm, warm like the noonday sun, and she felt mellow, mellow like the soporific sound of the rain singing on the pane. She felt light and airy, light and airy like the way the pink flower in the meadow responded to breeze and breath. She felt loved.

"I love you," he whispered. "Tracy, I love you so much."

The pleasure ripples ebbed. She opened her heavy lids and looked into the eyes of her lover.

He smiled, brushing damp hair from her cheek with his thumb. "That was beautiful...so beautiful."

"I didn't mean...it's been so long...you felt so good..."

His fingers stilled her lips. "Don't spoil it."

As reality enveloped her, she noted that his fingers shook...and that beads of perspiration, beads of consummate restraint, now dotted not only his upper lip, but also his forehead, yet he made no move to satisfy his own enormous need. Curling her arms about his neck, she brought his lips to hers. "Together," she whispered as her hips once more began the dance of love.

Cole moaned and lost himself in the heaven she was offering. Minutes later he cried out her name.

She held him as his body shuddered in release then felt her own body spasming. When at last he eased from her and rolled to his side, taking her with him, they were both depleted and deliriously satisfied.

Slowly he smiled. "We did it."

Not "you did it." Not "I did it." Not "I did it for you," which he might have had every right to say. But "we did it." The one word echoed in Tracy's heart.

"I love you," she whispered, through a glistening of tears.

For the second time within a few days, Cole wept.

SOME HUNDRED MILES AWAY, Thomas Lovell entered into the final throes of passion. As climax neared, the woman beneath him moaned a lover's encouragement and wrapped her arms more tightly around him. In his drink-drugged mind, he heard nothing, felt nothing, until at that precise moment, when body reigns supreme, he cried out a name.

"Lisa!" he uttered, the sound ripped from his throat, torn from his heart. Within moments the blessed oblivion of sleep and drink claimed him.

The woman lay perfectly still then slowly edged from beneath the man's slumbering weight. She sat on the side of the bed for long ponderous moments. Her body still racked with unfulfilled needs, she rose, dressed and let herself out the front door.

The April night was pretty, she thought. It would have been even prettier had her name been Lisa.

THE PHONE RANG. Cole jumped, grabbed the receiver in midring, glancing over to see if the noise had awakened the woman beside him. It had. Tracy stirred and opened her eyes just in time to see Cole put the phone to his ear. She also saw his impatient frown.

"Yeah?" he said brusquely. The sight of Tracy's sleep-hazed eyes on him softened the frown, and he impulsively leaned over, angled the phone out of the way and brushed her lips with his. Against the warm flesh of her mouth, he whispered, "Good morning."

She smiled, stretched felinely and brought her hand to rest in the deep pile of black hair on his chest.

"This is he," Cole spoke into the receiver. "Oh, yeah, Richard, how are you?" Cole paused, listening, and suddenly his frown was back. "When? No, of course, I understand." Again he paused. "I understand, Richard. No apology necessary. I know it's your job." There were several more seconds of quiet in which Tracy, without even knowing the cause, began to feel Cole's distress. Propping herself on her elbow, she watched him. "Of course I want to go through with the plans we discussed," Cole added, his eyes on Tracy's exposed breasts. "I'll assume the loans. Just call my lawyer and accountant and get it straight with them. And thanks, Richard, I appreciate your call." With that, Cole stretched, recradled the phone and tunneled his fingers through his night-tousled hair. He said nothing, just sat staring into empty space.

"What is it?" Tracy asked softly.

His eyes shifted to hers. "The bank's foreclosing on my uncle's land."

"When?"

"This morning at ten."

"There's nothing you can do?"

Cole shook his head. "That was the president of the bank. We went to school together, and he'd promised he'd let me know beforehand."

"He can't stop it?"

Cole smiled indulgently and dragged his finger down the side of Tracy's cheek. "That's not the way business works, baby. Richard has to answer to a board of directors. He did all he could by forewarning me."

Bits and snatches of the conversation flowed back. "You're going to buy Chigger's land, aren't you?" she asked, already knowing the answer.

"Yes," Cole said simply. "That way it'll stay in the family, and Uncle Chigger can continue to work it. I'd give it to him if he'd let me, but his Lancastrian pride won't allow that. He'll insist on leasing it. But he *will* have a living, and maybe in time he can buy it back from me." He gave a deep soulful sigh and passed his hand over his face. "But I can't do this for every farmer losing his land. Dammit, I can't save everybody!"

Tracy's hand settled on his arm. "Maybe not everybody, but you're doing what you can. You're going to be reelected and continue to fight for fair farming legislation. Cole, you will make a difference. You *will*."

Cole drew her hand from his arm and to his lips. He kissed the palm with a tenderness that tore at Tracy's heart. She loved him. Oh, God, how she loved him!

"Cole Damon," she whispered, "distinguished congressman, orator-extraordinaire, champion of the defeated, liberator of frightened women."

"Did I liberate you?"

"Yes."

"No more demons from the past?"

"When I close my eyes," she whispered, "all I see is you. All I feel is your body loving mine."

She saw him swallow low and slowly, saw him fight to control emotions that suddenly overwhelmed him. Easing flat on his back, he reached for her, and spreading his legs, fitted her between them. They lay belly to belly, she with her cheek on his chest, the crown of her head just beneath his chin. One of his hands cupped her head, the other sculpted the rise of one hip. That part of her that was most feminine fit flush with that part of him that was most male. He was aroused, ready to love her.

For a long while they just held each other, each listening to the heartbeat of the other.

"Last night," Cole finally breathed into her hair. "It was...it was..." The night seemed to defy his meager descriptive ability, so he abandoned the attempt and said instead, "I've been with my share of women, Tracy—I've even been married—but I swear before everything holy that I never made love until last night."

The words were poetry, his voice the music that set it to song. She raised her head, and her wide, honest eyes found his. "I loved Dennis...."

"I can live with that as long as you love me...."

"No," she interrupted, her fingers at his lips. "I loved Dennis in the only way I knew to love then, but last night you taught my heart a whole new way. What I feel for you makes what I felt for Dennis seem...seem shallow and so very inconsequential." Her blue eyes glazed. "I love you so much it scares me, Cole."

His eyes savored every precious inch of her face; his ears relished every loving syllable she'd spoken. "Don't," he whispered, dropping his mouth to hers. "Don't cry...don't be scared." Tenderly, his hands at her waist, he pulled her upward and, arranging her legs on either side of his, pushed downward to settle her fully on the heat of his arousal. As had happened thrice during the night, he filled her completely, solidly, as if nature had somehow destined her for him. "Just love me," he whispered as he eased her hips into the now familiar rhythm. "Please love me."

A long while after love's tender fury, their bodies still intimately joined, Cole spoke. "Will you go with me to Uncle Chigger's?"

Tracy raised her head. "Do you want me to?"

"I always want you with me," he replied, wiping at a bead of moisture that was trickling between her love-tender breasts.

"Then I'll go."

"And will you campaign with me?" His gaze moved from her breasts to her eyes. "I have to hit the road next week. Will you go with me?"

Tracy's heart split in two. "No," she said decisively.

Surprise and hurt flitted across his face. "If it's your writing, you can do it on the road. I wouldn't interfere...."

"Cole, my love, are you blind?" She inhaled deeply then deeper still. "I'm a woman with a past. You're a man with a future. Don't you see that I can destroy that future? If it comes out that you're seeing a woman who seduced..."

"That's crap!" he thundered. "You were raped."

"I couldn't convince a jury!" she cried, deliberately lowering her voice. "What makes you think I could convince your constituency?"

"I don't give a damn..."

"You have to give a damn, Cole. You have to be reelected. If someone like Lovell, if Lovell..."

"Screw Lovell!" Cole cried, anchoring her face with both his hands. "I've waited all my life to love like this. I want to be with you."

"After the election..."

"I'm sick of political tomorrows. I made those mistakes with Lisa. I'm concerned with now. Today. This minute."

"Tomorrow is a reality, no matter how much you want to believe that it's only Mickey Mouse time." Her eyes begged. "Please, Cole. Don't ask me to hurt you."

Their eyes held. Strength warred with strength. Heart warred with heart.

"We'll discuss it back in Washington," he said finally.

"My answer will be the same."

"You're forgetting I'm an orator," he said with a half smile.

"You're forgetting I'm in love with you," she said with not even a hint of a smile.

This time when they made love, it was with quiet desperation.

TRACY STOOD BY HER ANSWER. But then, it was a decision that both she and Cole found, if not easy, at least tolerable all during the remainder of April, simply because their schedules were so hectic. He spent almost the entire month in Pennsylvania, "stumping" the small towns and larger cities in his district and calling on those outside his district for the purpose of seeking statewide support and contributions. The three times he flew back to Washington, D.C., he was in important congressional meetings, meetings that didn't even allow time for him to see Tracy before having to fly out again. She said she understood, and she did, but increasingly she longed to see him, to just be with him. Repeatedly Cole begged her to come to him. Repeatedly she refused and threw herself into her work with such fervor that Nathan the Mouth couldn't find enough assignments to keep her busy.

By the end of April, patience—Tracy's and Cole's—was wearing as thin as late-winter ice.

"What time is it?" Tracy asked Hank, who sat with his feet propped on her coffee table, a can of beer in one hand, a copy of a men's magazine in the other.

He turned over his wrist and glanced at the expensive latest-in-technology watch that told the hour in four cities. "You want the time in Paris, London, Tokyo or D.C.?" he asked with a wide grin.

Tracy pushed aside an empty chocolate-chip-cookie bag and brushed incriminating crumbs from her lips. "Have I ever told you that you can be a real pain in the ass?"

Her friend chuckled. "I prefer to think that's one reason our friendship has survived. This honest rapport we have with each other."

Tracy gave another honest directive as to where he could stuff his sarcasm.

He simply laughed again, teased that she was touchy and announced, "It's nine-thirty." A sudden seriousness prevailed over him. "What time does he usually call?"

"Ten, ten-thirty," she answered, giving in to that impatient feeling that assailed her every evening right before Cole called.

"You're in love with him, aren't you?" Hank asked.

"Yes," she said simply.

"Are you sleeping with him?"

Had it come from anyone else, she would have refused to answer the question, but she knew Hank's interest came only from the heart. He knew about her past.

"Yes."

He smiled. "Good." Dragging his feet from the coffee table, he stood. "I gotta go. You want this?" he added, indicating the magazine.

"Hardly. I find it difficult to get excited about a naked woman whose only goal in life is to make love on the Serengeti Plain with a herd of gazelles jumping over her." She was referring to the centerfold's bio.

"Yeah. Me, too," Hank replied tonelessly.

Tracy's brows rose in exaggerated disbelief. "Is this Hank "Playboy" Yeats talking?"

"I think the playboy's fallen in love," he said seriously.

Tracy studied the vulnerable-looking, tall, thin man dressed in blue jeans. Slowly she smiled. "My congratulations . . . and my condolences."

His lips edged into a wry expression. "I heard that."

"Why aren't you with her instead of here with me?" Tracy asked.

A look of sadness swept across his eyes. "Marisa thinks that we're spending too much time together. Funny, I thought we weren't spending enough."

"Oh, Hank . . ."

"Not to worry," the photographer said with a confidence that didn't quite tell in his eyes, "I'll bring her over to my way of thinking."

Tracy walked Hank to the door then reached up to kiss his cheek. They stared at each other. Neither said a word. But then, good friends speak in a quiet language.

THE PHONE RANG AT 10:17. "Hello?" Tracy asked, her heart pumping in anticipation.

"I love you."

She closed her eyes and pulled the phone closer. "I love you," she whispered. Long moments passed. "Where are you?"

She heard the shuffling of papers. "Let me find my itinerary."

"That bad?"

"Believe me, that bad. I guess I'm in Kirkwood." There was another long silence. To two people, Kirkwood, Pennsylvania, seemed like a million miles from Washington, D.C. "Tracy..." Cole's voice was low, ragged, skirting the edge of desperation. "I'm going crazy without you."

MAYBE HE WAS GOING CRAZY, Thomas Lovell thought as he stared down at the photographs spread across the ill-made bed of the second-rate motel. Outside the window, a red neon sign proclaimed Cozy Cabins, Kirkwood. Every other letter of the sign had burned out and was as conspicuous as a missing tooth. The sign cheapened the motel more effectively than the drooping drapes and cigarette-burned carpet.

Picking up one of the photographs, Tom Lovell stared at the image of the handsome dark-haired man. It was a photograph he'd taken that evening at a political rally. He swore. Why were there people that fate kissed with kindness? Cole Damon had everything: good looks, money, charisma, and this son-of-a-bitch election sewn up unless a miracle happened. A pain shot through Lovell's heart. The man had also had Lisa.

"Lisa," he whispered. The word fell like a sacred prayer on a heathen altar. An image of sun-gold hair, laughing green eyes and a lithe body beneath his fired through his mind. He'd been different with her. He'd been going to get a real job, a job with a respectable newspaper, the kind he'd had before succumbing to the money-lure of the *Tattler*. She'd had faith in him. She'd told him that he had the soul of a poet. And he'd been sober with her, not stinking drunk seven nights out of seven. He'd been sane with her...not crazy.

Crazy. Was he going crazy? Or was following Cole Damon only his way of staying alive? Without his hatred of Damon, he felt dead. Obsession or not, he had to be near the man. Only then did he feel alive. Alive. Though possibly crazy.

CHAPTER TEN

"I'M SENDING THE PLANE FOR YOU." The tone of Cole's voice brooked no opposition, but then, it was an opposition that Tracy wasn't certain she had the emotional strength for. May had reached the midway mark, and still they hadn't seen each other since the glorious weekend at Cole's farm.

"That's not a good idea," Tracy said into the phone with a total lack of conviction.

"Be at the airport tomorrow at two."

"We really ought to think about this," she said, trying to inject some sanity into the insane moment.

"Petey will meet you and drive you to the farm."

"Cole..."

"I have one night...one night I can spend with you."

"What if someone knows..."

"I don't care."

"I do."

"Tomorrow at two," the strained voice insisted.

"Cole..."

"I need you. For God's sake, come to me!"

Deep in her heart she knew that she shouldn't be doing this, Tracy thought the next day as the small plane landed in Lancaster, Pennsylvania. But even deeper in her heart, she knew that she had no choice. She couldn't stand another lonely night with only his voice to snuggle next to. She had to feel flesh against flesh, heartbeat against heartbeat. Love words had to be exchanged at a distance no greater than touch.

Petey Jernigan did, indeed, meet her and drive her to Cole's farm. En route, he explained that Cole would arrive later that afternoon. After settling Tracy in and announcing that dinner was already prepared and had only to be reheated, the foreman left for Neffsville. It was obvious that they were being given time alone. It was probably just as obvious, Tracy thought, that they needed the time. How else could one interpret the satin and silk look in her eyes every time Cole's name was mentioned?

Impatiently she wandered the house—the living room, the kitchen, the dining room, Cole's bedroom. It was here, she noted with a blush, that Petey Jernigan had placed her luggage. Okay, she thought. She knew it had been obvious. A man and woman did not meet in a quiet secluded place to discuss the state of world affairs. They just met for affairs. Affairs best not seen.

A sadness crept over her at the harsh realization that of all the women in the world, she might be the very worst for Cole. It would have been far more prudent if he'd fallen in love with someone else. Someone whose past was not suspect. The thought restlessly drove her from the house. She stopped at the barn, fed Lady Macbeth a handful of oats then headed for the meadow. Their meadow.

Sunlight rained earthward, warming soil and creatures, and in the air hung the sweet, sweet smell of spring, the sweet, sweet trill of birdsong. Golden-yellow buttercups swayed in a faint late-afternoon breeze, while miniature violet-blue flowers marched across meadow and field like a peace-loving army. She bent, snapped up a fresh blade of grass and tickled it across her lips. The world suddenly seemed so far away, and the only reality was a blade of grass and a green spring meadow...and the man walking toward her.

Tracy's heart began a fast, jazz-discordant rhythm; her breath conversely slowed to a waltzlike pace. The blade of grass tumbled to the ground. As crazy as it seemed, she fell in love all over again.

Slowly, his eyes riveted to hers, Cole advanced toward her. A breath of May breeze teased a forelock of his jet-black hair; the same breeze flapped the legs of his brown slacks and the collar of his white shirt. His tie and suit coat had been abandoned somewhere, probably back at the house from where he'd obviously just come. Step by step, through grass and weeds and field flowers, he closed the distance between them.

He stopped mere inches from her and started to smile. The smile never materialized. Instead he simply groaned and yanked her into his arms. They held each other, both of them afraid that if they lessened their grasp the moment would prove to be a dream and vanish. Neither tried to find words—each simply sought the other's warmth. When Cole's mouth finally possessed hers, it was with savage splendor, tender majesty. They kissed, they caressed, in the subtle, bold way of lovers.

Without a word, Cole removed her pullover then began to unbutton her blouse. He found the creamy rise of a breast, a wispy hint of lace. She began to unbutton his shirt. She uncovered a wedge of tan skin, a dark frothing of black hair. They tugged at each other's waistbands to free them from the confines of clothes. Minutes later, she lay on the soft, fresh-smelling grass and watched as Cole lowered himself over her. Slowly they made love. The sun beat down its warming praise; the breeze murmured its windy approval. Man and woman whispered only in sighs and moans. And quickened breaths. And suddenly released groans of ecstasy. Then all was silent except for heartbeats.

Still buried deep inside her, Cole sought her eyes. A smile suddenly teased the corners of his masculine mouth in a very devilish grin.

"Hello," he said primly. "How are you?"

The proper greeting, considering their present positions, sent a sudden giggle gurgling up from Tracy's throat. But the giggle stopped in mid-deliverance, replaced by a choking noise that sounded suspiciously like the advent of tears. Tears that erupted in cyrstalline pearls that seeped from her eyes. Burrowing her face in his warm bare shoulder, she cried.

"I . . . I . . . missed . . . you."

Cole held her, rocking her gently, soothing her with words from his own unsteady lips. "Shhh. Don't, baby. Don't cry. We're together now."

Once more they made love.

And again and again, they made love that night. Because neither of them seemed able to get enough of the other. Sometimes the loving was silent and serious. Sometimes they talked and teased all during their pleasure. Sometimes they made love on the sofa, sometimes on the floor, sometimes in bed, and once on the bathroom vanity. Tracy teased that they'd become decadent. Cole told her that it was a strange comment coming from a woman with grass stains on her back.

As their time together ran out, the teasing disappeared and was replaced by somber spirits and long faces. Cole begged her to stay with him. Tracy begged him not to ask.

All the way to the airport, Tracy fought her tears, wondering when she would see him again?

Cole, dry-eyed and miserable, sulked all the way back to Larry Seeger's makeshift campaign headquarters. When would he see her again?

As Tracy was boarding the plane and Cole was trying not to think of her doing so, Thomas Lovell was studying his new photographs. The woman was pretty, he mused. And familiar. Wasn't she the one who'd been with Damon at the bar? Maybe. Maybe not. Frankly he didn't care about Damon's love life. All he wanted to do was to end his political career. Which he would somehow, someway. Because he owed it to Lisa.

JUNE ARRIVED. Back to their schedule of not seeing each other, Tracy and Cole spoke each night on the phone. It was an arrangement that was growing increasingly unsatisfactory. In fact, by the end of June, volatile was the only word for Cole's and Tracy's emotional status. It was as if they were waiting for some gigantic firework to go off. By tacit agreement, their nightly phone conversations were kept on asexual grounds. Both declared their love at the end of every conversation, but their needs were avoided entirely. That neither of them was sleeping worth a tinpenny damn was never mentioned, though curiously, each knew that the other wasn't. And somehow, as is always the mark of true love, the other's needs were most important. Cole stopped asking Tracy to join him. For that she was grateful. Because had he now asked, she wasn't at all certain she could have resisted. She was a woman in love. A woman who wanted nothing beyond being with the man she loved. With that in mind, the future was losing its power. And that Tracy couldn't allow to happen.

THE SOUND OF FOOTSTEPS striking concrete echoed in the quiet Pennsylvania evening. His suit jacket slung over his shoulder, his tie askew, his hand tucked deep into his pants pocket, Cole deliberately slowed his stride to match that of his rotund campaign manager's. The men had just eaten and were headed back to their motel rooms for the night. It was four minutes of ten, hot, and, at least for Cole, an inexplicable expectancy hung like thick draperies in the air. It was the kind of night when one made that emotional journey that took one to the end of one's rope.

"The campaign's going exactly as planned," Larry Seeger was saying. Cole heard his words as if they were being delivered from a faraway mountaintop. "Though we got more opposition from those church groups than I expected. The Moral Majority has certainly had its impact on politics these days. Don't you think?"

"What?"

"The Moral Majority's had an impact," Seeger said, answering his own question and taking Cole off the spot. "Thank God, you're squeaky clean."

Squeaky clean. Cole wondered what Larry Seeger would say if he knew that he was in love with a woman whose past was less than ideal for a politician. And furthermore, he wondered what Seeger would say if he told him that he personally didn't give a damn about Tracy's past and that he'd see any man in hell who did. The only thing keeping her from his side right this moment was her own stubborn insistence.

"I wish I could remember who that church representative is and where I'd met him before," Seeger said.

Cole looked in Larry Seeger's direction. The man had made virtually the same comment when he'd been introduced to Tracy those many months ago when she'd come to the office for the interview. It was because of that comment that Tracy had asked Cole not to tell Seeger about their relationship. She was afraid that he'd seen some of the negative press and would eventually remember her background. And, of course, that possibility was always there. Seeger's mind made elephants look forgetful. Cole didn't care if he did remember, but Tracy did.

In the far distance heat lightning zigzagged across the sky. It punctuated Cole's restlessness and made him feel somehow that the evening was circling around him, just waiting for its chance.

"Now that Lovell's smear articles have levelled off," Seeger continued, "I'd say you're in first-rate shape. Incidentally, rumor has it that he's about to get his ass fired at the *Tattler*."

This remark did snag Cole's attention, and his dark eyes sought Seeger's crystal-gray ones. "Oh?"

"Apparently he's missing a lot of work. Not meeting deadlines. And drinking too much."

"Too bad," Cole commented and genuinely meant it because he believed the waste of a human life was a tragedy. Once again, though, he wondered why Tom Lovell had singled him out as a target for his malice.

The two men stopped in front of Cole's room. Digging in his pocket, Cole produced a key, inserted it in the lock, and said, "See you in the morning."

"Yeah. Three more days and then a break."

"Yeah," Cole replied, hoping somehow he could last three more days. Right this moment, three more hours were in doubt. "Well, good night." Moving into the room, he shut the door and heard Seeger's muted footsteps moving next door. He had just thrown his coat over the back of a chair and was reaching to finish unknotting his burgundy tie when he heard a sharp rapping. Stepping to the door, he opened it. Larry Seeger stood in the doorway with a wide grin on his chubby face.

"Harper Sterritt. Two years ago in Spokane, Washington."

Cole looked blank.

"The church representative's name and where I met him. I knew it would come to me." He then walked off with a smug smile plastered across his mouth.

With a flick of his wrist, Cole closed the door, stood absently looking at the framed checkout schedule, and cursed.

Stripping from his dress clothes, he showered and slipped into a pair of jeans. They were the jeans he'd worn the first time he'd made love to Tracy. The thought practically destroyed his sanity. God, he missed her. Never in his life had he had this kind of aching need. But it was more than sexual, and that's what made it so powerful. He had an all-consuming need to just be with her. He'd had no idea that love could hurt so badly.

With this thought torturing him, he plopped onto the bed and stretched for the phone. He prayed that the sound of her voice wouldn't drive him completely over the brink.

TRACY STEPPED FROM THE SHOWER and reached for the towel. With a patting pressure, she smoothed the terry over her feet, her legs, her thighs, then with an abnormal haste she drew the towel across her hips, her stomach and the tawny-gold curls of hair that mounded her femininity. She dabbed at her back, her shoulders, her breasts. A gentle serrated sigh filled the foggy bathroom; an image of Cole's hair-sprinkled hand caressing the rounded flesh that the towel now molded filled her mind, while shooting sparks of fire gravitated to one hot body spot. Was she going to make it through the next few days? she wondered. Or would Cole find her certifiably insane when he got home?

"Certifiably insane," she muttered, "if you don't try to help yourself."

With self-assistance in mind, she flung the towel to the edge of the tub. She flicked off the bathroom light—killing the image of the misty-eyed woman in the mirror—and stalked into the bedroom. She walked to the chest of drawers. Rummaging through her gowns, she found nothing that appealed to her. All were too hot. It was the height of June, when bodies went limp from heat and humidity. Finally she found a chemise, decided it was the slight covering she needed and slipped it over her raised arms. It slithered over her body like satin and fell to just below the tuck of her hips.

She cut off all the lights except the faint lamplight, crawled into bed, and checked the clock. It read tenthirty. Cole would call any minute. The thought both excited and depressed her. How could she keep this overwhelming need from her voice?

The music box was tinkling its message of love and time, tomorrow and today, when the phone pealed its soft lover's call. At that moment Tracy would have recklessly traded all her and Cole's tomorrows for just one tonight.

"Hello?" Her voice was strained, as though it had been filtered through dense clouds.

"Hi." It was one word, one syllable, yet the moment Tracy heard Cole's voice, she knew it was different. There was a rawness to it. There was also a silence, as if he were dredging up the strength to continue. "Whatcha doing?"

Going crazy from missing you. "Waiting for you to call. What are you doing?"

Dying. By slow, punishing degrees. "Waiting for the day to end so I could call you."

"Did you have a good day?" she asked the way she always did.

"It was okay. Yours?"

"Okay." Silence ensued. Tracy ran her arm beneath her hair, pushing it up and off her neck and fanning it out against the pale-blue pillow. "It's hot here," she added, as if action spirited thought.

"It's hot here," Cole replied, burying his ink-black hair into the softness of the white pillow and bending his knees in an upward pose. Silence followed. "Is that the music box?"

"Yes. Can you hear it?" The question was stupid, she realized. Of course he could hear it. Otherwise he wouldn't have brought up the subject.

"Yes." His answer was equally inane. There was another silence, this one long and heavy as lead. "If I could be two places at one time, Tracy, I'd be with you. Tomorrow and today." It was more than the repetition of the song's lyrics. It was the baring of one man's soul.

"Are you all right?" she whispered.

"No." The word was ragged, rife with rent emotion. "I miss you like hell."

A thousand needs stormed her body, chief of which was her need to just be with him. She closed her eyes and sighed inconsolably, "I miss you."

"Where are you?" he asked, his voice not a whisper but not full-throated, either.

"In bed."

His breath escaped in an uncontrolled hiss. "What are you wearing?"

"A chemise."

"What's a chemise?"

"Sorta like a teddy."

"What's a teddy?"

Tracy's lips quivered in the tiniest of smiles. "Can I assume that this means you're not that familiar with women's lingerie?"

"I never paid that much attention to it...until you. Describe a chemise."

Instinctively Tracy's eyes slid to the garment that semi-encased her body. "It has little straps..."

"Like the blue gown?" he interrupted.

"Yes. Only thinner. And this one is ivory." The word, conjuring up the ivory slip he'd first seen her in the night he'd learned of her past, caused Cole to moan. "With brown lace over...over the breasts."

Cole's inconstant breath fluctuated even more. "Is the material soft?"

"It's sorta satiny."

There was a tortured sound as air moved through a tight throat. "And how long is this sorta satiny chemise?"

Her heart pounded a wild runaway rhythm that almost caused the fabric under discussion to flutter. "It stops just below my...my hips."

Cole's heart joined hers in its rash cadence. "What you are wearing under it?"

"Nothing," she breathed.

A trillion tingles, fire-hot and omnipotent, raced over her body, centering in one exquisite core. A trillion aches congregated in Cole's body in a spot strained so tight that painful was the only word to describe it.

"Where are you?" She knew she shouldn't ask, but she'd been driven beyond the point of caring.

"In bed. I'm wearing jeans," he volunteered. "The ones I was wearing the first time we made love."

The vision in her mind was cruelly clear. "Are they...snapped?"

"No."

How could one word so shatter her composure? She wasn't even conscious that she had moaned. "Cole?" Her body felt hot; her body felt cold. She felt as if she'd taken all she could.

"What?"

"I know I'm not supposed to say this, but..."

"But what?"

"I need you." The words tumbled out urgently.

He swore harshly.

Both lay a hundred plus miles apart with eyes closed and bodies heated beyond the capabilities of June. Cole's wrist was thrown across his forehead, damp from passion, while Tracy clung to the phone as if it were her only contact with reality. Both were lost in love, lost in need of the one they loved.

"Touch your lips," Cole commanded softly, hoarsely.

"What?"

"Put your fingers on your lips." He could feel her hesitation. "Do it," he begged.

She inched the pads of her fingers upward. Her lips trembled beneath her touch; her breath seeped out in an uneven stream.

"Are you touching them?"

"Yes."

"What do they feel like?"

"I don't know."

"Tell me," he rasped.

"Soft...I guess...and wet...and they're trembling."

He moaned. "I love your mouth. It's so sweet...so pretty...so soft under mine. I wish I were kissing you. God, I want to kiss you! That's all I can think about— my mouth on yours. I want to fill your mouth with my tongue...I want your tongue to fill mine...I want to taste you...I want to suckle your tongue...I want..."

"Please," she pleaded. "Don't. This is insane."

"Touch your breasts."

"Cole..."

"Touch them," he pleaded. "Touch them for me. Touch them the way I would if I could."

Slowly she eased the hand at her lips downward... until her fingers brushed against the pointed tip of one breast. Satin slicked over sensitive skin. Ice-hot tremors erupted, and Tracy sighed.

"Does that feel good?" Cole whispered.

"Cole..."

"It's all right. We're just making love a different way. Does it feel good?"

"Yes," she whimpered, unable to stop herself from palming the fullness of her breast and kneading in a reserved rhythm. She closed her eyes and bit at her lip. "Oh, yes."

"Are you touching your bare skin?"

"No. I can't."

"Of course you can. There's nothing wrong with that. Ease down the strap, Tracy." He heard her breath pounding against the receiver. He fought to control his own rough breathing. "If I were there, I'd pull down the strap, I'd push the fabric aside, and I'd take your breast in my hand. Oh, baby, it would feel so good... to you and me. Then I'd rub my thumb back and forth to make the nipple hard... hard like a rose-colored pebble... then I'd kiss it and draw you into my mouth and..."

The sensual sweetness of what he was saying enflamed her body to a fever pitch, and she was helpless to deny what he was asking of her. She eased the strap downward.

"Are you touching your breast?" he whispered.

"Yes," she answered, feeling the bare peak harden beneath her fingertips. Her whole breast seemed to swell. "It feels good. Oh, Cole, ... it feels so good."

"I'm glad." He took a deep, uneven breath. "I'm going to make you feel even better."

A faint shadow of what he meant flitted through her mind. "Cole, I want *you*. I want us to be together. I want..."

"Tracy, I can't be with you tonight. Please, please, let me do this for you. Let one of us feel good, anyway."

"No, I..."

"Take your hand..."

His instructions were explicit, breath-stealingly explicit, but tenderly given. They were the instructions of a lover. Her lover. The man she loved. Slowly, hesitantly, she obeyed his soft, pleading whispers... and surrendered a little each step of the way at the pleasure he caused to be unleashed.

"Relax. Do what I say. Let me make you feel good." His breathing had grown as shallow as a country creek. "Move slowly... slowly... that's it. There's no hurry."

Her voice was a broken string of cries and moans and whimpers. Her body felt hot, in need, and empty... so empty.

"Easy, baby," he soothed when he sensed the end was nearing.

"Cole..." Writhing, Tracy arched her hips into the irresistible sound of his voice. Never in her life had anything been so sensual, yet, curiously, she fought against completion. This wasn't the way she wanted release. Yet release tempted, tempted... with just the sweet, steady call of his voice.

"It's okay, baby. Let it happen. For both of us."

"Cole..."

"Don't fight it. Just enjoy."

Suddenly release came like a quick shower of gold pouring down on her damp body.

"That's it," Cole encouraged, his voice strained beyond recognition, his body more taut than it had ever been. "I love you. Do you hear me? I love you."

"Cole...Cole..." Her voice was strangled. She gasped, and then all was quiet. Slowly she rolled to her side and curled into a ball. A hundred miles away, Cole rolled to his side, hoping it would ease the ache. It didn't.

"Are you all right? Did it feel good?" he asked finally.

"Yes. But I think I'm blushing." Unconsciously she hid her face with its softly satisfied smile in the pillow.

Cole's lips twitched at her sweet naiveté. "Why?"

"Do you know what I just did?" There was a groany quality to the question. She dug her face farther into the pillow.

"Exactly what I told you to do. That makes it making love."

"Technically..."

"...we made love." He expelled a long, deep sigh. "Of course, to be real honest, I don't feel much like it."

For the first time his predicament registered in her mind. "Oh, Cole, I'm sorry. I didn't think. I..."

"Hey," he said, stopping her, "I knew what I was doing. I'll live." He rolled back to his back. He took the exquisite ache with him. "Maybe."

"Come home," she suddenly whispered.

Her plea was like fingers tightening around his heart. And the fact that she'd never asked it before only curled those fingers more snugly. "Three days, baby. In three days."

"Cole?"

"What?"

She hesitated then swallowed. "It felt good. I mean, it was satisfying, but emotionally..." Her voice cracked. "I want you. I want you beside me, inside me. I want you holding me. I want you touching me, kissing me...please come home. Now." She knew it was an unfair request and one that couldn't be met, but she couldn't help but ask.

There was a deep silence. Never had the distance from Pennsylvania to Washington, D.C., seemed so great. Never had either of them felt so helpless.

"Baby, I can't," he said at last in a choked voice. "In three days. I promise in three days. Tell me you understand."

"I understand," she whispered. And she did. It was just that the empty feeling she had was so overwhelming that she thought it would engulf her. In many ways, a partial release had been worse than none.

Ten minutes later they hung up. It was as if talking to each other was a torture too keen to be tolerated. Tracy lay quietly on her bed. Cole lay quietly on his. Finally she fell into a restless sleep. He wasn't so lucky. At eleven-thirty he got up, marched to the bathroom and turned on a cold shower. It was as the chilling drops fell on his still-aroused body that he made the decision.

CHAPTER ELEVEN

THE DOORBELL RANG at ten minutes to four. Tracy bolted to an upright position, listened once more to the frantic screeching of the doorbell and turned on the lamp. As the muted light spilled across the room, the bell shrilled again.

Who in the world? she thought, knowing immediately by the flurry of musical chaos that it wasn't Hank. The knowledge that someone else was ringing her doorbell before daylight sent her heart into a fear-charged cadence. She looked about for a robe, saw none, and as the bell squealed again, she padded in her bare feet and chemise out onto the landing. Deliberately leaving the stairway cloaked in darkness, she began to slowly feel her way down the stairs.

She was at midjourney when the caller substituted knocking for ringing—a jarring sound of a hand banging on wood that almost shook the house. Tracy hesitated. The caller grew impatient. The knocking gave way to shouting.

"Tracy! It's me. Open up."

Cole!

Surprise, relief and total happiness threatened to buckle Tracy's knees right there on the murky stairwell. Suddenly she couldn't get to the door quickly enough. Once there, she fumbled with the twin locks until both she and Cole were near screaming, but at last the door swung open.

With the darkened room behind her and the inky blackness of night behind Cole, they couldn't see anything more than shadowy silhouetted forms. But it was enough to recognize each other.

Instinctively she took a step toward him. "Cole," she breathed, the word so wispy, so airy, that it flew higher than clouds on a summer day. "What . . . what are you doing here?"

A broad-shouldered form stepped from the darkness of night into the darkness of the entryway. A suitcase was dropped inside just before the door closed, and a duffel bag was carelessly chucked onto the hardwood floor. Two hands reached for Tracy.

"Finishing what I started," Cole promised as he hauled the woman before him into his starved embrace.

One second the hot, humid night air was breathing against Tracy's bare legs, and the next second there was the bold scrape of denim against them. Her satin-covered breasts flattened against a wide hard chest. Just as Cole's mouth came down to claim hers in sweet savagery, his hands slid from her waist to sculpt the roundness of her bare bottom beneath the chemise. Cole groaned. His hands molded the curved fullness of her hips, kneading the tender flesh in his greedy palms. The ivory chemise rode upward, and when Cole pulled her intimately into the cradle of his legs and ground himself into her, it was strained denim colliding with a bare mound of soft womanly flesh. Tracy moaned at the exquisite burst of firelight that shot through her and crumpled against him. Scooping her up into his arms, his mouth fastened to hers, he started up the stairs.

"Is this a chemise?" he breathed against her lips.

"Yes," she whispered, teasing the tip of his tongue with hers.

"Thank heaven I didn't know. Thank heaven..." Her tongue, slipping inside his mouth, silenced him.

Once they were upstairs, he put her down in the middle of the bed. The hem of the chemise tangled at her waist. The gilded light from the lamp glowed down on her, making her legs, her shoulders, her exposed stomach appear the color of honey and peaches. The dark nest of curls looked like a topaz treasure waiting, begging, to be found. Cole simply stared at the beautiful perfection before him. Slowly he eased from the side of the bed and, his eyes never leaving hers, he began to shed his clothing. With each piece that fell away, Tracy's breath grew more and more shallow. At last he stood before her, naked and glorious and fully proud. Tracy could hardly breathe.

"I want you so badly," he said with the thickness of desire.

She held out her hand.

When he came to her, it was all fire and fury, a fire and fury neither had ever experienced before. Neither could touch enough or taste enough of the other. Lips devoured, hands ravished, teeth nibbled and bit, bodies shimmied and slid. Tracy's nails stroked the swollen brown buds hiding in the deep furry woods of his chest; Cole kissed and tongued the turgid peaks of her breasts through the chemise then quickly tired of the satin barrier. Tossing the garment onto the floor, he lowered his warm mouth to her even warmer breast. Tracy twisted and writhed and thought she would die from pleasure. Cole tormented and touched and didn't care if he did die of such exquisite torture. He bestowed kisses to her breasts, her belly, the sweet crater of her navel, the tender skin of her thigh.

"Soft, warm, sleep-warm," he mumbled as his hands separated her legs. His lips worshiped her in intimate lover's ways—soft, gentle kisses and daring movements of his tongue and fingers that robbed her of all sanity.

"Cole," she whimpered, digging her feet into the mattress to arch her body into the heat of his mouth. She reached wildly, blindly, for him. He let her find him. Moving over her, positioning and parting, he dove deeply into her.

"Ah, God," he groaned, feeling himself fill every womanly inch of her, just as she felt herself wondrously filled to overflowing. It was the satisfaction long desired by both. Gently, fiercely, thoroughly, he thrust, taking them from fury to something so wildly consuming that both were mindless in moments.

The end came swiftly on the surging tide of passion and the softest of love words. A cry of his name. An echo of hers. Heat that shamed the June night. A sweetness to be always remembered. Wet brows. Slick bodies. Clouded eyes. And lips that kissed in a smoldering afterglow.

"Hold me," she begged afterward. "Just hold me."

He held her the way he had not been able to hours before. Stretching across her to turn off the lamp, he pulled her back flush against his furred chest, his arm draped tightly about her waist.

"Do you have any idea," he breathed near her ear, "what it did to me to hear you beg me to come home?"

"I'm sorry. It wasn't fair of me. But I wanted to see..."

"I wanted to see you, too," he whispered, kissing the baby-soft spot just behind her ear. "Go to sleep now. We'll talk in the morning."

She had thought sleep impossible, but her mind and her body, both sated by the man lying beside her, had no alternative with the fatigue weighing so heavily on them. Within minutes she slept.

Cole couldn't sleep. He wanted to endlessly savor the feel of the woman in his arms. Nothing in the world was so soft...nor so precious...nor so perfectly loved by him. And she was his. In that inexplicable way that a man knows a woman is his. And it felt good. So damned good! So worth waiting for all these lonely years. She stirred and sighed, a sound of peace and contentment. Her hips nudged him, as if even in sleep she was searching for a greater closeness. At that movement, he hardened according to nature's designated plan, but he felt the reaction to be more spiritual than sexual. Moving his hand onto her hip, he slowly angled her leg forward and, inching downward, eased himself up and into the still-moist cavern of her body.

"Cole?" she mumbled.

"Shhh. Go back to sleep. I just wanted to be closer."

She adjusted her hips and trailed her hand to touch their joined bodies, sighing softly, sleepily, "Nice."

"Nice," he repeated into the crown of her head and surprised even himself by drifting off to sleep.

TRACY WOKE ALONE. Her first thought was that she had dreamed Cole's presence. Her second thought, as her nostrils caught a whiff of an aromatic fragrance, was that dreams don't make coffee. She stretched, and then she knew for certain that she hadn't dreamed the night or Cole. Her love-tired body clearly said that it had been the object of one man's possessive loving. She smiled. It was the best possible feeling to wake up to.

Slipping into her old pink robe, she headed for the bathroom. There she found Cole's duffel bag on the floor and his shaving gear spread on the vanity. The sight warmed her. Minutes later, she padded barefoot down the stairs and across the living room. She stopped at the kitchen door and watched the man leaning against the cabinet. He was engrossed in reading the morning paper. Cole wore jeans and the plaid shirt he'd arrived in, except now it hung outside the jeans and was unbuttoned from top to bottom. A wide slit of tan skin and black hair teased Tracy's eyes. His hair was tousled, his feet bare. He'd never looked sexier.

"I thought I had dreamed you."

At the soft sound of her voice, Cole glanced up. The look in his eyes said that he couldn't quite believe how beautiful she was. "Come here," he commanded huskily as he laid the paper on the cabinet. "Let me show you how real I am."

She crossed the room to him. He pulled her into his arms. She smothered her face in his chest. He laid his cheek against the top of her head. They simply held each other for wonderfully long moments.

"Did I tell you last night that I love you?" he whispered.

"With every touch," she whispered back.

He left a kiss in her hair before nuzzling in search of her face. He kissed her forehead, her eyebrow, the tip of her nose then dropped his mouth onto hers in a sweetness beyond compare. His lips were warm and greedy. "Good morning," he said finally.

"Good morning," Tracy responded. "I thought you weren't coming home for three more days."

A dark opaqueness flashed in his brown irises. "How could I not come home after that phone call?" His hand gently caressed her cheek. "God, Tracy, do you have any idea how much I wanted you? How much I wanted to be with you? How much it hurt to hear you begging me to come home?"

"I didn't mean to upset you," she apologized. "But I wanted you, Cole. Not just ... not just a release."

Strong arms pulled her closer. "I know. And I'm glad. Do you know that I have a pilot who thinks I'm crazy?" Cole asked.

"And what does your campaign manager think?" It was a casual enough question, with a not-so-casual wait for an answer.

"That I went home to tend to personal business." His head angled and dipped; his lips brushed hers. "Very personal business."

"Are you staying?" she whispered. This time she held her breath.

"I'm staying...for three..." His lips slid onto hers. "Whole..." Teeth nibbled the inner softness of her mouth. "Days."

"That's an eternity," Tracy murmured.

"Yes. And we'll do whatever you like—shopping, the movies, eating out..." The sudden look in her eyes caused him to stop. "Tracy, our not being seen together is stupid. You're a part of my life, and..."

"Not until after the election."

"Tracy..."

"Please don't spoil our time together," she pleaded. "Let's just be together here...at my house."

Cole studied her. "Whatever you want," he said quietly.

That day they unashamedly spent in bed. That night they prepared spaghetti, which was eaten with a green salad but without wine because Cole refused to leave Tracy's side or have her leave his to go purchase a bottle. Immediately following dinner and the cleanup, they went back to bed, where they again loved long into the night. Both enjoyed a sleep of blessed contentment.

Saturday was so hot that D.C. residents—at least those whose brains weren't soggy from the humidity—would have sworn the sidewalks bubbled. Cole decided that what he and Tracy needed to combat the high temperature was an orgy-supply of pistachio-swirl ice cream. She agreed. She also volunteered her car. As Cole was going out the back door, he asked her to come with him, but just as he knew she would, she declined, saying that she'd stay home and get the steaks ready to broil. Cole didn't push her, but he hurried like hell to get to the ice cream shop and back home. He walked through the door at exactly six-thirty.

"Ah, the ice cream man cometh," Tracy proclaimed, looking up from the spinach salad and thinking that it seemed like a year since he'd left the house.

A pinkness that was somewhere between the color of roses and coral blushed her cheeks, while her eyes were widely blue and slightly hazed. Her lips showed a hint of a swelling, suggesting excessive kissing. She looked like a woman who'd been thoroughly loved. Not thoroughly enough, Cole thought.

"You're so literary," he said, banding his arms about her waist and burying his face in the side of her neck. His breath tickled. Tracy giggled and scrunched down her head. "You're also sexy."

She turned around, linking her arms around his neck. She was securely pinned between the unyielding cabinet and the even more unyielding body of Cole Damon. "Am I?" she whispered. "Sexy?"

His eyes roamed over every aspect of her face and finally settled on her mouth. That mouth instinctively parted. "Oh, yeah," he practically growled. His lips captured hers in a way that gave substance to his answer. The kiss was slow, passionately slow, with lips wide and wet, and when it was finished, two bodies were trembling... more than aroused.

"I'm melting," Tracy whispered, fanning her breath against his mouth.

"Me, too," he whispered back.

She smiled. "And the ice cream... it's melting. Don't you think you ought to get it into the freezer?"

"What I really think is that I ought to get you into bed," he said as his mouth nipped hers again.

"You're insatiable."

"You don't seem to be having any trouble keeping up."

"Touché," she answered with a sultry smile that was delivered by love-pouty lips.

"Why don't we hurry and eat and... go to bed?" Cole proposed.

"If I remember correctly, you just got out of bed."

A roguish grin sauntered onto his lips, settling sexily in one corner. "Yeah, I know. Positively inspiring, isn't it?"

A half hour later, he set the table while she finished broiling the steaks.

"You know anybody who drives a dark blue Chrysler?" Cole asked, arranging the silverware.

"I don't think so. Why?"

"There's one parked up the street. Looks like a man is just sitting in it. I think it was there yesterday, too."

Tracy turned the steaks one last time to achieve the medium-rare both wanted. "The woman up the street has a steady boyfriend. I've never paid any attention to his car."

"Ummm," Cole replied absently.

When Tracy turned around, there was a devilish smile on her face. "Maybe sex researchers have the house staked out. Waiting to see if we're going to survive."

Cole grinned and delivered the old joke that if they didn't survive, it would take every undertaker on the East Coast to get the smiles off their faces.

Two hours later, though, a scowl replaced his grin. Staring through a slit in the living room drapes, he could still see the car parked at the curb several houses up. The sight left him with a funny feeling. His apprehension lasted until his eyes lighted on the newly bathed and sexily gowned Tracy.

When they woke Sunday morning, the room was swimming in sunshine and sadness. Though both were careful to say nothing, it was as plain as the clock by the bedside that they had only another twenty-four hours to spend together. It was equally obvious that that knowledge was already beginning to take its toll.

The toll grew higher as the day wore on. It was heaven played out on the stage of hell. Each sweet kiss became miserably sweeter because of its soon-to-be absence. As did each touch, each caress, each lover's look. By midafternoon the house could have rivaled a tomb with its silence. To fill in the screaming void, Cole flipped on the television to a channel showing an old movie.

He sat in the corner of the sofa with Tracy snuggled between his legs. They spent more time watching their hands, which were laced together and resting on Tracy's stomach, than the screen.

She swallowed, already fighting the pain of separation.

He swallowed, wondering how in God's name he was going to leave her.

Slowly she turned in his arms. Their eyes met, locked. They silently pleaded for time to stand still. Suddenly they were leaning into each other and kissing with a wildness that was painful, though neither of them noticed.

"Cole..." she breathed in an uneven rhythm as her lips were flattened under the weight of his.

"Don't. Don't say it," he pleaded. "Just love me."

In seconds they were naked, in seconds they were lovers joined as intimately as lovers can be and in seconds both cried out their bittersweet pleasure. Then they lay quietly, memorizing the feel of the other.

Hours later, as they tried to choke down hamburgers, Cole spoke. "You're not eating."

She shrugged. "Too much ice cream yesterday, I guess."

With that, she got up from the table and began to load the few dishes into the dishwasher. Each motion she took seemed surreal. It was almost as if she could hear the hands of her Mickey Mouse watch taunting her. So loud was the passage of time that she never heard the glass she dropped crash onto the kitchen floor. She felt it slip from her hands, she saw its million crystal shards at her feet, but she never heard the sound. What she did hear at last was her own crying. It started with a gulping sound in her throat, and she felt her shoulders heave, then heave again, and suddenly the tears were flowing, warm and salty rivulets that dripped from cheek to chin to linoleum where they mingled with the shattered glass.

Cole wrapped her in his arms. He held her until her tears were spent, held her until his muscles ached, held her until the stinging in his own eyes subsided. When the tears were but sniffles, he pushed her from his shoulder and looked down into her emotion-torn face.

"Go on upstairs and shower. I'll clean this up." When she hesitated, he urged, "Go on." She did as he instructed because she didn't have the strength to resist.

Fifteen minutes later Cole cut off the downstairs lights and peered out between the drapes. The dark blue Chrysler was still parked curbside. There was a twinge of that funny feeling again, but this time it had to take second place to his hurting heart.

Tracy was just stepping from the tub when Cole entered the bathroom. Their eyes met, hers red and swollen, his the deepest of brown-black. Those brown eyes lowered, taking in every inch of her body in absolute appreciation. Reaching for the towel, he spread it wide. She stepped into it, and he folded it about her. Just as he folded her once more into his arms.

"We have to talk," he said, finally pushing her to arm's length.

She instinctively knew what about and didn't think she had the strength to hear what he was going to say. She fastened the towel about her and moved into the bedroom. Cole followed.

"We're in love, Tracy," he said softly. "We need to be together."

She picked up the brush from the dressing table and roughly pulled it through her hair.

"We're miserable just contemplating saying goodbye," he added when it was obvious she wasn't going to reply. He waited this time, forcing an answer.

"I can hardly deny any of that, can I?"

"Then why deny our being together?"

She threw down the brush. "You make it sound so damned simple."

"It is."

"It isn't!" she cried, instantly hating the tone of her voice. Why was she screaming at him? This was the man she loved! "It isn't," she repeated more rationally. "And you know it."

Cole's patience, like hers, was as threadbare as a years-old coat. "All I know is that you're willing to throw away the reality of now for a possible tomorrow. Tracy, now is all we have, and you're a fool if you think otherwise. One sure today isn't worth sacrificing for a thousand might-be tomorrows."

"Don't . . ." She held up her hand.

"Don't tell me 'don't'!" he cried. "Tell me you'll go back with me."

"Cole . . ."

"I don't know when I'll be able to see you again. July and August are heavily committed. They're the last thrust before the election."

"Then we'll have to settle for the phone," she said, her heart breaking.

He said something vile about the telephone that would have spun Ma Bell's head. "I want you. Not some goddamned voice! I'm sick of making love to a goddamned voice!"

"Then don't call!" she shrieked, feeling her composure shattering like the glass had shattered such a short while before.

"Is that what you want? Me to stop calling?"

She closed her eyes and thought of long, miserable nights. "No. No. I want . . ." She stopped.

"What do you want, Tracy?"

She opened her eyes to find that his gaze had gentled on her. "I want a past that won't jeopardize your future."

"I don't give a damn about your past. And I don't think the Pennsylvania voters will, either."

"But I give a damn about your future. Cole, you have goals, plans, worthwhile things to accomplish." She raked her fingers through her hair. "I'm no saint, and I'm as selfish as the next person, but I can't sacrifice you for me, others for us."

"I'm not giving you up, Tracy. At some point we have to go public."

"We'll see."

They stared at each other. Finally Cole said in a flat voice, "You're not coming with me, are you?"

"No," she whispered. Her knees felt weak, her stomach sick, her heart empty.

Cole, too, felt weak, sick, empty. But he also felt a keen sense of admiration, which only made him love her more. Cruelly, that made saying goodbye all the harder.

That night they made love, but not in the conventional sense. He simply entered the hardness of his body into the softness of hers... and held her... and told her that he loved her more times than there were stars in the black velvet sky. And when black faded to the iridescent gold and pink of early dawn, he left her... as he'd found her. Alone. And lonely.

IT WAS HELL. It was also the end of September. July had dragged into August, August into breezy September, and each week of that preautumn month, Cole thought the campaign was winding to a close. But each time he thought that, Larry Seeger, demanding despot that he was, would think of one other appearance that Cole simply had to make. Both Cole and Tracy were numb, numb with wanting, numb with caring, numb with loving at a distance. They saw each other exactly twice during the three months, and both times their meeting was hurried and unsatisfactory. The rest of the time they spoke to each other by phone. Long, lonely calls in the night, when all they had were sighs, sweet words and promises.

Cole was constantly irritated, an irritation he tried hard not to take out on the well-meaning people around him. Sometimes he even succeeded. Tracy, on the other hand, had gone past irritation, long past. She now lived in the world of desperation. And desperation sometimes led to impulsiveness. It was what she feared most—that one night he'd beg her to come to him... and she would.

"I'm miserable," she mumbled into the foamy crest of her second beer. It was the last day of September, a Monday, a blue Monday, made bluer by the fact that Cole had said the night before that he still had no definite date as to when he was coming home.

"Ha!" Hank Yeats snorted into his third beer as he rearranged his stockinged feet on Tracy's coffee table. "Lady, you don't know what misery is. I'd have to get better to be suicidal."

"Why does everyone think his crow is the blackest?" Tracy scoffed.

"Because mine is."

"It is not."

"It is!"

"It is not!"

Green hazel eyes met blue, resulting in the byproduct of laughter.

"Are we getting drunk?" Tracy asked, giggling.

"I hope so. Our adventurous spirits need to tie one on."

As if on cue, both swigged down another deep swallow of beer. Both also returned to a despondent silence.

"Dammit, Trace, life isn't fair!" Hank's voice boomed seconds later as he sloshed his beer onto the table and stood. He rammed the tips of his fingers into the back pockets of his much-faded jeans and stalked to the living room window to stare outside. Night was slowly closing its inky curtains about the city.

"No," Tracy agreed, thinking not only of her friend but also of herself. She shifted, slumping her spine into the sofa. "No, life definitely isn't fair."

"I'm the one," Hank said, "who's avoided commitments at every turn. So what do I do? Meet a woman I want to commit to, and dammit, she won't commit to me!'' He slipped his hand from his pocket and rubbed his bronze head absently. "Marisa says she loves me, and I know she does—I can feel it—but she's scared of making a permanent commitment. The word marriage actually makes her shake.''

"Do you have any idea why?'' Tracy asked, her heart aching for her best friend.

He glanced over his shoulder and shook his head. "She won't talk about it, but I think she's been burned. Bad. She says she'll live with me, but she won't marry me. She keeps telling me to forget about tomorrow and to concentrate on what we have now.''

"It sounds as if she's worked for Cole too long,'' Tracy said on a deep sigh, adding, "Cole says that time is only a comic illusion.''

Hank Yeats crossed the room, reseated himself and chugged down a third of his beer. When he looked up, his eyes were mirrors to the uncertainty in his soul. "Do you think they're right, Trace? I mean, about living only for today?''

"I'm not the person to ask,'' Tracy said, feeling tears sprinkling her eyes and fighting them back. "I'm so miserable tonight that I'd probably agree to anything. If I could just see him . . .'' She sniffed back the beginning of tears. "I'd agree to anything.''

Hank reached out, took her hand and held it in his. It was one of those times in life when the questions outweighed the answers, and the only thing that made that inequity tolerable was a friendly hand to hold.

Later that night, Tracy stared at the ringing phone. Please, she prayed to some nebulous god, don't let him ask me tonight. Don't let him beg me to come to him.

With trembling fingers she delivered the receiver from the phone to her ear.

"Hello?"

There was a silence so long, so heavy, that Tracy felt herself drowning in it. She knew what was coming. She felt it in every fiber of her lonely body, felt it in every heart-cell that loved Cole Damon.

"Come to me," the dark masculine voice implored.

Tracy eased to the side of the bed and graciously accepted defeat.

CHAPTER TWELVE

THOMAS LOVELL SAW HER the moment she stepped from the cab. From behind the wheel of his dark blue Chrysler, which was inconspicuously parked in the Holiday Inn lot, he watched the woman leave a tip, grab a small suitcase and walk toward the lobby of the Harrisburg motel. Although she wore sunglasses with lenses as big as saucers, he recognized her. Instantly. She had the same long legs and good looks that he'd photographed any number of times when she'd opened her door for Damon. To prove the point, he riffled through a dozen photos strewn across the front seat and produced one bearing a recognizable image. He had taken it the month before when the congressman had dashed into D.C. for a one-nighter. Yeah, it was the same woman all right. Probably here for another one-nighter.

He raked his drink-shaking fingers through his disheveled blond hair and sighed a long "damn." There was nothing about an affair with which he could hang the congressman. After all, the man was single, and single men dated, even went to bed with women. At least half of the voters of Damon's district would approve wholeheartedly, and as for the female half, well, hell, it *was* the eighties. No, Lovell thought, he couldn't ruin the man's political career because he was seeing a woman.

Lowering his eyes to the photograph still in his hands, he studied the feminine image. Looking for what, he wasn't quite sure. But slowly, like the smoke-gray clouds presently taunting the October sky, something began to nag at him. And it kept on nagging. The photograph of the pretty woman, her face unshielded and open to the world... His mind kept contrasting that image against the hidden face of the woman who had just walked into the motel. The sunglasses. It had something to do with the sunglasses. And it was something more than the fact that she chose to cover her eyes on a chill and cloudy autumn day. The truth was that the sunglasses invoked a memory. A memory of another photograph? He wasn't sure, but he was going to toy with the memory and see where it led.

TRACY HOPED THE PATH she'd taken led to room 161. The desk clerk had just flicked his wrist toward the right and had instantly busied himself with some paperwork, which had been fine with her. At least he hadn't stared as if it were obvious that she was here to meet a lover. She had asked for the key just as Cole had told her to do, prefacing the request with Cole's suggestion to tell the clerk that she was part of his campaign entourage. Actually that had been his second suggestion. The first had been to announce to the clerk, and anyone else within hearing range, that she was the woman whom Cole Damon loved and she'd like a key to his room...and to hold all his calls for the next eighteen hours. Tracy had insisted on an alternate suggestion.

Room 147...151...154...She glanced from the room numbers down to her watch. Cole would be leaving his luncheon at about two. It was already twenty past one. The thought of seeing him so soon made her heart beat faster.

Room 161.

Tracy stopped, looked around as if she had burglary on her mind and inserted the key. She pushed open the door. The room was empty—as Cole had promised it would be—and it had already been freshly tidied for the day. Tracy quickly shut the door behind her and leaned back against it. She let the dark, sanctuary-coolness settle about her.

Suddenly, standing in Cole's motel room, the reality of what she was doing struck home forcefully. The bottom line was that she shouldn't be here. She shouldn't be jeopardizing Cole in this selfish way. She shouldn't... She peered through the sunglasses and her eyes strayed to one of the double beds. On it lay one long-stemmed red rosebud. Tugging the sunglasses from her eyes and abandoning them to a table, Tracy stepped toward the rose. She picked up the single flower, bringing its satiny ruffle-edged petals to her nose. A rich sweet fragrance whispered a sensual "hello." A loving "hello." A golden glow washed wavelike across Tracy. True, the bottom line was that she shouldn't be here, but she had to be.

"WHAT TIME IS IT?" Cole asked.

Larry Seeger glanced down at the military watch that was a holdover from his days as a major in the air force and almost stepped off the narrow sidewalk that trailed to their motel rooms. "Fourteen-thirty hours. I thought the luncheon went great. I think we can count on that money, don't you?"

Cole translated the time to two-thirty. "You think you could cancel that interview for tonight?"

His campaign manager looked instantly displeased.

"Don't say it, Larry. I know how important you think it is." He could have added that everything about the campaign was compulsively important to the man beside him but refrained. "Look, I've had it. I need some rest."

"Aren't you feeling well?"

"I have a headache," Cole lied, assuaging his guilt by adding to himself that half of the statement was true. He *did* have an ache. Several, in fact. He ached just to see Tracy. He ached to hold her. He ached to tell her he loved her and then spend the next few hours proving the truth of it.

"You got something for it?" Seeger asked.

"What?"

"The headache."

"Yeah. I got everything I need," he said, stopping before room 161. "Why don't we call it a day? I'll meet you in the lobby at ten in the morning. If you want, reschedule the interview for then."

It was obvious that Larry Seeger disliked the summary dismissal of him and his carefully laid publicity plans. "Yeah. In the morning. I'll spend the evening with your correspondence." Hiking his lazy-fitting pants back up around his excessive waist, the man lumbered on down the sidewalk and disappeared around the corner of the building. Cole heard him shuffling up the steps to his second-story room and sighed in relief.

He inserted the key. *Was she here?*

Tracy heard the key being jabbed into the lock. *Was that him?*

He turned the key, praying she hadn't changed her mind.

The turning of the key sounded loud in the still room, and she prayed he wasn't sorry he'd begged her to come.

He pushed the door open and stepped inside. She pushed away from the edge of the bed and stood. Their eyes met.

After what seemed forever, his eyes still locked to hers, he closed the door. But neither moved. It was as though neither could.

Tracy's eyes roamed over every beloved feature of his face, from his wide brow, fringed in coal-black and wind-tousled hair, to his firm, strong chin. He wore a charcoal-gray wool suit, a pale pink shirt and a gray knit tie. But it was the look he wore in his eyes that kept drawing hers back to them. It was the look of love. Simple. Unadorned. Unadulterated.

Those loving eyes were worshiping the image before them, worshiping and sending signals to Cole's brain that translated to both beautiful and sensual. They were sending images of honey-tinted hair brushing the tops of her shoulders in a wild, seductive freedom. They were sending images of a white satin gown, a gown whose bodice was primly fastened by a row of tiny pearl buttons that slit the fabric from throat to midchest. Prim buttons that lost all their properness, sitting as they were in see-through lace that ran in a diamond pattern from throat to just below the indentation of her navel, stopping only to discreetly conceal the beginning of coarser tawny hair. Her hips were lovingly hugged by fingers of rippling satin. Her lips were glossed to a whispered shade of the red rosebud she held. Her eyes were the blue of daytime skies and nighttime promises.

"I wish..." Cole's voice cracked. "I wish you could buy moments in time that you could relive. If you could...I'd buy this moment. You've never looked more beautiful." He said this as his eyes coasted to the dusky pearl nipples clearly peeking through the webbing of lace. "I've never loved you more, and I've never needed your love more."

She took a slow step toward him, the hem of the satin gown flaring out as if in the wake of royalty. "Even if you could buy a moment," she breathed in a voice softer than the fabric swaying about her body, "neither of us could afford this one." She stopped mere inches from him, her head tilting upward, her eyes on his. "It's priceless," she whispered.

"Yes," Cole repeated, "priceless." He reached out a hand. It trembled, and he almost brushed his fingers to her cheekbone. He stopped short of making contact. "I'm afraid to touch you," he said, his voice rasping. "I'm afraid when I do, I'll lose control."

"That's all right," she whispered, deliberately stepping into the arc of his arms and gliding her arms, the rose still in her hand, around his neck. "I already have."

At the feel of her body, Cole groaned helplessly and crushed her to him. His lips slanted over hers with the pressure of desperation. The kiss was primitive, rough, uncontrolled...and Tracy returned it with the same primordial fury. The rosebud fell to the floor.

Slowly and with all the will he possessed, Cole gentled the kiss. The tip of his tongue met with the tip of hers to pursue a sweet lesson in braille, while his hands slid restlessly, but now tenderly, over her back, over the womanly swells of her hips. Arching her into his lower body, he felt her softness mold against his aroused strength. When she provocatively rotated her hips, a moan slipped through his lips. Tracy felt a rush of power.

Drawing her lips from his, she sought his eyes, which were now dark with unsated passion. Her hands unhurriedly glided up the front of his shirt, and she guided the jacket from his broad shoulders and down his arms. She tossed it to a nearby chair. Next she unknotted the gray knit tie and slowly pulled it from his neck. She unbuttoned the first button, followed by the second button and the third. She lowered her lips to kiss the inch of black-haired skin. Another button, another, another, each followed with a kiss, and then she slid both hands, palms flat, inside his shirt and raked it apart. Her head angled, and her lips claimed a coffee-brown nipple. Cole closed his eyes.

She kissed the tender-budded flesh, kissed it again then lazily ran the tip of her tongue across it, moistening both nipple and the curling hair that surrounded it. Then she started to pull her lips away.

"No," he grated harshly, his fingers tunneling through her hair to hold her mouth where he wanted it. "No, don't stop. I need..." He never said exactly what he needed. But Tracy knew.

She kissed, tongued, nipped softly with playful teeth. At the same time her fingers moved to his other nipple to bring what pleasure she could in the form of stroking and gentle abrading. She pulled gently at the swollen pebble-peak.

She brought too much pleasure. His fingers still tangled in her hair, he dragged her lips to his with a gentle savagery. "Remind me someday to make slow love to you," he murmured around a kiss.

"When do you think that'll be?"

"When we start spending time together like normal people." Three kisses later, lifting her into his arms, he crossed the room and put her down on the bed. With no delays he finished undressing and eased to her side.

Pulling her wrist to his mouth, he kissed its vulnerable underside where a tiny pulse beat in a riverlike blue vein, before placing her hand at her side. His finger moved to draw a seductive design on the breast pushing plumply against the transparent lace. He grinned.

"Naughty," he whispered.

She smiled. "I bought it to arouse you."

"It worked. Though you could have gotten the same effect wearing a tow sack."

As he spoke, he began to unfasten the tiny pearl buttons but had to stop once because his fingers shook so badly. Finally he mastered them. Parting the lace, his large hands caught her breasts as they tumbled forward. They were hot and swollen, with nipples knotted in a plea for attention. Which he gave them. He lowered his head, and his lips, his tongue, his teeth played the same love games that hers had earlier. With the same result. Tracy moaned and anchored his head with her fingers speared in his hair. As he sucked gently but boldly, his hand slid the length of her body, down her belly, past her navel, over the triangle of lace to find the sinfully wonderful feel of satin. He eased that satin between her parted legs, between the petals of her feminine softness. She cried out as the silken fabric rubbed over the hard pearl of her desire. Dewdrops of her moisture instantly beaded the gown and wet Cole's fingers. His eyes found hers.

"We'll observe the amenities next time," he whispered in a rush as he pushed the hem of her gown upward until it rested at her waist. Raising himself over her, he merged his lips with hers as she guided him between her legs.

"This," he moaned as he thrust into her, "is the only home I have."

"WILL YOU MARRY ME?" Cole asked long minutes later after their heartbeats had returned to a semblance of normalcy.

Snuggled in the strength of his arms, just as his body was still tunneled in the warmth of hers, Tracy tilted her head upward. "What?" she asked breathlessly.

"My proposal can't come as a surprise."

No, it didn't, she realized, then realized something else. She'd never really let herself think about the permanence of their relationship, wholly because she wanted a future with him so badly—just the way Hank wanted a future with the woman he loved. With Cole, it was a future she had been afraid to consider. With her past and his political plans, she was still afraid to consider it.

"Let's talk about marriage after the election is ov—"

"No," he said, turning quickly, pinning her beneath him. "We're going to talk about it now." The look in his eyes gave no quarter. "I've been patient, Tracy, damned patient, but my patience has worn out. I have to have an answer now."

She placed the tips of her fingers to the hollow of his cheek. "Cole, I . . ."

"No discussions. No postponements. A simple yes or no."

She hesitated.

"Will you marry me?"

"Have you considered all the ramifications . . . ?"

"Will . . . you . . . marry . . . me?" he asked again, and this time she heard the fearful tremor in his voice. He was afraid she'd say no. Her heart burst with the love she felt. And her eyes misted.

He read that as her answer and hung his head in rejection.

Raising his head with the gentle pressure of her fingers to his chin, she brought his eyes back to hers. His eyes were hazy, as well, and filled with black pain. "Yes," she whispered, praying to a merciful god that it was the right answer, an answer that wouldn't ultimately hurt the man she loved. "Yes, I'll marry you."

Tracy would always remember the slow way realization stole across Cole's dark brown irises. Cole would always remember the heady feeling that suddenly surged through his veins.

"Cole," she whispered, tempering the moment, "have you thought of the problems? I mean, really thought . . ."

"Yes," he interrupted, now fighting tears of another kind. "We'll work them out. Together."

Together. He'd made that promise once before, and together they had solved a problem she'd thought insurmountable. She let herself believe they could again. Because to go on living, she had to believe.

"You're going to be my wife," Cole said, as if in disbelief.

"Yes," she whispered, "and you my husband."

They spent the entire afternoon, the long night, the short morning, in celebration. But even as they celebrated, Tracy fought back the niggling fear that being married to Cole was just too good to be true.

THE MORNING SUN STRUGGLED to break through the gray clouds and bestow its golden harvest on Harrisburg. It was a lost battle. The silent war, however, went totally unnoticed by Tracy and Cole, who still remained within the cocoon of the motel room.

Stunning, she thought, not about the sun but about Cole, who stood before the mirror, his legs bent at the knees to accommodate his tall frame. He grimaced and tried once more to knot the scarlet-red tie. It went impeccably with the pristine white shirt that went gorgeously with navy slacks and a navy blazer.

"Stunning," Tracy spoke softly. Her head rested in the palm of her hand, while her naked body still lay cuddled in warm sheets and warmer memories. Two pairs of eyes met in the mirror. "You look stunning," she repeated.

"I was hoping," he said, a smile crawling over his lips, "that was a critique of last night's performance."

"I haven't the strength to critique last night's performance," she volleyed back.

He turned, sauntered toward the bed and sat down. Tracy slipped her head from the prop of her elbow and back to the pillow. Passion-mussed hair spilled about her very lovely face. He bent his head and placed his lips on hers.

"Nor do I," he whispered, "but I think our performance fell somewhere under the heading of fantastic."

"Umm," she mumbled in agreement, silently wondering just how many times they had made love. "And the Hill thinks you're a great orator."

Both Cole and Tracy grinned. Cole's grin slowly faded in the light of what would soon be happening. "This is the last time we're going to say goodbye." The knuckle of his finger grazed Tracy's well-loved bottom lip. "I'll be home this week...with or without my campaign staff. Enough is enough. In the meantime," he added, "start making wedding plans."

"Cole..."

"I know," he interrupted, "after the election. Which is fine," he conceded. The smile slipped back to his lips. "But I would remind you that that's next month. The seventh of November, my love."

"Don't you think we should wait..."

"We are. We're not going to rush. I'm prepared to wait fifteen, even twenty minutes after the polls close."

Tracy's lips started to quirk into a smile, but the smile was lost in a sudden attack of doubt.

"We'll work everything out," Cole reassured her. "Together. As husband and wife."

It was she who pulled his lips back to hers. She needed his strength, his confidence. Both had meant the kiss to be light, easy, the kind you could part on, but two bodies betrayed their good intentions. Cole moaned, slipping his hand beneath the sheet as his tongue slipped into her mouth. His fingers trailed over the roundness of her hip, the flat of her belly, the golden triangle of hair and beyond...

"I could make love to you again," he growled as he pulled his lips from hers and his hand away from the sweetest temptation he knew.

That she could let him make love to her went without saying.

"What time does your plane leave?" he asked, purposely setting them on another course.

"In an hour and a half," she said breathlessly. "When do you leave?"

He looked at the clock by the bed then back at her. "Now."

Tracy tried not to look as if despair had just claimed her heart. "I'll see you later this week."

"I love you," he whispered.

"I love you," she whispered back.

He didn't kiss her. She was glad. She was also glad that he didn't look back from the doorway. It made his going a little easier.

Forty-five minutes later, showered and dressed, she, too, left the room. She was again wearing the oversize sunglasses that seemed inappropriate for the overcast day. Inside her suitcase were the remnants of a red rose.

CLICK. CLICK. Thomas Lovell snapped the pictures just as Tracy walked from the motel and folded herself into the back seat of the cab. He watched as she quickly disappeared from sight. She'd still been wearing the sunglasses...on a day that didn't warrant them. And those sunglasses still sparked the faintest hint of familiarity. Why? Why the sunglasses? Why the familiarity?

He didn't know, Lovell thought, reaching for a cigarette and lighting it. He inhaled deeply and seemed to lose a curl of white smoke somewhere in his chest. Something wasn't right. He sensed it in the gut. Which is where all reporters sensed the best stories. For some reason, Congressman Damon and his lady friend were playing it low-key. Very low-key. In fact, they'd been playing it low-key all along, and he just hadn't seen the signs until now. The two of them shied away from being seen together in public. There had to be a reason. And he was going to find that reason. He was also going to find out why the woman and her sunglasses suddenly looked so familiar.

COLE WAS DELAYED. He was angry with Larry Seeger for booking him at two fund-raisers without consulting him first. Tracy was angry with the powers-that-be for continually keeping them apart. Cole promised that he'd be home on the tenth. Tracy set about waiting as impatiently as one lover always awaits another. And as she waited, she worked herself to a frazzle. She told herself it was only to pass the time, but in her heart she knew that she was covering up a blizzard-cold fear. She was scared to death that something, someone was going to stop her from becoming Mrs. Cole Damon.

GREEN EYES. A sorceress's green eyes that sparkled with magic. Blond hair, rich, thick, twining about his fingers. A smile, wide and tempting and calling to everything male in him.

Thomas Lovell restlessly rolled to his side, emitted a muffled sleep-cry and let himself drift back into the dream.

She was brightness to his darkness. She was hope to his hopelessness. She was pregnant...pregnant...pregnant...

"Why didn't you tell me?" the dream-man asked the dream-woman.

"I...I wanted to be sure first," the woman hedged.

The man suddenly looked distraught. "It is mine, isn't it? You haven't been sleeping with..."

"Of course not," the woman shot back quickly. Maybe too quickly.

Relief swept across the man's face, and he slid his hand down to the woman's still-flat stomach. He smiled, a smile that smoothed out lines of dissipation and made him look young and vibrantly alive. It was a smile that immediately proclaimed that he was handsome.

"We'll get married. I'll start looking for another job. I know you don't like my working for the *Tattler*. And we'll need a house, a house big enough for a nursery..." The man stopped. The woman's green eyes weren't sparkling. "What is it?"

The woman turned away and stared out the window. "He...he won't give me a divorce."

"What do you mean?"

"He said it wouldn't be good for his career." She looked back over her shoulder. "Maybe...maybe it would be better if we didn't see each other again."

"No!" the dream-man screamed with the lips of the man sleeping on the bed. "No!"

Thomas Lovell came instantly awake. Moisture beaded his forehead, and some dark, desperate emotion encompassed his body. He shifted to sit on the side of the bed and buried his face in his hands. After a few restoring breaths, he rose and went to the bath-

CHERISH THIS MOMENT

room where he splashed water on his face then walked to the bureau in his bedroom. He stared down at the photographs of Tracy Kent. Tracy Kent. He'd managed to learn the woman's name and the fact that she was a free-lance writer and that she consistently did work for the *Political Monitor*. Beyond that, he knew nothing. After almost a week of intensive research, he knew nothing beyond her name, her address and her occupation. And he was damned if he knew how he was going to find out more.

His eyes fell to a copy of the *Political Monitor*... just as an idea fell into place. Reaching for the magazine, he flipped open the pages to the publishing information and picked out the name of the editor in chief. Moving back to the bed's edge, he snatched up the phone, and, after an exchange with the long-distance operator, was soon listening to clear, crisp rings. When a secretary answered, Thomas Lovell spoke.

"I'd like to speak with Nathan Jeter, please."

There was a pause while the connection was made. "Jeter here."

"Mr. Jeter, I'm..." He lied and gave the name of a prominent editor of a prominent magazine. "I'm trying to locate a writer who does free-lance work for you. The name's Tracy Kent."

Nathan Jeter recognized the editor's name. "Yeah, sure, Tracy does a lot of stuff for us. She's first-rate. Let me give you her address and phone number."

Lovell didn't bother to copy either. He was staring at the information that Jeter was rattling off. "Thanks. I'm interested in having her do something for us."

As if remembering her insatiable work appetite of late, Nathan Jeter commented, "Probably going to catch her at a good time."

"Listen," Lovell added, starting on his fishing expedition, "she's not originally from D.C., is she?"

"Huh-uh. She's from New Jersey. Trenton. Been in D.C. about a year and a half."

"That's what I thought." He let a second or two pass before brazenly dropping the line that almost always guaranteed another name he could trace when trailing down a woman. He had the all-too-high divorce rate to thank for the comment's usual success. "Too bad about her marriage."

"Yeah," Nathan the Mouth answered, "but then, Dennis Webber was a jerk."

Webber. The name, like the sunglasses, instantly connected with some memory in Thomas Lovell's mind. Tracy Webber. That sounded familiar. Real familiar. And so did Trenton for some reason.

"Anything else?" Nathan Jeter asked.

"What?"

"Anything else I can do for you?"

"No. No, thanks."

Seconds later both phones sat recradled. Nathan Jeter suffered an instant pang of guilt at mentioning Dennis Webber's name, but he quickly let the guilt die. What the hell! The guy already knew about Tracy's marriage.

Hundreds of miles away, Thomas Lovell still sat on the side of the bed, staring down at the name scrawled across the writing pad. Tracy Webber. Suddenly the image of a woman wearing dark sunglasses came to mind. That same woman was emerging from a courthouse.

"No," he said softly, thinking that it couldn't be the same woman. Could it? Jumping from the bed, he grabbed up a jacket and raced from the house. For the first time in a long while, he prayed, never stopping to realize that the dark prayer he asked for would never find favor with a benevolent god.

An hour and a half later, Thomas Lovell located the back issue of the *Washington Tattler* that he was searching for. The article—his own—was accompanied by a photograph of a woman with dark glasses, leaving a courthouse. The woman's name was Tracy Webber.

EXHILARATION PUMPED through Lovell's body as he slipped two photographs into a manila envelope. One of the photos was of Tracy Kent opening her front door to Congressman Damon; the other was of the same woman leaving the Harrisburg motel. The envelope was quickly sealed and addressed to Congressman Cole Damon. A flourish of the pen labeled the envelope personal. The post office would later postmark it as mailed on October 9. Lovell smiled, a smile that was neither sane nor insane. He was going to destroy Damon, he thought. But before he did, he was going to play with him. The way a cat played with a mouse right before he pounced.

"I'M HOME," the voice announced.

"Cole." The word was uttered through Tracy's smiling lips.

"Or rather, I'm at the office. Hold on a minute." Tracy heard muffled chatter then again heard Cole's voice coming through the line. "You wouldn't believe the work on my desk. There are at least five thousand letters that need my signature, and there's a stack of mail a mile high."

"Didn't your staff keep up with the mail while you were away?"

"Yeah. Most of it. But not the personal stuff. Larry goes through that."

"He gets to open your love letters, huh?" Tracy asked with a grin.

"I assure you the only thing personal will be a request for money to support a favorite charity. Maybe someone asking me to a party. And a dozen people wanting me to support their cause in Congress. But," he added, obviously grinning, "if there was a love letter would you be jealous?"

"Would I have reason to be?" she teased back.

The moment grew serious. "Not in the least." Cole paused. "Actually I do have a love letter in my pocket. Two tickets to Martinique. I thought we could honeymoon there. Is that okay?"

Tracy's eyes misted. "More than okay." She hesitated, willing her voice to be normal, which it wasn't when she said, "Oh, Cole, I've missed you. I can't believe you're home."

"I'm not, really," he said, seductively reminding her of the comment he'd made when they were last together.

A hot flush of blood rushed through her body. "And when do you think you'll really be home?"

"Tonight. In fact, about seven-o-three."

Tracy giggled and swiped at a happy tear. "That precise, huh?"

"I'm working here until six-thirty then allowing about thirty minutes to get to your house, another minute walking from the car to the door, kissing you, carrying you up the stairs, my clothes, your clothes...yeah, I'd say about seven-o-three on the dot.''

"You're crazy."

"Yeah, but do you love me?"

"Absolutely," she whispered, adding, "unequivocally, totally, insanely, with all my heart..."

"Hold the thought," Cole interrupted softly. "I'll see you tonight."

Tracy hung up the phone and leaned against the kitchen counter. A smile claimed her lips; a song jumped to her heart. Cole was home. She suddenly felt as if everything in the world was right.

LARRY SEEGER TRASHED the first three letters, put the fourth aside to show Cole, while the fifth he acted on by marking the date of an important event on Cole's social calendar. The sixth piece of mail was a manila envelope. Slitting open the top, he drew out two photographs. And frowned. He immediately recognized the woman. She was the one who'd interviewed Cole for the *Political Monitor*. The one who had looked so familiar.

Several facts became apparent. The woman and Cole were obviously involved. And, unless he were mistaken, the second picture had been taken at the motel in Harrisburg. Cole's headache suddenly made sense. Though little else did. Why was the relationship under wraps? And wasn't it obvious that someone had just unwrapped it? But for what purpose had the photographs been sent?

And why, dammit, couldn't he remember where he'd seen the woman?

He stared at the photos, stared at the woman, stared at her pretty face. It was an intelligent face. A familiar face. Suddenly his jowled face blanched. His heart stopped. A trial. That trial. His first thought was that if this got out, Cole was dead at the polls. His second thought was how could Cole have done this to him?

CHAPTER THIRTEEN

WHEN THE DOORBELL RANG early that afternoon, a smile spread across Tracy's lips. She had known, with the certainty of long days spent apart, that Cole wouldn't wait until that evening to see her. He couldn't wait, any more than she could wait to see him. Shutting off the typewriter, she made a mad dash down the stairs and to the door. She pulled it open, a beautiful smile of greeting on her lips, her heart scampering a wild welcome. At the sight of the heavyset man standing on the porch, his hand caught in midact of smoothing the sparse layer of hair over his balding head, Tracy's smile vanished, though her heart increased its riotous beat.

Clear crystal-gray eyes collided with startled blue. "Ms Kent, I'm Larry Seeger. Congressman Damon's campaign—"

"Yes, I know," she interrupted. A small voice at the back of her mind asked what he was doing here. Another voice answered that maybe she didn't really want to know.

Uncomfortable seconds passed before Larry Seeger asked, "May I come in? I'd like to speak with you." Tracy hesitated, not really understanding why, just knowing that it felt right. "It'll only take a minute."

"Yes . . . yes, of course," she said, stepping back to allow the rotund man entrance. He stopped just inside the doorway, and neither he nor Tracy offered to move farther into the room, though his presence, square-shouldered and militarily crisp, intimidated in such a way that he seemed to fill not only the room but also the entire house. Tracy felt another wave of discomfort. A sudden frightening thought overrode that wave, however. "There's nothing wrong with Cole...Congressman Damon, is there?"

"No," the man assured her.

She relaxed, though only slightly.

"Ms Kent," the man said with a heavy sigh, "I'm going to come straight to the point."

"I wish you would."

He thrust forward a manila envelope. It was the first time she'd noticed that he was carrying anything. She instinctively took what he offered.

Addressing the puzzled look on her face, he said, "This came in today's mail."

She reached inside the envelope and pulled out two photographs, both black and white, both of her. One had been taken in almost the exact spot at which she was now standing—that photo showed Cole's broad back as well—while the other photo was of her leaving the Harrisburg motel—sunglasses, suitcase, furtive look and all. Her first reaction was a feeling of violation, not unlike the feeling she'd had when she'd been raped. One was a violation of her physical being, the other a violation of her privacy. Her second reaction was anger, tempered with perplexity. Her eyes darted from the pictures to Larry Seeger. "I don't understand."

"It appears that you and the congressman are...involved". There was no denying the censure dripping from the word. "And that someone has found out."

"Who?" Tracy asked, though she suspected even as she was asking that the man would have no answer.

"I have no idea who sent the photographs, but rest assured that it's no one who has the congressman's best interests at heart."

"Does Cole know..."

"No. I take care of his personal mail."

She vaguely remembered a discussion of that very fact only a few hours before. It seemed like so long ago now.

"Ms Kent..." Larry Seeger paused. "I'm a blunt man. Forgive me if that bluntness is offensive. I know of your background. I know about the trial. I know about its outcome." Tracy's knees weakened, and a cold sweat sheened her forehead. "I'm not being judgmental as to your innocence or guilt, but I am telling you that, guilty or innocent, you'll kill Cole at the polls."

Tracy's knees completely gave way beneath the length of her denim skirt, and she stepped back then eased herself down to sit on the second step of the stairway. She told herself that this wasn't really happening. The sound of Larry Seeger's voice confirmed that it was.

"Voters are a curious breed," she heard him adding, as if from far away. "They expect perfection in an imperfect world. They..."

On and on he droned. Over and over Tracy's mind repeated one fact. One unalterable fact. She wasn't perfect. Her past wasn't perfect...wasn't perfect...wasn't perfect...

"Ms Kent?"

Her eyes refocused.

"Do you hear what I'm saying?"

"Yes," she whispered then repeated more audibly, "yes."

"Cole Damon is the brightest political mind to hit D.C. this decade. His future is unlimited. What he can do for Pennsylvania, this country, is beyond measure. Nothing must stop him. Nothing, Ms Kent." His eyes hardened to a flinty implacable gray. In that moment Larry Seeger looked like the formidable opponent that he was. "Do I make myself clear?"

Tracy swallowed and drew in a wavering breath. "Oh, yes," she whispered, feeling a thousand emotions at once—denial that this was happening, a numbness already setting in to deal with the fact that it was, hurt, and a reactive anger. "You want me...to give him up." The words were unsteady, as if they'd been nearly impossible to say.

Grim lines tightened about the man's lips and eyes. "I don't think you ever owned him to give him up. He belongs to only one thing. Politics. And however enamored he is of you at this moment, I don't think in the long run that he'll thank you for destroying his career."

"And what makes you so certain that these photographs haven't already destroyed his career?"

"They may have, but my guess is that someone is toying with the congressman. The pictures may never come to light. But if they do, we can always deny an involvement. That is, if you're no longer part of the scene. The first picture may or may not be the congressman. A man's back isn't much to make an identification from."

"And the second picture?"

"You could have been in Harrisburg to do another piece on the congressman, couldn't you?"

"You've thought of everything," Tracy said, unable to hide the sarcasm from her voice.

"That's what he pays me to do. That, and to protect him . . . even from himself."

A pain tore through Tracy's heart to think that Cole needed protecting from himself for loving her. It was a pain, sharp and searing and like none other she'd ever felt.

"Ms Kent, do you love him?"

Tracy didn't answer verbally. But then, she didn't have to. Her love was written in the haunted look on her face.

Larry Seeger read it there and capitalized on it. "Then don't destroy him. Nor what he's worked so hard for." He riffled in the inside pocket of his jacket and produced an envelope. "Here, take this," he ordered. Her eyes dropped to the envelope. She made no move to reach for it. "Go on. Take it. Get away for a while and think about what I've said. There's enough money here to . . ."

Tracy's eyes flashed fire. "You're insulting, Mr. Seeger," she said softly but firmly.

The envelope dangled from his fleshy fingers before he finally slid it back into his pocket. "Suit yourself . . . but if you love him, get out of his life."

Seconds, minutes, hours seemed to pass before Larry Seeger finally turned, opened the door and vanished into the sunny and cool October afternoon. He left Tracy sitting on the second step of the stairway, holding two photographs.

She would never know just how long she sat there. The clock struck a new hour, though, and the sun slanted at a new angle. *Who in hell did he think he was to come here and tell her to get out of Cole's life? What kind of godlike mission was he on to manipulate people's lives?* Over and over Tracy questioned herself, but the answer, hard as it was to accept, was always the same. Whoever he was, whatever godlike mission he thought he possessed, Larry Seeger had been right. She *could* destroy Cole's career. It didn't matter whether she was guilty or innocent. Her past could nullify his future. As she'd always known it could. And even if Cole never resented the destruction—which he might—wouldn't she always?

The truth was that Cole's career mattered more than her happiness. For Cole could make the world better, and it was his destiny to do so. In the way it was her destiny to love him. *"If you love him, get out of his life. If you love him... If you love him..."* She closed her eyes, knowing what she must do—and knowing that she must do it without seeing or speaking with Cole again. If she did either, she'd never have the strength to walk away. Never.

Rising to her feet, she walked zombielike to the kitchen and lifted the receiver. She started to dial a number, but her fingers trembled so badly that she had to start again. As she waited for the phone to ring and be answered, her eyes filled with tears.

"Yeah?"

"Hank?" she whispered in a tremulous voice. "I have to go away."

HE SHOULD HAVE KNOWN that he couldn't wait until that evening to see her, Cole thought with a grin as he slammed the car door, raced up the sidewalk and bounded up the steps in two athletic leaps. The sight of the snow-white envelope taped to the front door stopped him short. With a hunch that was inexplicable but powerful he knew that he wasn't going to like what he read. He knew it with such certainty that a sick feeling instantly settled in his heart.

With the tape squealing an ominous prediction, he stripped the envelope from the door and pulled the folded sheet of paper from inside. He forced himself to read the letter.

My darling Cole,
In my heart of hearts, I always knew that you were too good to be true. I always knew that we would never be married. It was only in your arms that I allowed myself to believe. Something happened to bring reality sharply back into focus.

You tell me that now is all that matters. I wanted to believe that, truly I did, and maybe I was beginning to, but no today can be lived in a vacuum. Tomorrow, God willing, will be a reality that must be dealt with. Your tomorrow belongs to politics because you, Cole, belong not to just one, but to many. You matter. Please believe me when I say that I love you more than words can ever express . . . and I will love you as long as there is breath in my body, spirit in my soul. It is because I love you so dearly that I must say goodbye. Please, I beg of you, don't try to find me. I can't bear to say this face-to-face. I'm not that strong.

Please know always that if I could be two places at one time, I'd be with you . . . today and for all eternity.

Remember me,
Tracy

The words blurred. Even then Cole didn't realize that he was crying. "No," he whispered, the sound more animal than human. "No," he repeated, the timbre of his voice rising as desperation sunk in its fearful talons. "No!" he roared, his fist striking the door in pain and frustration.

His mind whirled with a thousand questions. *What had happened?* He had just spoken to her hours before. *When had she left?* He tried the door and sent the doorbell into a frenzy of chiming. There was no answer, just as he knew there would be. *Where was she? Where in God's name was she?* A feeling of utter helplessness, total desolation, invaded his body, leaving his head light, his heart heavy. Never in all the weeks of separation had he felt so impotent, so lonely. Then, even though they had been apart, he had known where he could find her. Now she was lost to him, swallowed up by a world that was suddenly cold and empty and larger than it had ever seemed before.

He forced himself to take slow breaths of air into his lungs. *Think, Damon. Think. Where would she go? To her parents? Maybe. Where else? And who might know where she went? In whom would she confide?* The last question brought an immediate answer. *Hank Yeats! Why hadn't he thought of him sooner?* The letter in his hand, Cole raced back down the steps and to his car. He then drove hell for leather to find a pay phone. With each illegal increase of the speedometer, he prayed that Hank would be listed in the phone book.

He was. Within ten minutes Cole was climbing to the third story of a modest apartment building. He stopped at the door of apartment 35. He knocked first then pounded when the knocking brought no answer.

That, too, was fruitless. His knees bent, Cole slid to the floor, his back against the hallway wall that could have used a fresh coat of paint. He'd wait—all night, the rest of his life, if he had to.

And wait he did. Without a watch, Cole could only guess at the time, but he reasoned after some hours' wait that it must be close to seven. Surely Hank would be home soon. Surely.

Chill shadows darkened and lengthened like svelte and supple dancers in the autumn evening as the hours came and went.

Where was she?
What was she doing?
Was she as miserable as he?
Where in hell was Yeats?

Two things crossed Cole's mind simultaneously. Both made him feel like a fool. He could find out the time by the clock in the car... and Hank Yeats might be spending the evening with Marisa. Both conclusions impelled him toward the car.

At 11:18 the car sped toward Marisa's apartment, whose location Cole remembered from the double date months before. It had been the night he had learned of Tracy's past, the night they'd cried together, the night he'd held her until she'd fallen asleep in his arms. *Would they ever cry together again? Laugh together? Love together?* The thought that they might not threatened to rob him of all sanity. It was a sanity he might lose, anyway, if Hank Yeats wasn't at Marisa's.

THE WOMAN IN HIS ARMS was warm, the kind of warm that nourished body and soul. Hank eased his lips to Marisa's temple and left a kiss, at the same time settling himself more comfortably in the sofa's corner and pulling her more snugly to him. She snuggled willingly.

"You all right?" she whispered. Her husky voice sounded more masculine than feminine, as if it were comprised of bourbon and sand. It was a voice that unfailingly ensnared his attention.

Hank's arm tightened about her waist. "Yeah," he answered, guessing that he was all right, though he certainly had no way of proving it for a fact. It had been an emotional day, one that had scanned the heights and skimmed the depths. It had been eighteen hours of no emotional middle ground, and that had made it a tiring time.

The day had begun with the biggest decision of his life. He'd called Marisa early that morning, after days and weeks of deliberation, and told her that he would move in with her—without the marriage vows that he wanted, without the guarantee of a tomorrow. It hadn't been what he'd wanted, but he'd reasoned that if he were living under the same roof with Marisa, he'd be in a better position to persuade her. Eventually he'd overcome her fear of marriage. Eventually she'd be his wife. He was settling for her now, with his tomorrow hopefully on the horizon.

Then had come the afternoon. And Tracy's call. He'd never forget her voice, nor the way she'd looked when he'd met her at the airport. People less dead were buried everyday. It had broken his heart to see his friend suffering so. And she had been suffering. More than he'd ever seen her suffer before. More even than in the aftermath of the rape and divorce. He'd wanted to do something, say something, but all he'd been able to do was hold her, all he'd been able to say was that he cared. Then he'd watched her board the plane,

watched her sacrificing her today for Cole Damon's
tomorrow.

"She'll be all right," Marisa said softly, reading her
lover's mind.

Would she? This time he wasn't so sure. But he *was*
sure that he needed to lose himself in the woman now
turning in his arms.

Marisa smiled and brushed her lips against those
peeking from his dusky beard. "I love you," she
whispered, her breath mingling with his. "I'm glad
you're here."

His lips nipped at hers. "You eventually will marry
me. You know that, don't you?"

Her eyes met his, and some deep emotion flamed in
hers. "I know that if anyone can talk me into it . . ."
The thought was lost in the meshing of two mouths.
Just as the kiss was lost in the sudden, near hysterical
buzzing of the doorbell.

Hank and Marisa instantly drew apart. The look
they exchanged asked the question, "Who?" Hank
glanced at his watch. It was twenty minutes to twelve.
Easing Marisa from his arms, he stood up then crossed
the room and peeked through the peephole. He saw an
agitated Cole Damon. Hank's reaction was mixed. On
the one hand, he couldn't say that the congressman's
appearance surprised him; he'd expected him to get in
touch sooner or later. On the other hand, he wished it
had been later, though there was nothing he could tell
him without breaking a promise to Tracy. He had the
feeling that he'd just been caught in the middle. The
feeling was uncomfortable.

When the door opened, two pairs of male eyes met.
Undeniable relief flashed in Cole's. "Thank God

you're here," he rasped. He looked as though he might collapse.

"Congressman," Hank acknowledged, inviting the man to enter by stepping back. Cole did. And his eyes quickly found Marisa's. She still sat on the sofa, her expression saying that she understood completely why her boss was there.

"I'm sorry to disturb you," Cole said to the woman. "I know it's late."

"It's all right," she answered. "We weren't asleep."

Cole made the distant observation that the two were living together. He silently applauded. Right this moment, he wished every pair of lovers could be together. That wish in mind, his eyes moved back to Hank's. "Where is she?"

All in all, the question was simple but brimmed with passion. Hank heard in the three words every negative emotion known to man—fear, hurt, loneliness, and such desperation that it momentarily shook his resolve. He had the human need to end this man's suffering by telling him, no questions asked, no verdicts rendered, what he wanted to know. At the last moment he stopped himself. Only because of Tracy.

Cole saw Hank's hesitation. "At least tell me if she's all right," he pleaded.

"She's all right," the younger man said then qualified his answer, "As all right as she can be under the circumstances." He spread his fingers wide and agitatedly ran them through his cinnamon-colored hair. "Hell," he grunted, "she's not all right! She's hurting. Bad!"

Another light died in Cole's already lifeless eyes.

"I'm sorry," Hank said, instantly apologetic. "It isn't your fault."

"Whose fault is it?" Cole said, now choking out his words. "Hank, do you know what happened this afternoon?"

Hank did know. Quickly he searched his mind to see if he'd promised Tracy to keep it a secret. He didn't think he had. Yet he was certain she wouldn't approve. He was...

"Tell me!" Cole shouted. "For God's sake, tell me!"

Hank studied the man before him. Cole Damon, always the perfect picture of a man in control, was on the verge of coming apart. His hair was tousled from too many sweeps of nervous fingers, he needed a shave, his clothes were rumpled, and his eyes were wild.

"Your campaign manager came to see her," Hank said, the pent-up anger he'd felt when Tracy had told him about the visit now obvious.

"Larry?" Cole asked in disbelief.

"Yeah. I think that's the creep. He told her that if she loved you she ought to get out of your life, that she was going to screw you up at the polls."

Cole said nothing. He couldn't find any adequate response. Partly because the situation was unbelievable, partly because there was a pounding in his temple that made thinking difficult. Finally a facsimile of a reply surfaced. "Why? Why would...why would he tell her that?"

Hank told him about the photographs.

Cole cursed darkly.

Hank told him about Larry Seeger's knowledge of Tracy's past.

Cole cursed again.

The room grew quiet. His hands on his hips, Cole hung his head and stared at a spot on the floor. Finally he raised his head and spoke to no one in particular. "Oh, Christ, what she must have felt."

"Yeah," Hank replied roughly.

The room grew silent again as three people lived through the imagined pain of one.

"Where is she?" Cole asked softly but with the strength of a hurting lover.

"She asked me not to tell you," Hank said.

"Where?"

"I promised her I wouldn't."

"I'll beg if that's what you want me to do, Yeats."

Hank heard the sincerity in Cole's words, saw it burned into his brown irises with the black heat of pain. He would beg. Cole Damon would beg. Just the way he himself would beg to know where Marisa was. Hank looked at the woman sitting on the sofa, the woman watching him with such sweet intentness, the woman willing him to answer. Yes, he thought, love reduced one to begging. Or maybe it was that love elevated one to begging.

"Please..." Cole begged in a thick voice.

Hank's eyes shifted back to the man before him. He imagined himself standing there asking about Marisa. "Martinique," he replied. "She flew to Martinique."

Marisa smiled lovingly at Hank, while Cole savored the beauty of the answer. It eased his pain just a little to know where he could find Tracy. He would ease the pain a lot when he flew to Martinique.

"When?"

"This afternoon at five."

"Do you know where she's staying on the island?"

Hank shook his head. "She said she'd call in a day or two and let me know."

"I'll find her," Cold said with a confidence that anyone would have believed. He then turned and started for the door.

"Damon?" It was the first time Hank had strayed from Cole's political title. Cole turned, his eyes instantly meeting Hank's—man-to-man. "If you hurt her, I'll break your neck."

The threat didn't offend. In fact, it made Cole think all the more of Tracy's friend. "If I hurt her, Yeats, I'll expect you to."

COLE WALKED INTO HIS OFFICE the next morning. A revised plane ticket was in the inside pocket of his olive-green corduroy blazer, and he was carrying a suitcase. As his long legs clipped out the distance through the outer office, his intense eyes grazed Marisa's. A knowing look was exchanged.

"Hold my calls," he told her.

"Yes, sir."

Larry Seeger had observed Cole's entrance, the suitcase, and the look in his eyes. He hoped he knew what had put the unsettled expression on the congressman's face. He hoped Tracy Kent had slipped from his life, a fact that repeatedly unanswered phone calls to her house tended to support. He was about to probe conversationally and ask what was wrong, when Cole said brusquely and formally, "I want to see you in my office."

Seconds later, a frown puckering his brow, the stout campaign manager closed the door behind him. He advanced only partially into the room—maybe out of an innate sense of self-preservation. Cole stood, his hands buried in his pants pockets, staring out the far window.

"Are you going somewhere?" Seeger asked, his eyes moving from the suitcase to Cole's broad back. It was the only thing that confused him.

"Yes."

No additional information was offered, forcing Seeger to add, "Do you really think that's a good idea? You have a full calendar this week and a luncheon..."

Cole pivoted. "You're fired."

Larry Seeger's face went blank then blanched to the color of an ashen dove in winter snow. "What?"

"You're fired. Get your things and get out."

Seeger immediately assessed the situation. Cole knew about his visit to Tracy. "Listen to me," he said, stepping forward to stand in front of the desk. Cole had walked to the desk's other side. The two men stood face-to-face. "It had to be done. Someone knows about your relationship, probably knows about her past, as well. She'll kill us at the polls."

"Not *us*, Larry!" Cole barked, placing his palms flat on the desk's surface and leaning forward, his eyes flashing a dark fire. "*Me!* If she kills anyone, she'll kill me at the polls!"

Larry Seeger took a step backward, as if willed there by Cole's wrath. A wrath he'd never experienced before.

"That was your first mistake, Larry. Assuming my win was your win, my career, yours. Your second mistake, and biggest, was interfering in my personal life."

"Your personal life, as it affects this campaign, is my domain," Seeger parried, his face now rouged with strain, his voice tinted with anger.

"The hell it is!" The words screamed through the walls and reddened the ears of Cole's two secretaries. Startled, both women looked at each other then hastily busied themselves at tasks that neither was paying the slightest attention to.

"Cole, for God's sake, be reasonable. We're in the middle of a reelection campaign . . ."

"I am being reasonable, Larry, or I'd kick your butt so far out of D.C. that you'd never work again." Cole forced himself to take a deep, calming breath. "The truth is that you're good at what you do. You just overstepped the line, and that I won't tolerate. I won't tolerate you, or any one else, telling me how to run my life. And no one, *no one*, hurts Tracy."

"I thought she understood," Seeger said, groping for anything that might help his cause. "I thought she was in full agreement. I thought . . ."

"I doubt seriously," Cole cut in, "that you gave it any thought one way or the other what she thought or felt."

"Cole, think of what you can do for the country."

"Aren't you more concerned with what I can do for your career? Isn't that what's always concerned you most? Every step up the ladder for me is the same step up for you, isn't it?"

"You're being unfair."

"I wish I was."

Desperate, Seeger tried one last-ditch appeal. "Cole, come on. No woman is worth wrecking your career for. And what do you really know about this woman? She may very well have coerced a man into having sex with her then hollered rape. The jury wasn't satisfied . . ."

"Get out," Cole ordered, his voice lethally quiet, his eyes smoldering. "Get out before I change my mind about being reasonable."

The two men glared at each other. Cole fought the nearly overpowering urge to plant his fist in Seeger's over-abundant stomach. Suddenly with a starched motion that belied his excessive weight, Larry Seeger whirled and marched from the office. Cole slumped into the chair and buried his face in his hand.

The worst was over. Everything was going to be all right now, Cole promised himself. He had spent the night phoning hotels on the Caribbean island of Martinique, and sometime around the hour that night dies into dawn, he had located Tracy. Every nerve in his body had screamed for him to call her, but he hadn't. There had been altogether too many phone calls in their relationship. If he had his way, they'd never again be far enough away from each other that they couldn't communicate in a whisper.

And as for the campaign . . . well, it would just have to take care of itself. Whoever had sent the photographs . . .

Cole glanced up to see a flustered Marisa standing in the doorway. "I'm sorry, Congressman, but there's a man who insists . . ."

That man pushed past her and stumbled into Cole's office. His hair was strawberry-blond and erratically combed: his eyes were blue but not quite focused, as if they turned so deep inside that they could no longer see fully what was before them. His walk was unsteady, maybe from fatigue, maybe from too little sleep, maybe from too much liquor.

Cole recognized the man instantly. He also knew instantly who had sent the photographs. The only thing he didn't know was why. It was what he now asked.

"Why, Lovell? Why go to all this trouble?"

CHAPTER FOURTEEN

"YOU REALLY DON'T KNOW, DO YOU?"

As Cole watched the man advance, he made the mental observation that, with firing Seeger and confronting Lovell, his day was off to a lousy start. He also admitted that he obviously wasn't the only one having a renegade day. So was Lovell, if appearances were accurate. He noted that the empty-eyed man before him was precariously teetering on an emotionally thin tightrope. And probably had been for a long while, with the threat of falling off becoming more and more of a reality.

"No," Cole answered, at the same time nodding to Marisa to close the door. "I have no idea." Even as he said the words, he felt his hackles rising. Whatever the reason, it damned well wouldn't be good enough. No reason was good enough to attack a man's honest career.

Without an invitation, Lovell slumped into the chair across from Cole's desk. Their eyes locked. Lovell's, though vacant, burned with purpose, while Cole's expressed an impatient and guarded interest. "The answer is very simple, Congressman." The word was emphasized snidely and with the slightest liquor-tainted slur. It was also pronounced in a distinctively British accent. "I'm going to ruin your bloody career. I'm going to take something from you the way you took something from me." The matter-of-fact way the statement was delivered made the threat particularly powerful.

Cole frowned. He also asked the obvious. "What did I take from you?"

"Lisa." The name was spoken quietly, reverently, as if there were no other way Lovell could speak it.

The answer stunned with the potency of a staggering, bloodless blow to the head. Cole's eyes narrowed, his mouth slackened. "Lisa?" What in the name of all that was righteous did Tom Lovell have to do with Lisa?

"We were lovers," the blond-haired man answered the silent question, his voice once again as soft as silver threads of silk.

Disbelief rippled in chilling cold waves across Cole's body and mind, but even as the waves were crashing onto the shores of his soul, he reluctantly realized the possibility of what Lovell had just announced. Lisa Damon had been a woman who craved attention, an attention she hadn't gotten in full measure from her husband. Wasn't it altogether possible that she had turned to someone else for it?

Cole felt the needle-pricking of his pride. That was immediately followed by guilt, guilt that his pride had been the only thing injured. He felt no real hurt that his wife might have taken a lover...not the shattering kind that a husband should feel at his wife's betrayal. In contrast, if the same situation involved Tracy, he would find it absolutely devastating. Because he couldn't even bear the thought of it, he forced his attention back to Lovell.

When Cole's eyes refocused on the man before him, he found Lovell staring down at a photograph of Lisa.

The photograph had been slipped from a folder that the man had been carrying. On the desk were now scattered black-and-white photos of him and Tracy. Cole opened his mouth to express his malignant opinion of having had his and Tracy's privacy invaded, when the abstracted look on Lovell's face, the absent way his fingers were tracing the features of Lisa Damon, silenced his words.

"She was so pretty," Lovell said, his finger slipping over a cheekbone that bespoke a classical beauty. "Wasn't she?" He glanced up with tear-glazed eyes that begged for Cole's agreement.

"Yes," Cole said quietly. He wanted to hold on to his anger, but felt it turning into pity.

"I could never understand what she saw in me." He smiled slightly, an irresistible bad-boy smile that made Cole realize what many women might see in him. Even Lisa. Particularly Lisa. "We met at a party about three years ago. Barbara Hershel's party."

Cole remembered the party vaguely. A swim party, he thought. Both he and Lisa had gone and, as always, they'd fought on the way home at what she had considered his less than total attention. She'd accused him of talking politics all evening. Which he guessed he had. Lovell's voice snagged Cole's wandering thoughts and dragged him by the heels of guilt from past to present.

"She told me I was writing below my ability. She told me I had the soul of a poet." His smile was now self-derisive, a sneer really. "She was right. At least about writing below my ability. I didn't start out that way, though. I used to work for a prestigious London newspaper." He mentioned the name of the newspaper, and Cole silently agreed on its prestige. He also wondered what had prompted Lovell to leave it, and actually heard himself asking the question.

"Money," Lovell answered bluntly. "Bloody money. It's frightening, isn't it, how principles can be bought? What am I bid for one sterling set of principles?" he mocked as if he were at an auction. "A thousand? Ten thousand? The promise of a monthly salary that allows a have-nothing kid to drive a Porsche and live better than he ever had?" Lovell trained his eyes on Cole. "The *Tattler* may not be journalism at its best, but it pays well for your principles. It gives you premium dollars for your scruples." Cole saw the man's hand tremble as he laid Lisa's picture on the desk. "I was going to get a decent job for her. I was going to start all over again. Make something worthwhile of myself." His eyes darkened. "Did I tell you she said I had the soul of a poet?"

"Yes," Cole said, pity blossoming to full flower. "Yes, you did."

"Do you have a drink?" Lovell asked suddenly. It was a little after ten o'clock in the morning.

Cole shook his head. "Only coffee."

"No, thanks," Lovell answered, giving a mirthless laugh. "I can't run the risk of sobering up." He leaned forward conspiratorially. "Too many demons when you're sober."

Cole suspected that sober or drunk, the man lived with soul-thirsty demons.

"You say that I took something from you," Cole said after a few seconds as he rolled back his chair and rose, "but it seems you were the one to take something from me."

"No," Lovell replied in a tormented whisper. "You took my future...and left me only with a past. A dead past."

"How?"

"Lisa and I were in love. We wanted to be married. But you wouldn't give her a divorce." His voice trembled as his hand had earlier and probably as his hand still would if it weren't so tightly clenched in his lap.

Cole zeroed in on Lovell's last comment. Lisa had never asked for a divorce, and he'd had the feeling that if he'd ask, she would have balked. In fact, it had crossed his mind that she had sensed their marriage coming apart, sensed his growing wish to be free and had deliberately allowed herself to get pregnant to stop it.

"...baby."

Cole's head whipped toward the sound of the word.

"I wanted my baby."

The words thundered in Cole's ears.

"Did you really think I'd let you raise my baby as yours?" Lovell asked, his eyes cloudy with hurt and anger. "What kind of man would deprive another man of his child simply to protect a political career?" His cloudy eyes began a misty rain. "She was going to break off with me. She thought it would be best for everyone. But it wouldn't have been best for me. Or my child. And she wanted to be with me. She did. She told me so." Lovell buried his face in his hands.

Cole felt as if his breath had been clubbed from his chest. *Dear God,* he thought, *had the baby been Lovell's? Had the child that he'd mourned a thousand times not even been his to mourn? Had the nights of hell, memories of "what ifs," been for nothing?* He felt a surge of anger so scalding that it threatened to all but overpower him. The anger was solely directed at Lisa. "How...how do you know the child was... yours?"

Lovell's eyes found Cole's through a veil of misery. "She wasn't sleeping with you. She told me she wasn't..." He stopped, his face paling to a sickly pallor. "She wasn't, was she?"

In that moment a lot of wayward pieces fell into probable place, and Cole's first inclination was to shake Lisa Damon senseless—whether she be in heaven or hell—for playing two men so ruthlessly against each other. How could she have been so insensitive? He knew, though, in the clearest corner of his heart that Lisa had loved him—it had been a love he had guiltily not been able to return—but she obviously had become involved with Lovell as a way to supplement the attention she wasn't getting at home. He doubted very seriously that Lisa had wanted a divorce; she'd certainly never asked for one. He further suspected that she was trying to break it off with Lovell. Maybe because she was tired of him. Maybe because she discovered she was pregnant. As to who had been the father of the baby, it wouldn't have surprised him if Lisa herself hadn't known the answer to that. The thought made him sick and once more angry with Lisa Damon.

"No," Cole lied, refusing to strip the man of the only thing he had left—memories of a woman who deserved neither him nor Lovell. "We weren't sleeping together."

Lovell looked pathetically relieved.

Cole said goodbye forever to a baby that may or may not have been his.

"You do understand why I have to destroy your career?" Lovell asked in a tone curiously solicitous of Cole's feelings.

"I understand why you think you do."

"That's the only thing you have that means as much to you as Lisa meant to me."

Cole realized, with heart-sickness, the one-time truth of that accusation. Thank God, it was no longer true!

"Can I call someone to come for you?" Cole asked, realizing that the man before him needed help.

"I'm going to ruin you with these photographs . . . and the fact that your girlfriend has a past. For a while I thought I was going to have to be content with those articles in the *Tattler*. They weren't very much . . . just hints of personal gain . . . but then I started following you . . . and I knew I'd seen her somewhere . . . would you believe I'd written her trial article myself? Don't you think that's fate? It must be fate."

Fate. Was fate what Cole should blame for this insane fiasco taking place in his office? He couldn't very well blame a dead woman—at least he could only up to a point—and he certainly couldn't blame a man who was more of a victim than even he himself was. But sweet heaven, he did have the scorching and very human need to blame someone or something. His fists curled into balls. Fate sounded as good a scapegoat as any. Hell, why not fate?

No, he thought on a deep, labored sigh. That wasn't good enough. Politics was the real culprit. Just as it had always been. Just as Lisa had told him it was. He'd long ago admitted that she'd been right, but had he really believed it? Really believed in that place in the heart that will hear no lie?

Cole turned to stare out the window, realizing even as he admitted politics' complicity in the matter that there was something or someone that was even more to be blamed. And that someone was himself. It had been his insatiable ambition that had brought him here. Because of it he'd made Lisa suffer, and he was responsible, at least in some fragmented way, for Lovell's present state, and he was the reason that Tracy's past was going to once more be laid open for all to judge. Christ, how had he hurt so many people without meaning to?

Cole picked up the phone and beeped the outer office. When Marisa answered, he said, "Call a cab for Mr. Lovell. And get a second one for me."

"I have to do this, Damon," Lovell said, almost apologetically now. "I have to ruin you."

The phone still in his hand, Cole passed it to the blond-haired man and pressed the button of his private line. "Give it your best shot, Lovell. I have a plane to catch."

Seconds later, as Lovell's unsteady voice connected with the *Tattler* office, Cole walked from the room. He left Thomas Lovell believing the lie that Lisa had loved him. Cole carried with him the certain knowledge that Tracy did love him—enough to sacrifice her happiness. One man was lost in the past, the other in the pursuit of a lifetime of todays.

TRACY FELT MISERABLE. That is, when she felt anything at all.

It had been almost twenty-four hours since she'd arrived at Lamentin Airport on the Caribbean island of Martinique, twenty-four of the longest, loneliest hours of her life. They had been hours like none other she'd ever lived through, hours frighteningly empty and pitifully purposeless. They had been hours in which she'd gone through the motions of living, but there had been a gray deadness to the ticking away of the seconds, the minutes. And worse, a deadness to the beat of her heart.

Occasionally a moment of clarity would steal through the miasma of her emotions, and she would feel sharp, rending pains of separation, a callous cutting at her heart to know that never again would she see Cole. At those times she pleaded for strength and prayed that an emotional death would once more quickly claim her. Thankfully, it always did. Regretfully, however, the pain always returned.

The way it had right at that moment.

Tracy swiped at the slow tears pearling beneath the sunglasses that unnecessarily sheltered her eyes from a swooning sun. The sunglasses were worn solely to camouflage her swollen eyes. Sniffing, she shifted her position on the chaise lounge and willed the respite of sleep. She hadn't slept all night. Or more correctly, she'd slept only in fitful snatches that had in the long run seemed more debilitating than no sleep at all. But even as she begged for this most natural anesthesia, thoughts of Cole sprang to life.

The knot in Tracy's stomach tightened, making her feel that ruthless fingers were tearing at her flesh. Fresh tears rushed to her eyes and scalded their red, aching rims.

Stop it! she silently screamed as she threw her legs to the side of the chaise lounge and rose. Grabbing a powder-blue wraparound, she tied the skirt at her waist, and the gauzy fabric settled over her white swimsuit, stopping at midcalf. She started off down the beach. She'd walk until she was ready to drop, and maybe then she could go back to her room and sleep. Maybe then thoughts of Cole would mercifully leave her alone.

Damp sand squished beneath the force of her feet, leaving prints that were pure and perfect until the sea rolled inward to obliterate them in one quick invasion. In contrast, the rhythmic, timeless sea-melody sang of constancy, a constancy much prized in a world that seems to pride itself on change.

Tracy walked onward. To her right the sunset striped the sky in colors of baby pink and lavender, vermilion and salmon orange, while to her left the hotel was swathed in blankets of crimson poinsettias and purple bougainvilleas. Overhead a white bird screeched.

Poinsettias, she thought, turning and heading back the way she'd come. She and Cole had spoken of Martinique's poinsettias on their first meeting. They had planned to honeymoon here among them next month. They... Tracy deliberately abandoned the thought, wondering if there was anything left in life that wouldn't remind her of Cole. Or anyone, she thought as her gaze settled on a dark-haired man walking slowly along the beach toward her. Before she could stop herself, her heart turned over. She called herself a fool and admitted that dark hair and a totally masculine physique were not the sole property of Cole Damon. She diverted her eyes.

She watched the sea, watched and heard the way the waves crashed against a far boulder, watched and felt the way the water hungrily, coolly, licked at her toes.

She glanced up. The man was coming closer, and he was still headed in her direction. He looked more like Cole than ever. Dark hair had given way to definite black, while the features were taking on an appearance of familiarity.

Tracy's heart again went wild. Again she glanced away. *What's wrong with me?* she thought. *It can't be Cole.*

She glanced back quickly because she couldn't help herself. The man even walked like Cole.

Don't do this to yourself, she pleaded.

The man's shirt was rolled up at the sleeves . . . just like Cole always wore his. The man's corduroy pants were inappropriate for a tropical climate. As if he'd just flown to the island. From Washington? Those pants molded thighs firm and recognizable. His shirt's vee at the throat revealed wisps of black hair, hair that a voice inside her insisted she knew the feel of. Dark eyes became Kahlúa brown.

The man stopped. Ten, perhaps twelve feet away.

Tracy's breath stopped.

Sky-blue eyes, hidden behind dark shades, met dusky brown eyes. Tracy's heart pounded against her ribs, violent reverberations that caused her head to feel light. Was she hallucinating?

"Cole?" she whispered, fearfully, prayerfully, in need of confirmation.

The confirmation came in the form of two rasped words. "Come here."

Tracy thrust herself against him, and they wrapped their arms around each other's body so crushingly that both felt their breath snatched away. Tracy buried her face into Cole's shoulder, spilling forth unchecked tears that wet his shirt in seconds, while Cole tunneled into that spot where neck and shoulder so temptingly meet. He let her cry, just as he let himself bask in the warm knowledge that she was at last where she belonged. In his arms.

"I thought..." She sniffled and tried to speak. "I thought I'd never...see you again."

Cole pushed her from the shelter of his shoulder and stared down into her face. Tears streamed from beneath the wide, shielding frames of her sunglasses. He reached impatiently for them. "Take these damned things off so I can see..." His words were cut short by the sight of the ravages of a day's crying. Tracy's eyes were red, the lids swollen punishingly taut, dark hollows beneath them, pale shadows above them. He swore with a vileness that was made tender by his tone. Tossing the sunglasses to the sand, he gently raked the pads of his thumbs across her lids. "My God, what have you done to yourself?" he whispered. She automatically closed her eyes and luxuriated in Cole's healing touch, in the balm of his voice. His lips replaced his thumbs and bestowed warm kisses to her lids. His tongue caught the teardrops that still clung to her thick, spiky butternut-colored lashes. "I swear," he promised in a gravelly voice, "that I'll never again be the reason why you cry."

The word never was sobering. It implied a future. A future that Tracy could be no part of. Though it was the hardest thing she'd ever done, she pulled away from him. Caught off guard, he let her go.

"Why did you come after me?" she pleaded, even chastised, as she focused her eyes on the spot where sea and sky speak of union.

"If you're walking out of my life, you're going to have to tell me to my face."

Didn't he understand that that was what she ouldn't do? she thought as panic clutched at her.

"Is that what you want, Tracy? To walk out of my fe?"

He knew that wasn't what she wanted. She'd told im that in her note. How cruel could he be in mak- g her say the words out loud!

"Is it?"

She didn't answer.

"Is it, Tracy?" Cole asked, his voice rising to a pitch at demanded a response.

She whirled, and her glassy red eyes impaled his. No! You know it isn't!"

"Funny," he said with a calmness that was made all e richer in contrast to her upset, "that isn't what I ant either."

"Cole, please, you don't understand...."

"I do understand," he answered. "I understand ore than you." His words were cryptic, and they erved the purpose he'd intended. At her look of in- erest, he added, "Seeger no longer works for me." racy's eyes widened. "I fired him this morning."

A thousand questions raced through her mind, but ot the question of why. She intuitively knew that. omehow Cole had found out what had happened. ven as she listened, he confirmed her thoughts.

"I won't tolerate anyone messing in my private fe." His voice hardened. "And he's lucky I didn't ounce his butt out of politics for what he did to you."

Tracy's eyes again filled with tears, tears of happi- ess at Cole's defense of her, tears for the remem- rance of how helpless she'd felt at Seeger's visit, tears ecause in her heart she knew that Seeger had been ight.

"He's right," she said as she swept back a teardro
that was burrowing into a corner of her mouth. "H
was only trying to protect you...."

"He was protecting himself," Cole broke in, non
too charitably.

"But the photographs. Someone..."

"Lovell," he supplied. "Lovell sent the photo
graphs. He'd been following me, us, for weeks."

Tracy tried to be shocked but somehow she wasn't
Thomas Lovell was too much the kind of man who'
do just that. There had been something about him th
night she'd seen him in the bar that told her the ma
was troubled. Maybe severely. "Why?" she asked
because she had no idea.

"In his own words, he wants to ruin my politica
career."

Again the question was a startled, a simple "Why?'

Cole explained in the fullest of terms everything tha
had happened in his office that morning. Tracy lis
tened with growing disbelief.

"Lovell and Lisa?" she asked at length. Cole nod
ded. "Did you...did you know?"

"No."

"Oh, Cole," she whispered, taking a consoling ste
toward him.

He placed the palm of his hand against her tear-
damp cheek and smiled softly. "It's all right. Neither
Lovell nor Lisa can hurt me."

Tracy wasn't altogether sure that was true. She'd
seen the look in his eyes when he'd spoken of the baby;
she'd seen the pain he would always live with at never
knowing whether it was his.

"Tracy..." Cole's voice had softened to the sound
of a sprinkling spring rain. "He knows about your

ast. About the trial.'' He paused, letting his words
nk in. "Tomorrow morning you and I may...you
nd I *will* be smeared across the front page of the *Tat-
er*, and after that, probably throughout Pennsyl-
ania and conceivably on any other major news
ublication that deems the story notable enough.'' A
ained expression dulled Cole's eyes. "I'm sorry that
ecause of me your past is going to be dredged up
gain.''

Tracy said nothing. Waves crashed. A bird cawed.
omeone from a distant sailboat laughed. Suddenly
racy laughed, too—the hysterical sound of emo-
ons snapping. "You're sorry because my past is
oing to be dredged up again.'' Her laughter rose to a
nrill note. "I'm ruining your career, and you're sorry
ecause my past is going to be dredged up. I'm de-
troying everything you've worked so hard for, and
ou're sorry...'' Laughter turned to convulsive tears.
Cole reached for her and pulled her into his arms. She
ollapsed against him and cried.

"Shhh,'' he whispered. "Don't, baby. Please
on't.''

"I knew...this would happen,'' she sobbed. "I
new it would. I knew from the beginning.'' She clung
o him as her body heaved with pain. "Oh, Cole, I
on't...I don't want...to hurt you.''

"Then don't,'' he said, cupping her tear-tattered
ace in his palms and staring down into shimmering
lue eyes. "Don't walk out of my life. If you do...''
He swallowed from emotions strong and powerful.
"You'll kill me. No, worse. You'll leave me alive but
estroy my reason for living.''

"But...''

"No buts." Her tears now made runnels tha braided in and out of his fingers. "I made so man mistakes with Lisa. I let my ambition..." He traile off as if the words had been bitten back by remorse "Tracy, winning that election means nothing to m without you. Don't you understand that?"

"But I may have just...caused you to lose it."

"I don't care.

"But I do!"

"Then your priorities are all wrong."

"Cole, I'm ruining your future!"

"I don't have a future!" He closed his eyes, tryin to regain his composure. Slowly he opened them "I've tried all along to tell you that. I don't have a fu ture, you don't have a future, none of us do. You can live for tomorrow because it always shows up in th form of a today. What's going to happen will hap pen. If the people of my district don't want me as the congressman on November seventh, there's nothing can do about that. I can be responsible only for now live only in the now. *Now*, Tracy!" His hands tigh ened on her cheeks. "I'm not offering you tomorrow It's not mine to offer. What I'm offering you is to day. Every today I have for the rest of my life. Pleas stop running from the past, stop looking to the fu ture, and live with me in today." Delivering the speec he'd rehearsed a dozen times as the plane had made i way to Martinique, his eyes filled with tears. "Please, he pleaded. "I can promise you nothing but to day...today and my love."

Tracy's mind reeled under the weight of Cole words. Was he right? Was tomorrow that illusive thin that everyone used up his life waiting for? She kne of the past. It hurt. At least hers did. She knew als hat today without Cole would hurt. She'd just spent twenty-four hours without him...and had thought she would die. A string of todays without Cole, each blurring into another until her life, all her tomorrows, was over, would hurt with a power she might not be able to survive. And yet, staying by his side, where he wanted to be, might cripple his career. Did she have the right to tamper with Cole's destiny? Even as she watched a tear seep from the corner of his eye, she knew it was a question that she'd never have the answer to.

"I know a man," she whispered as she reached out and trapped the tear coursing down his cheek, "who says that time is a comic illusion...that it really doesn't exist at all."

Cole waited. And prayed. Another tear rolled from his eye.

"I have no idea whether he's right or wrong. I only know..." Her voice shook at the forceful emotions sweeping through her body.

"Only know what?" Cole prompted with a voice that wasn't even as steady as hers.

"I only know that I can't live without him...that I can't tell him...goodbye."

If the world thought it strange that two people stood crying on the shores of paradise, the world kindly refrained from comment. Cole's comment was a low groan as his mouth sought and found Tracy's. Tracy's comment was a whisper of his name as her lips rejoiced at the weight of his. The kiss was slow and passionless—passion would come later. Now was the time for the spiritual binding of vows.

"I love you," she whispered.

"I love you," he replied.

Their words of love danced in the air, merged with the sunset and were finally carried into forever by the timeless sea.

EPILOGUE

WHEN THE PHONE RANG, Cole jumped. The woman wrapped in his arms awoke instantly, as well. Though they both had pretended otherwise, they'd been waiting for the call all through the night. Now their eyes met briefly before Cole reached for the receiver and silenced the second ring.

"Hello?"

"Sorry if I woke you," Hank Yeats's voice apologized, "but I have no idea of the time difference between Washington and Martinique."

Cole instinctively glanced at the clock by the bed. "It's almost five here," he announced, his heart beating a rhythm that had little to do with the dawn about to break through the sky.

"How's the weather?" Hank asked, a hint of devilry in his voice.

"Ah . . . probably somewhere in the eighties today."

"We're getting cold."

"Are you?"

"Yeah, sure are," Hank supplied. "But then you can expect D.C. to be cold in November, right?"

"Did you?" Tracy whispered, now wide awake and propped expectantly on an elbow. The sheet had slipped to her bare waist, and her heart was almost visibly beating a rapid tattoo.

"Right," Cole answered as he shrugged at Tracy. He also silently promised to throttle Yeats when he next saw him.

"By the way," Hank broke in, "when are you coming back—" there was a meaningful pause "—Congressman?"

Congressman!

A slow smile broke across Cole's mouth. Victory flowed in his veins. "Day after tomorrow. And I'm going to kill you first thing."

Hank laughed.

"You won!" Tracy screamed, recognizing the smile for what it was.

She lunged at the distinguished and newly elected congressional representative from the state of Pennsylvania, almost knocking him from the bed. He yelped as his arm gathered her about the waist and pinned her tightly to his nude form. Somehow he managed to keep them both from toppling to the floor of the bridal suite. The quick vibration did mysteriously knock one of the room's twenty-five pots of poinsettias over. Each marked a day of marriage; each had been given by Cole and was treasured by Tracy. And spread out on the room's desk was a multitude of telegram congratulations. It seemed as though everyone in the world was happy with their marriage—Cole's family, her family—Ruby Kent was still shedding tears of joy—and politicians whose names Tracy had only read in print. There was even a congratulatory message from the president of the United States.

"I take it that's the congressman's wife receiving the good news," Hank said with a grin in his voice.

"You're right, and I can honestly say it was the most hazardous part of the campaign."

Hank laughed again. "You won by a landslide, sir. You stomped Adams's ass." There was a pause before he said sincerely, "Congratulations."

"Thanks, Yeats. And thanks for calling."

"My pleasure. Tell Tracy hi."

"Will do. And tell Marisa that she's still got a job."

"I'll do that right now."

The line went dead. Cole recradled the receiver then turned his full attention to the woman beside him.

"You won," she whispered, staring up at him with a smile and adoring blue eyes.

"I won," he answered, staring down at her with eyes filled with love.

"I didn't . . . I didn't ruin anything." Cole had been right. The two of them had made front page news, though not in as many papers as they might have. Ironically, Lovell had made news, too, in the form of a small announcement in the *Tattler*. It seemed he had returned to England. For psychiatric help, Cole hoped.

"You could never ruin anything," Cole said, leaning down to kiss the end of her nose. When he drew back, his eyes raised to hers. They had suddenly turned serious. "Tracy, as long as I'm in politics, we're both fair game. Some ambitious reporter may drag your past out from time to time. Is that going to bother you?"

Her fingers feathered across his lips, lips soft and warm, lips that knew every way there was to say "I love you." "Do you believe my innocence?"

Cole kissed each fingertip then kissed the simple gold band encircling the third finger. A similar gold band was on his left hand. "Implicitly."

"Then I don't care what anyone else thinks."

She scooted upward, her breasts moving against the dark spirals of hair matting his chest, and sealed his mouth with hers. As always happened, both were instantly lost.

"I'll never get enough of your mouth," he whispered, slipping his tongue once more past the wet satin of her lips.

"I have a confession," she said moments later after his attention had shifted to the curve of her neck, the linear plane of her shoulder, the globed fullness of her breasts.

"What?" he breathed as he pushed her breast upward and took one rosy peak into his mouth.

She whimpered. "I've always...oh, that's good...I've always wanted to make it with a newly elected congressman."

Cole released his treasure. His eyes found hers. There was an instant light in his. "What a coincidence. I've always wanted to make it with the wife of a newly elected congressman."

Tracy's lips tilted at the corners. "Then I'd say that this is an opportunity just too good to be missed."

"I suspect you're right," Cole said, adoring her breasts again with his eager tongue as he boldly trailed his fingers over her stomach and through the tawny delta between her legs. Tracy gasped as his fingers spread wide the petals of her womanhood and probed gently, seductively. Moments of magic made her moist, and Cole, his lips possessing hers, eased into the valley of her legs and pushed his hard sex into the softness of hers. He wanted to claim, and she wanted to be claimed.

"Cole, let's have...a baby. Soon." Tracy whispered.

Cole's hips stilled. His eyes mated with hers.

"Give me a baby," she begged, her hands going to cup his morning-shadowed face. "Your baby. Our baby."

Cole closed his eyes...and once more heard a baby's laughter. This time, it didn't hurt. He felt no regret, no pain. Only a hint of sorrow that Lisa's baby had never known life. When he opened his eyes, his dark brown irises were moist. "I love you," he breathed. "More than you can possibly ever know."

Her hand at the back of his neck, she drew his mouth to hers. "Oh, but I do know," she whispered. Her hips arched against his, re-creating the sweet rhythm. Cole succumbed to their lovemaking. And to the thought of their eventual child.

Minutes later both were hurled into the most sensual sphere of existence. It was a journey they made together. It was a journey that would never grow old, even though they would. Sated, their bodies moist from love and loving, they lay side by side. The congressman and his lady.

Slowly Cole smiled.

Slowly Tracy smiled.
Outside, the sun smiled a good morning.
Another today had just been born.

No one Can Resist . . .

HARLEQUIN REGENCY ROMANCES

Regency romances take you back to a time when men fought for their ladies' honor and passions—a time when heroines had to choose between love and duty . . . with love always the winner!

Enjoy these three authentic novels of love and romance set in one of the most colorful periods of England's history.

Lady Alicia's Secret by Rachel Cosgrove Payes

She had to keep her true identity hidden—at least until she was convinced of his love!

Deception So Agreeable by Mary Butler

She reacted with outrage to his false proposal of marriage, then nearly regretted her decision.

The Country Gentleman by Dinah Dean

She refused to believe the rumors about him— certainly until they could be confirmed or denied!

What readers say about
HARLEQUIN SUPERROMANCE.T.M.

"Bravo! Your SUPERROMANCE [is]... super!"
R.V.,* Montgomery, Illinois

"I am impatiently awaiting
the next SUPERROMANCE."
J.D., Sandusky, Ohio

"Delightful... great."
C.B., Fort Wayne, Indiana

"Terrific love stories. Just
keep them coming!"
M.G., Toronto, Ontario

Harlequin Superromance

COMING NEXT MONTH

#214 CLOSE TO HOME • Rosalind Carson
Amnee Bristol will always be treated as the boss's
daughter if she stays at Bristol Skis. But her plans to
escape are nearly undermined by the company's
golden boy, Lee Forrester, who is determined to keep
her very, very close to home....

#215 A PRIMITIVE AFFAIR • Sharon Brondos
The funny, charming but unpredictable
Ian Bradshaw is all wrong for the conservative Wall
Street financier Elizabeth Marlowe. They have
nothing in common. So why are they falling in love?

#216 FIREBRAND • Rosemary Aubert
Since a brief meeting fifteen years ago,
Jenn McDonald has harbored a fantasy about the
young, charismatic mayor of Toronto, Michael
Massey. Now her dream has a chance of becoming
a reality.

#217 A TIME TO LOVE • Jocelyn Haley
Jessica Brogan has her life neatly under control—
until the unexpected happens. She suddenly finds
herself the heroine of a foiled kidnapping and the
object of a stranger's passions.

Can you keep a secret?

You can keep this one plus 4 free novels

One of America's best-selling romance authors writes
her most thrilling novel!

TWIST OF FATE

JAYNE ANN KRENTZ

Hannah inherited the anthropological papers that could
bring her instant fame. But will she risk her life and give
up the man she loves to follow the family tradition?